D0853104

DISCARDS

Isaac's Torah

ALSO BY ANGEL WAGENSTEIN

Farewell, Shanghai

Isaac's Torah

CONCERNING THE LIFE OF ISAAC JACOB BLUMENFELD

through

TWO WORLD WARS, THREE CONCENTRATION CAMPS

and

FIVE MOTHERLANDS

— a novel —

ANGEL WAGENSTEIN

Translated from the Bulgarian by
Elizabeth Frank and Deliana Simeonova

HANDSEL BOOKS

an imprint of
Other Press • New York

Originally published in Bulgarian as *Petoknizhie Isaakovo* by Izdatelska kushta "Khristo Botev," Sofia, 2000.

Production Editor: Yvonne E. Cárdenas
Text design: Natalya Balnova

This book was set in 11.5 pt Bembo by Alpha Design & Composition of Pittsfield, NH.

10 9 8 7 6 5 4 3 2 1

Library of Congress Cataloging-in-Publication Data

Wagenstein, Angel.
[Petoknizhie Isaakovo. English]
Isaac's Torah : concerning the life of Isaac Jacob Blumenfeld through two world wars, three concentration camps, and five motherlands / Angel Wagenstein ; translated from the Bulgarian by Elizabeth Frank and Deliana Simeonova.
p. ; cm.
ISBN-13: 978-1-59051-245-6
ISBN-10: 1-59051-245-6
1. Blumenfeld, Isaac Jakob, 1900—Fiction. 2. Jews—Ukraine—Fiction. 3. Jews—Ukraine—Social conditions—20th century—Fiction. I. Frank, Elizabeth. II. Simeonova, Deliana. III. Title.
PG1039.33.A37P4813 2006
891.8'134—dc22

2005034311

Publisher's Note:
This is a work of fiction. Names, characters, places, and incidents either are the product of the author's imagination or are used fictitiously, and any resemblance to actual persons, living or dead, events, or locales is entirely coincidental.

If the Lord had windows, they would long ago have smashed His panes.

Isaac's Torah

Instead of a Foreword

Except for the title of this work, if I may call it that—because it is nothing more than a conscientious transcription of another's memories and reflections—I have not invented anything, since any intervention of mine in the narration would be like a liter of vinegar in a cask of good wine, and any embellishment like a pinch of yeast and salt that could only spoil the sanctity of Easter bread. Everything you will peruse a little further on, my dear and unknown reader, even the most incredible twists and caprioles in the destiny of Isaac Jacob Blumenfeld, was told to me by the man himself, from the beginning, in the renowned and prestigious Russian Club, in Sofia, and later at his home in Vienna, at Margaretenstrasse 15.

Mr. Blumenfeld used to supply a Bulgarian firm with sewing machines and other equipment for making ready-to-wear clothes, and he looked me up on his own, because he had seen, on television, somewhere in the West, a film based on a screenplay of mine about the fate of the Jews. I thank Fortune for this meeting, because it has enriched my life with yet another friendship, and by what else does a man become enriched if not by friendship, love, or wisdom?

I want personally to thank as well Isaac Blumenfeld, who never stopped being astonished by my interest in his life, on behalf of which he gave me access to surviving letters and the scanty traces of things like diaries, documents, and snapshots, testimonials to the abominations of one epoch, but also because of which he made me feel that this planet has never lacked good joyous people with sad, intelligent eyes. Such, for example, as Sarah Blumenfeld, here in this little old snapshot, who left with her children for the mineral baths, and arrived, not there, but at the gas chambers of Auschwitz. Such as, staring at me from a photo unglued from a document, the good rabbi Shmuel Ben-David, probably much like the many other inhabitants of the little town of Kolodetz near Drogobych—Jewish, Polish, and Ukrainian—who turned into smoke passing through crematoria chimneys and now shepherd the white flocks of clouds through the limitless blue meadows of God. Here also is a certificate in English stamped with the seal of the Eighth Corps of the North American Army, which testifies that Isaac Jacob Blumenfeld was liberated from the camp Flossenbürg (Oberpfalz), Germany, and that he was permitted to set off with the American military forces for Vienna. There is, as well, a slip of paper serving as a paid baggage receipt, filled in with violet ink and sealed by the prosecutor of Yakutsk, certifying that citizen so-and-so was freed on October 7, 1953, from the camp in Nizhni-Kolymsk, northeastern Siberia, and must therefore be considered completely rehabilitated by reason of lack of evidence of crime. There are also five documents, according to which Isaac Jacob Blumenfeld was, consecutively, an Austro-Hungarian subject, a subject of Zhech Pospolita, that is, the Polish Republic, a Soviet citizen, a person of Jewish background residing in the eastern territories of the Reich and deprived of citizenship and every kind of civil right, and, at last, a citizen of the Federal Republic of Austria.

I gaze with love and sorrow at the little portrait of this plump, freckled person, with a wreath of reddish hair that sticks out from the bald spot on his head, who made me swear not to publish even one page of his biography as long as he was alive. And here, today, is a telegram from Vienna with black borders. I read it through the blurring filter of my tears and vow neither to keep anything back nor to add one word to the new Torah, or, as you might call it, the new Pentateuch of Isaac Jacob Blumenfeld.

ISAAC'S INTRODUCTION

A Letter to Rabbi Shmuel Ben-David

Grüss Gott! Cheshch, pani i panovie! Zdrastvuite, tovarishchi, and Shalom Aleichem! In other words, peace to you and to your home. If you ask me how I feel, I would honestly reply: thank God, excellent, because things could be even worse. But even if you don't ask me, I'll still tell you—because have you ever seen a Jew who can keep to himself what he's already decided to say?

I'm not young anymore, I'm sitting on my terrace in Vienna—my wonderful eternal dream of Vienna—I'm drinking coffee and reflecting on various matters concerning Life. Around my completely bald pate, a golden wreath of hair, which was once, if you remember, copper-red, is shining against the descending sun. A more poetic writer would compare it to the halo around the head of a saint, but as I consider myself a sinner, who survived by chance the fall of Sodom and Gomorrah, it rather reminds me of the ring around Saturn. Because what is that ring if not remnants of old worlds, planets broken into shards like clay pots, asteroids, national myths—"eternal" truths and revelations, ground into ashes and dust—which turned out to be less durable and more poisonous than an old can of fish, Reichs that were supposed to last for millennia, while they couldn't even count to twelve, empires smashed to bits that turned into midget-states, and cruel maniac dwarves, self-proclaimed immortal emperors, dictators, fathers of nations, great leaders and prophets, who would poop in their pants if after their deaths they could only read what the grammar school history book says about them.

All these remnants from the past are circling not only around Saturn but also around my head, so that I can understand that, from the times of Nebuchadnezzar, enslaver of the Jews, till the present day, nothing much has changed, or as that genius bastard, who signed himself by the mysterious pseudonym "Ecclesiastes," put it, all is vanity, what was, will be, and what has been, will be done again: I saw everything that is done under the sun, and here—it's all vanity and chasing after wind. . . . That's what he said—or something along these lines.

Someday I'll try to tell you how my five most cherished dreams, which we've discussed more than once, were fulfilled. Now, at the sunset of my life, I know that for one human life this is no small thing—to live through five dreams-come-true, for which I should have thanked God and fate, if things were not a little strange: I feel shy about saying this, but those dreams were actually never mine. As a matter of fact, everything was the result of the political situation, and I was never interested in politics, just the opposite—politics was interested in me and kept setting for itself the goal, or as the government leaders would say, "the task of tasks and the main priority," of fulfilling my most cherished, as they insist and they're probably right, historic dreams, so to speak. They are five, as I've already mentioned, those dreams-come-true of mine, and five are the books of Moses, which proves without doubt that my tribe is God-chosen, and so destined to have its dreams realized. And therefore I, as a minute speck of dust from this tribe—or if you wish, a little ant from our ant colony dispersed around the world—have the right to my own piece, to a percentage or bonus, or something like shares from this joint venture of the God-chosen. On the other hand, when I think about what's happened to the Jews through the counting of the endless prayer beads of Time, and when I add up my own modest invoice, including Value-Added Tax, I will myself cry out, like that bard who roamed our lands under the name of Peace to You: "Thank you, God, for the high honor, but couldn't you have chosen some other people?!"

Please, don't look for any logic in my destiny, because it was not I who directed the events, but they who directed me. I was neither the millstone nor the water that turns it around, I was just the flour, and mysterious remain for me the ways of the Miller, glory to His name eternally and unto the end of time.

Don't look for logic either in the historic events that determined my destiny—they don't have logic, though maybe they have some hidden meaning. But is it given to man to know the secret meaning of the tides and of the sun and the early blooming of the snowdrop, of love and the mooing of the cow?

Don't make me, brother, begin the explanation of the political situation with that shot in Sarajevo that I am so fed up with, when some high school student with the strange surname of Prinzip shot our dear, beloved, unforgettable, et cetera, et cetera, and so on, Archduke Franz Ferdinand. Because the First World War was ripe as a festering boil in Europe's womb and was going to burst even un*prinzip*led, that is, even without the foolish shot of this Prinzip, as if, let's say, some German diplomat in Stockholm had slipped on a banana peel, dropped by chance by the French representative of the Michelin company. Please, don't look for logic either in the fact that my dear motherland Austria-Hungary and its unconquerable army, under the wise leadership of General Konrad von Götzendorf, raced to shove itself even deeper into the conflict exactly when even the last idiot could have guessed that we were already losing the war. Is there logic in the fact that all true subjects of Austria-Hungary most zealously wished for the breaking-up of the Habsburg empire into small states, suspicious ethnic unions and tectonic federations, waving national flags and wiping away their tears and snot while they listened to the performance of the "Hey, Slavic People!" song, and are now sobbing by the broken washtubs and remembering Austria-Hungary as the "good old days"?

Tell me, my dear brother, is there logic in all that? Or in the fearful joke of Greece and Serbia, who held hands like little brothers as they jumped into the bloody abyss on the side of the Entente, while Turkey, this eternal English spy, without a single known reason, turned against England, and Bulgaria sided with its enslaver of five centuries and leaped into the war against Russia, its liberator, which in its turn . . . et cetera, et cetera, and so forth.

The First World War is the first whale on which, as the ancient people say, my story will rest its foot. The second whale, of course, is the Second World War, and if now, as I'm stepping on it with my other foot, I start exploring the meaning and meaninglessness of this most frightful of all wars, I'll most probably be torn to pieces at the very beginning, because historic whales only very rarely swim parallel. In this connection, it will suffice only to remind you about those eternal and sacred national ideals, as a result of which during the First World War, Germany was a mortal enemy to Italy and Japan, and during the Second World War proclaimed them its blood brothers and entered with them into a similar eternal and sacred alliance.

Let's forget the grief from this most frightful war; it'll turn into a dull ache from an old rheumatism. It is characteristic of humans to forget the bad, because if they only think of death and of those they've lost, the plowmen will cease to plow, the young to make love, the children to repeat syllables and words—these golden beads on the string of thought. We'll forget the pain and then the meaning of wars will come down to that old, ancient anecdote, which you've probably heard a hundred times in a hundred different versions, but that I'll still tell you, because can you stop a Jew from telling a joke when he's already made up his mind to do so? So, somewhere in Galicia, a Jew and a Pole are walking from one little town to another. The Jew, who always thinks himself cleverer than the rest, and so, entitled to give them advice or to make fun of them, points to a smoking horse turd on the road and says: I will give you ten zloti if you eat this turd. The Pole, shrewd like any peasant, has nothing against making ten zloti. Okay, he says, and, frowning and gasping, he eats the turd. The Jew gives him the ten zloti, but soon feels sick to his stomach when he thinks that he gave away all this money for a stupid thing like that. So the next smoking horse turd he sees, he swallows hard and says to the Pole: will you give me back the ten zloti if now I'm the one who eats the turd? Okay, says the Pole. The Jew frowns and gasps but even so swallows the turd and gets his money back. They continue down the road, until the Pole stops, scratches the back of his head, and says: Listen, if you Jews are so smart, could you tell me why we ate those turds? This time the Jew says nothing—an extremely rare event.

So if you ask me about the meaning of everything that happened during the two wars and in between, I would in turn answer your question with a question that doesn't have an answer: Why did we, indeed, eat that shit?

I don't know, my dear brother, if you'll ever receive these lines of mine, because you too are like a leaf blown by the whirlwinds of destiny and chance, which you in your Marxist way consider an ordinary logical occurrence, and you Marxists so marvelously predict, and even more marvelously explain the reasons why your predictions don't come true. But who but Jehovah or rather Yahweh, whom you renounced (I'm not blaming you for anything, everybody is right for himself), was able to predict or could have foretold that you, the good rabbi of our little town by Drogobych, would later become a labor union activist and chairman of the Atheists' Club? Could anyone have foretold that our paths would cross again at the barbed wire of the Flossenbürg camp, and that they—these camp fences—a symbol and a road sign of the Epoch, would divide us at the crossroads—you over there, and me over here? Did anyone on earth, in hell or in heaven, know that destiny would be so generous to us, and instead of disappearing into the gas chambers or Jewish paradise, we would meet again—oh, joy, do you remember!—in the Gulag, somewhere in the middle of nowhere in Kazakhstan? But you, ZEK 1040-260 P, as a political case had to go to the left, to dig Stalin's White Sea-Baltic canal, and I, ZEK 003-476 V, as a war criminal and traitor to the motherland, was just coming from the bottom of the Archipelago, where I was the interpreter of captured barons, marshals, and et ceteras, bearers of the Iron Cross with Oak Leaves, who so intelligently, through common efforts, thank God, had managed to lose this war too. For me, the insignificant Jew, a private from the Austro-Hungarian army, and later on an honest Soviet worker in Sewing Workshop No. 6 (this was my father's atelier, Mode Parisienne, do you remember?), for me it was a high honor to serve the chevaliers of the Iron Cross with Oak Leaves. Learning that I was a simple soldier, they asked me to polish their boots and bring their metal cups of oily tea, though they never learned that I would dart behind the barracks and piss in that tea of theirs. One time Baron von Rodenburg, whom—do you remember?—the Russians caught in the lavatory of the Leipzig railway station, while he was getting into a housemaid's clothes so he could sneak out to the Americans, so this baron once said the tea tasted a little different that day. I mumbled that the night before we'd had turnip soup. He conceitedly asked what there could be in common between the turnip and the tea, and I dared mention that all the phenomena of our existence, Mister Baron, sir, are connected by a mysterious metaphysical link. The baron looked at me through his monocle and said: you're a smart-aleck Jewish philosopher. How right he was, this baron!

I don't know where you are now, my dear brother, but probably you are again in our little town—again a rabbi or a chairman of the local committee, or a neighborhood militiaman, it doesn't matter. Probably you have many children and grandchildren, let them be healthy and happy, I wish them a bright future, because this little corner of Europe so dear to our hearts is the crossing point of Slavic, German, and Jewish passions, and from such Hasidic incest springs a certain Chagall, or that Sholem Nahimovich Rabinowitz, that is our Sholem Aleichem, and at the neighbors', some great anti-Semite who in his own way brings glory to our native land. I hope the yeast that history uses to raise the children of today is better and that days of wisdom will come, days of joyous peace and brotherhood, so that in the coming years and centuries, all the way to Judgment Day, no one will ever again piss in someone's tea, amen.

Your old friend and brother-in-law,
Isaac Blumenfeld

ISAAC'S FIRST BOOK

How I Went to War, in Order to Bring Victory

ONE

Our tailoring workshop, "Mode Parisienne," was located on the main and almost only street in Kolodetz—a small town, *miastechko* in Polish, and *shtetl* in our language. We didn't have a proper display window, just a low pane with glued-on scraps cut out from Paris and Vienna fashion magazines, with elegant gentlemen in tuxedos and exquisite Viennese ladies in pink, though as far as I can remember we never tailored a single tuxedo or lady's pink garment. My father was mostly involved in turning old worn-out caftans inside out and was happy as a child when, at the fitting, in front of the mirror, the clothing, turned inside out for a second time, looked as if it were new—or at least this is what he'd say through his tightly pressed lips, which were holding an incredible number of pins. He was a good tailor and here's the place for me to mention his favorite story about how one time he'd tailored a red uniform for a dragoon from His Majesty's Lifeguards (I personally have never seen dragoons in our Kolodetz) and how the client was very satisfied as he looked in the mirror, but said, "I don't understand why you needed a whole month for a simple uniform when your Jewish God created the whole world in six days!" My father replied,

"But look at His work, Officer sir, and look at this wonderful uniform!"

I was eighteen years old, helping out my father in the workshop, screaking out Jewish songs on the violin for celebrations and weddings, and reading selected chapters from the Tanakh, in other words the Five Books, to the children at the synagogue school, in our language the *Beys Medresh*, every Friday. As for the reading—I was reading all right, and reading, as they say, with passion and heart, but I wouldn't claim I was a Kogan at the violin. I was learning to play with the good old teacher Eliezer Pinkus, God rest his soul, he was a kind man and remarkably tactful, but one time he couldn't hold it in any more and carefully said to my father: "Please, don't be offended but your Itzik has no ear for music . . . ," at which my father angrily asked, "But why does he need an ear? He won't be listening, he'll be playing!" And how right my father was, for now I was more or less playing, or rather screaking out, as I have already indicated, the violin that my dear Uncle Chaim gave me on my bar mitzvah, that is my religious coming of age, on my thirteenth birthday.

I was a dreamy boy, and traveled in my dreams all the way to Vienna, and it wasn't only once that my father Aaron, or Ari Blumenfeld, pulled me out of these sweet journeys by his wooden tailor's measuring stick, so that I would find myself all of a sudden back again in Kolodetz by Drogobych, sitting at the table, with a needle stuck in an unfinished sleeve. In my dreams I was always wearing one of those spiffy Parisian tuxedos from the magazines, stepping down from a fiacre, and extending my hand to help a lovely lady in a pink dress, then bowing to kiss this tender and soft hand, but always right at this moment my father would smack me on the head with the measuring stick and so I never learned the rest of this story, neither who this wonderful lady was nor why I was helping her step down from the fiacre. I probably saw this scene somewhere in the movies.

Now, I remember about the movies. Sometimes, in a horse cart, all the way down from Lemberg, that is, Lvov, Mr. Liova Weissmann would visit. A journalist, newspaper publisher, and owner of a movie projector, he was selling his newspaper *Yiddishe Heimland*, and in the evening he'd show films at David Leibovich's café. These were always films, or parts of films, about wonderful distant worlds, inhabited by divinely beautiful women, who lowered their eyelids when gallant cavaliers kissed them on the lips. We were uneducated and too simple to understand such high-class plots; moreover, Mr. Weissmann, in the ongoing war situation, was getting those films from God knows where, and their subtitles (at that time cinematography was silent and subtitled) were in Danish, Flemish, Swedish, and one time in Japanese or something like that—and in Kolodetz by Drogobych no one spoke those languages, especially Japanese. Only Avramchik the postman, who had fought in the Russo-Turkish war as a signalman, claimed he could understand Turkish, but unfortunately we never happened to get a Turkish film. And one time, I remember, we were watching quite a long piece that was turned upside down, when somebody tried to whistle in protest and to stomp his feet, but Mr. Weissmann angrily said that this is how the film was and he was in a hurry to get back before the night caught him. And so, the gorgeous ladies and gentleman were kissing with their heads upside down, which was quite amusing. Sometimes they showed military newsreels and then Liova Weissmann would comment in dramatic fashion, "Our unconquerable army is advancing irresistibly!" It didn't matter what direction the soldiers were going in—left to right, right to left, coming toward us or going away from us—the commentary was always one and the same: "Our unconquerable army is advancing irresistibly!" Quite some time later I happened to notice the fact that Mr. Weissmann would say this only when Pan Voitek, the policeman, was sneaking a look at the image on the screen.

To these celebrations of art, if I can call them that, the young girls of Kolodetz would come—among them our Jewish girls, as well as Polish and Ukrainian girls. Now we were living, I have to tell you, quite a communal life in general and we weren't divided by religion and nationality, but still, we courted our own women—otherwise either their mothers would give us dirty looks, or our fathers would grimly hint that we better not have any illusions that they'd okay a non-Jewish woman. This situation would always make us enthusiastically tell the story of the baptized banker Goldberg, who married his daughter to the son of the baptized factory owner Zilberstein, and happily announced: "I have always dreamed of having for a son-in-law a nice rich young Christian from a good Jewish family!" But of course this has to be a joke, because reality was quite different, and in Kolodetz there were no bankers and factory owners, just the opposite.

But we were talking about the cinema and the inhabitants of those distant fairy worlds in which people, apparently, had no other cares but to drink champagne and kiss afterward. In one such movie scene, just when the lady on the screen (the screen was a tablecloth with a coffee stain that was alternately situated either on her face, or the face of the gentleman)—just when the lady parted her lips for a kiss, I unconsciously reached out and took in my burning palm the little hand of Sarah, the sister of our rabbi Shmuel Ben-David. She didn't react, she was watching the movie with eyes wide open, and when, together with the actress, she lowered her eyelids, I then bent over and lightly touched her lips with mine. It lasted just a second; then, it seems to me, Sarah, realizing I wasn't the fellow on the screen, looked at me with indignation and slapped me on the face. There was a laugh, a mocking whistle, and at that moment Pan Voitek the policeman peeked into the café and Mr. Liova Weissmann, who had fallen asleep, woke up with a start and solemnly announced: "Our unconquerable army is advancing triumphantly!" In short, I had no luck, neither with the lady in pink from the fiacre, nor with Sarah.

In addition to the thrilling evenings with the films of Mr. Liova Weissmann, I was crazy about *Shabbos*—the holy, for the Jews, Saturday evening, and not only because the next day we didn't work. I loved it when the family was gathered all around the holiday table—all of us clean and combed, in white shirts of homemade linen, freshly ironed by my mother—my father, myself, my sister Klara and her fiancé Shabtsi Krantz, who was an assistant pharmacist in Lvov and we were very proud of it, and Uncle Chaim. We would listen to my mother's short prayer glorifying Adonai, the only God of the Jews, followed by the grand breaking of the steaming bread, candles burning in the seven-branched menorah and peace falling on all of Kolodetz. Even the Christians fell silent that evening, there weren't the usual drunken songs and Polish fights, but if you're not Jewish, you'd probably think our Saturday night was just a Saturday, right? Oh no. There's nothing the Jews do like other people, so don't wonder at the fact that our Saturday night is really Friday, and that's just how it is—take my word for it.

Then all of the next day—Shabbos—until sunset, the Jews don't do a stitch of work and even the poorest delight in it, breathing in the deep and joyous Saturday peace. Some go over to the shul for prayer, swaying dreamily and for a long time, to the rhythm of the incomprehensible ancient Hebrew poems, while others do this business more quickly and less thoroughly and go out on the main street to take a stroll and look at the world. Passing each other, they nod importantly and even solemnly, and in a Viennese manner doff their hats, as if it's been twelve years since they've seen each other and as if yesterday they didn't almost have a fight because this one's hens invaded that one's garden. The women warmly exchange greetings with "*Gut Shabbos*," and indeed everything is peaceful and quiet, and on that day they forget the rumors going around again about Cossack pogroms in Russia, and that they owe the grocer, that the horse is limping, and that all these things are a bad sign. And all through the day there is that Saturday peace, as you perhaps know, it's a sin to do any kind of work, to make a fire, and even smoke. In ancient times, they say, this would be punished by death, but later on, with the development of more humane ideas, the death sentence was overruled and the actual crime declared a sin with unpredictable consequences in the Other World. Look, I'm not bragging, but in one way or another, it's a great invention of the ancient Jews—this holiday. Before that no one even fathomed that we could do without working one day of the week. And so insistent were my distant ancestors in introducing their innovation that they forced even God to rush through his work in six days so that on the seventh, like a good Jew, he had to rest. When I tell you also that on Shabbos it's forbidden and a fearful sin to touch money as a sign of something diabolic and unclean (even though during the other days the Jews don't hold this rather extreme opinion), you'll realize the whole deep and wise meaning of the Seventh Day. There's even a joke on this topic, you probably know it, but I can still tell it to you:

Two Jews from two towns are arguing over whose rabbi is more powerful in his spiritual connection with God and hence, more capable of performing miracles.

"Ours, of course, and I will prove it to you," says the first one. "Last Shabbos our rabbi was going to synagogue when suddenly rain came pouring down from the sky. Not that the rabbi didn't have an umbrella, but on Shabbos any kind of work is forbidden—so how can he open it? He looked up to the sky, God immediately understood, and there was a miracle, you won't believe it: on the left side—rain, on the right side—rain, and in the middle—a dry corridor all the way down to the synagogue. What do you say to that?"

"What I say, of course, is listen to this! Last Shabbos, our rabbi was coming home after prayer and what did he see? Lying on the road was a hundred-dollar bill! Well, how could he take it, when it's a sin to touch money? He looked up at the sky, God immediately understood him, and there was a miracle: on the left side—Shabbos, on the right side—Shabbos, and in the middle, you won't believe it—Thursday!"

Speaking of Thursday! The first Thursday of May 1918, at 10:30 in the morning, something happened that other, more epic writers would describe as "a turning point in life," or maybe "an historic moment." At this turning point or historic moment, my father, Ari Blumenfeld, was measuring the right sleeve of the military jacket of the policeman, Pan Voitek, probably for some alteration, while at the table, sitting and smoking, was my Uncle Chaim, known as Chaimle—a bohemian, a rascal, and a very good man, the only one from the family who had been to

Vienna, and more than once, too—and I was sitting there daydreaming, that is, pretending to be at work. And right at this moment of the plot, the postman Avramchik comes in, or rather comes down—because Mode Parisienne was three steps below the pavement—with a yellow piece of paper in hand. "Big news for you!" said Avramchik.

"Good or bad?" my father asked, with fear in his heart, pins between his lips.

Avramchik looked in confusion at us, then at the paper, then at Mister Policeman, and was apparently unable to say definitively one way or the other whether the news was good or not. Then Pan Voitek took the initiative in his hands, as they say in the military news, and grabbed the paper. He read and offered this verdict:

"Good news! Your son Isaac Jacob Blumenfeld is mobilized Under the Flags of the Austro-Hungarian Imperial Army and has to present himself exactly seven days after receipt of this summons . . . and so on, and so on. Congratulations!"

"But he's still a child . . . ," my father whispered.

"His Majesty knows perfectly well if he's a child or a real man! Children don't kiss young misses in the dark during cinema projections!"

"Did you do that?" my father asked reproachfully.

"Without knowing . . . ," I said, and that was the actual truth.

My father slapped me symbolically, apparently with the purpose of impressing Mister Policeman. "Here, in front of Pan Voitek, and to teach you a lesson."

"Good," I said.

"And couldn't we do something . . . ," said my father, "connected with heart failure or something like that?"

"No, no!" said Pan Voitek abruptly. "Stop with these Jewish tricks of yours! Our motherland needs him! At this moment when victory has never been closer!"

"Closer to whom?" Uncle Chaimle asked his question with great curiosity.

The policeman opened his mouth to reply, but stopped to think and only after a long pause said, "The question is still being clarified."

"And is it good for the Jews?" Mama asked anxiously, coming up suddenly at the end of the staircase leading to our kitchen, from which wafted the delicious smell of borscht.

"In what sense, Mrs. Rebekha?" asked the policeman.

"In the sense of the situation at the front line."

"Good for us."

"For us?" Uncle Chaimle asked, surprised.

"I said for us, not for you."

We all knew that Pan Voitek was Polish and that the concept of "us," "you," and "them" in Austria-Hungary was quite a delicate question, in which Jews should not be involved, and that's why my father and uncle looked at each other, nodded wisely to each other, and almost simultaneously said, "Yes, right."

I remained under the impression that nothing was right.

TWO

Our rabbi Shmuel Ben-David was finishing the prayer when I entered the synagogue, in our language *Beys Tefile*, the prayer house. Don't think that this was an imposing holy temple with marble columns or things like that. It was a very ordinary room with whitewashed walls and a small wooden lectern in front of the faded drapes embroidered with sacred words and signs, from where on Pesach, that is, our Passover, they took out the Pentateuch. Our synagogue was not like the Catholic church with luminous saints in many-colored glass on the windows, with a crucified Jesus and a statue of the Holy Mother as well as a number of other colorful Christian things. Nor was it like the small Christian Orthodox temple on the other side of the river, with bright icons, gilded ikonostasis, and walls painted with different scenes that I loved looking at as a child. Theodore the priest used to pull us by the ear and kick us out, hissing viciously, "Off with you Jews from the temple of God! You, who sold Christ! Who crucified him!" We kids tried to explain to him many times that it was all a very big misunderstanding, because we had neither bought nor sold their Christ, but Theodore the priest would throw stones at us, sic his dog on us, and we had to postpone looking at those fascinating pictures until a more appropriate moment. But the synagogue wasn't like this. It was forbidden to have images, sculptures, and such in it, and everyone had to imagine Yahweh the way his heart prompted him and not get distracted by looking at biblical scenes, but just enter into a quiet and soulful conversation with God, and complain about his destiny (have you ever seen a Jew who doesn't complain about his destiny?). And Yahweh, whose name translated means The One Who Is, can also complain to you because life has become, let's say, expensive—a loaf of bread now costs as much as a whole bushel of wheat used to, even in heaven horse fodder isn't free, He's got loans outstanding to pay back that he took out for construction work during the time of the Creation and so on—the way any decent Jew would do when another Jew is bellyaching to him. Then the first one pours out all his own troubles and in this way avoids the unpleasant moment of asking the other one to lend him money. Yahweh was not born yesterday, the One Who Is, He's learned His job over a couple thousand years, or even longer. What's important is to gripe, even to weep a little—you get relief. But I've gotten off the subject myself, just like Solomon and Aaron, who were complaining to each other, each one afraid the other would ask to borrow money, and didn't notice that they had strayed from the road a little bit, and so, grousing all the while to each other, instead of reaching Vienna ended up in Warsaw.

This, by the way, is also the case with our great prophet Moses, who took us out from Egypt with the promise to lead us to the blessed land of Canaan, but he got into such a deep conversation with God, the way that only two Jews can, and got so carried away discussing one thing and another, that instead of getting us to Canaan, for forty long years he dragged our tribe all over the desert. Such an extensive exchange of thoughts, as they say. Moreover Moses, as you know, had a stutter, which in no way facilitated the dialogue. They even say that one time when he was a young man, the pharaoh asked him if he had always had a stutter.

"N-n-n-not always. O-o-o-only when I talk."

I don't know what exactly they discussed, but without doubt they must have complained to each other. They even say some desert bird flew over and shat, can you imagine, on the head of our prophet Moses. He touched his head, looked at his smeared fingers, and with bitterness said to Yahweh, "And for the A-A-A-Arabs, they sing. . . ."

But we were talking about the service at the synagogue.

After the prayers the rabbi Shmuel Ben-David came up to me. I had squeezed under my armpits one of the huge bound tomes of the Tractates of the Talmud and the Pentateuch with Commentaries, and I told him I wanted to return them because I had been called up. I said this not without pride, I admit—the young are fools, who believe that being summoned Under the Flags means that they acquire qualities that until now they've lacked. They don't understand that in military service they'll even lose the few qualities they had to begin with. And thus, full of unmerited pride, I went up to the rabbi—truth be told, not so I could say good-bye, but because he had a sister—Sarah.

The rabbi invited me to tea at their place and said he would surprise me with another piece of news. His one-story house was in the little garden of the synagogue; you could enter the parlor straight from the courtyard. And just as I went in, whom should I collide with but Sarah. My face flamed and it seemed to me that maybe hers did too. The rabbi asked his sister to bring tea.

So we sat there, the three of us, and drank tea. I didn't dare look at her, though I felt her looking at me; yet, when I lifted my eyes toward her, she immediately looked away. On the whole, as writers say, the atmosphere was tense. Rabbi Shmuel, as if noticing nothing, intently set about the ritual preparation of tea with the pedantry you could find only in that region of the world, breaking the sugar with little tongs, and spooning the sour cherry jam into three small scalloped gold-rimmed china cups.

"Do you know," said the rabbi, "that joke about the rabbi who was the only one who knew the secret of making exceptionally wonderful tea?"

Of course I knew it, but at that moment nothing could have been more helpful.

"No one could make tea like his, and he guarded the holy secret of its preparation. Although the governor himself stopped by to drink tea, even to him the rabbi refused to reveal the secret. When he was on his deathbed, the elders said: 'You're on the point of departing, Rabbi; you're not going to take the secret to the grave with you, are you? Tell us how to make your famous tea.' Then the rabbi ordered everyone should leave the room and only the oldest man remain behind. And into his ear he whispered with his last strength: 'Put more tea in the teapot, and don't be stingy. That's the secret.'"

We laughed; Sarah's and my glances met and immediately shifted away. I asked, "And what surprise were you going to announce?"

The rabbi reached over and took from the buffet a little yellow sheet of paper—exactly like mine. "And me too—I've been called up. As a military rabbi. In other words, God isn't going to leave you without a *tzaddik*, that's to say, without a spiritual guide."

I was honestly delighted. "This means we'll be together and together we'll go on leave . . ."

These words were directed toward Sarah and this time when I looked at her, she didn't lower her eyes, and her glance, I thought, showed concern.

"Or together we'll die," said the rabbi and quickly added, "I'm joking, of course. The war is already almost over and before long there'll be peace."

"And who, by you, will win?" I asked. "Our boys or theirs?"

"Which ones are ours?" thoughtfully said the rabbi. "And which ones are theirs? What does it matter already who the winners are, if victory will be like a short blanket. If you pull it up to cover your chest, you expose your feet. If you want to warm your feet, you expose your chest. The longer the war goes on, the shorter the blanket will be. And the victory will hardly warm anyone."

"I don't get it," I said.

"One day you will. When both the losers and the winners will pay for broken crockery. As the prophet Ezekiel says: 'The fathers have eaten sour grapes, and the children's teeth are set on edge.' Listen, I'll tell you a story about the pope and the chief rabbi of Rome."

He was truly incredible, our rabbi Ben-David. For every occasion in life he had in the drawer of his memory ready-made stories; where I come from we called them *khokhmi*, something like parables, full of wise sayings. He began to tell his latest *khokhma*:

"So the pope died, and the candidate for the new pope had, for his closest friend, the chief rabbi of Rome. The future pope said to him, 'I have examined, my friend, the papal archives from countless centuries. And the same ritual is always repeated over and over again. There is a procession of ambassadors and royal envoys from all over the world coming to the new pope with gifts and good wishes. And all through these centuries, the last one to come is always the chief rabbi of Rome with his ten devoted elders. Having said whatever he has to say, the rabbi then turns to one of the elders and takes a faded envelope made of old parchment and hands it to the pope. This fellow looks at it and with an expression of mild disdain hands it back to the rabbi. The Jews bow and leave. This is how it's been for centuries; this is how it will be this time. Tell me, my dear friend and advisor, what's inside this envelope?'

"'I don't know,' said the rabbi. 'I received it from my predecessor, may his soul rest in peace, he in turn received it from his predecessor, and so on, from the beginning of time. But what's inside this envelope, I swear to God, I don't know.'

"'Let's do this, my dear brother,' said the future pope. 'As soon as you, the Jews, have come through the procession, and you're always the last ones to do so, I'll retreat to the library. One of my cardinals will catch up with you and invite you to visit me. Bring the envelope, and let's see after all this time what's inside it, eh? After all, there's no such sin described in the Holy Book!'

"'All right,' said the rabbi, who was renowned for his freethinking.

"And so they did this. And when they were left alone in the pope's library and opened the ancient envelope—what do you think was inside it?"

"Well, what?" Sarah and I asked, almost at the same time.

"Here's what was in the old parchment: the unpaid bill from the Last Supper. Do you understand now what I was telling you before about bills that sooner or later have to be paid?"

I nodded wisely as if I knew.

Quite politely and even a little formally I said good-bye to Sarah, and thank you for the tea, and shook hands. The rabbi Ben-David saw me to the door. When I had just passed through the yard, right at the small gate to the street, his voice caught up with me.

"Itzik, so what was it you came for?"

I realized that in my confusion I had taken the Tractate and the Pentateuch, which I was supposed to have left with the rabbi. I turned back to hand them over to him and then I noticed the good, understanding little smile at the corner of his lips.

THREE

I was sitting at the edge of the ravine. Down below stretched out the fields of Kolodetz. A quiet stream capriciously wound this way and that between the blooming sour cherries and wild plums. Only someone who's never been in Kolodetz by Drogobych couldn't imagine this blessed bounty—the fields of rye already turning blue, the green of the young barley and the yellow of the blooming coleseed, the puffy buds of the fruit trees and just above them, the white clouds in the sky. And you don't really know whether it's the earth reflecting the celestial grace or the heavenly magnificence or is it God, made lazy and contented because of the great May sun, contemplating His own Image in the grand mirror of Nature. In the distance along the pathway, Ukrainian women—you know them by their snow-white kerchiefs—were striding along on their bare white feet, and their song—a Ukrainian maiden song—drifted up in fragments, torn into waves by the mild wind. As a white horse cart passed them by, the women waved, and the man in the cart waved back at them, and you will easily guess by his wide-rimmed black hat that he was one of ours and that as he passed he must have made some spicy remark, because their ringing laughter flew all the way up here.

Someone sat down next to me and put his arm around my shoulder, startling me. It was my uncle Chaimle. "Don't be sad," he said. "The soldier's service is like measles, tonsillitis, whooping cough—you have to have them at least once in your life. Are you going to light a cigarette?"

I looked at him in surprise. "You know I don't smoke."

"I can't imagine a war hero who doesn't smoke! Here, take one!"

I took a cigarette. Uncle Chaimle tried to light it for a long time with a big gas lighter until it blazed up with a smoky flame. I started smoking and coughing and we laughed happily through tears and smoke.

"Do you really love her?" suddenly asked Uncle Chaimle.

"Who?" I asked, confused.

"The one on whose account you got a slap in the face from your father."

"Two slaps," I said. "One from her, too."

"Uh-oh," said Uncle Chaimle. "So you don't have a sure thing there yet."

"I don't even think about it," I said with dignity. "It was just what it was."

"It shouldn't be just what it was. You're going to war, you're going to be conquering countries and continents. In the capitals you've conquered you'll be met by charming women with big heavy breasts who'll adorn your gun with flowers. . . ."

"Uncle, please," I said, embarrassed.

"You will not interrupt me and you will look me in the eye when I'm talking to you. Where was I . . . ? I'm asking you, where was I?"

I swallowed with difficulty. "At the big breasts."

"Exactly. Okay. I can't let you go unconsecrated to their warm bed. Tomorrow we leave for Vienna. This will be my gift."

I was beaming all over. "All the way to Vienna?"

But Dad didn't beam when that same night he said angrily, "But that's very expensive!"

"For you everything is expensive," said Uncle Chaim. "And this time I'm paying!"

We were sitting around the table, eating dinner.

"And from where do you have such a lot of money, Chaimle?" asked my mother.

"You're not supposed to ask where money comes from, but what it's for! I've got money to take your son to Vienna. To see our capital, before he goes for many long years in the trenches." My uncle seemed to have gotten a bit carried away.

"Long years?!" my mother cried out in horror. "But this war is going to end, isn't it?"

"You don't understand anything about poetry. In poetry they say 'long years.' Or, for instance: 'He rang the bell and it took an eternity before they opened the door.' Well, how much time do you think passed by? Two minutes!"

Uncle Chaimle stood up and said to me, "Tomorrow at eight sharp I'll stop by with my cabriolet to pick you up. If there isn't a delay, the train leaves at nine forty-five."

He reached into his small vest pocket for his watch, and at first, not realizing it wasn't there, by habit started feeling his pockets, searching for it. Then, a little guiltily, he said, "I must have lost it."

"The gold watch?!" cried out Mama.

"Well, so what if it's gold?" Uncle said abruptly. "They can also get lost, can't they? So, Itzik, tomorrow at eight!"

He grabbed his hat, mumbled a "Shalom," and sneaked out, embarrassed. Mama and Dad looked at each other: the source of the Vienna funds had been clarified.

FOUR

We were swaying back and forth in the third-class compartment. Uncle Chaimle was pensively looking through the window at the tangled telegraph wires and I was most likely drowsing, looking through the window, and then nodding off to sleep again. The compartment was full of soldiers, apparently on leave—some with crutches, some with heads all bandaged up. One of them asked my uncle what time we were due to arrive in Vienna. He courteously reached for his watch, and was searching for it again when he remembered that it wasn't there, and furtively glanced at me. I pretended to be sleeping. "About five o'clock," said my uncle.

This reminded me of that rabbi on the train to Warsaw who was asked the time by a young coreligionist sitting across from him. The rabbi looked at him, and, without answering, wrapped himself up in his coat and went to sleep. In the morning, just before the train arrived at the Warsaw station, the rabbi said, "You asked me the time, young man. Right now it is eight-twenty and we are about to arrive."

"And why, honored Rabbi, didn't you answer me last night?"

"Because the road is long, young man, and if I had replied, you would have started chatting with me. Later on you would have asked if I live in Warsaw and at what address. Then one thing would have led to another, and you would have asked whether I have a daughter. And then one fine day you would have dropped by me for a visit and asked for her hand. And I have no intention of marrying my daughter to a person who doesn't even own a watch!"

I looked again at my dear Uncle Chaimle, who was now taking his turn at a nap. With his big curly reddish sideburns, and his jacket with its large square-checked pattern and an old, stiff bowler resting on his knees, he could have passed for a respectable provincial merchant of wheat or cattle, though he wasn't one. He wasn't anything in fact. Without a definite occupation, he was always full of grand new plans that, in the distant future, were supposed to end with a move to America. "The difficult thing," he used to say, "is actually to land on the hard American soil. After that, everything goes like bread and butter. This isn't Tarnov for you. This is America!" He based all his hopes on one invention, unknown in our part of the world—the electric vacuum cleaner, all the rage in America. He managed to get hold of some of these items and announced that he was collecting advance orders, but nobody ordered one, not because the merchandise was bad, but because in Kolodetz in the early years of my childhood there was no electricity yet and only our dear emperor knew when they were going to bring it in. Uncle delivered fifty gramophones with funnels and a bunch of records with popular German songs. With the greatest pleasure he would demonstrate the quality of the gramophones to anyone who was interested, explaining that the gramophone as such would raise the culture of our whole native region. He changed needles and records, people gathered to listen, patted him on the back, asked for more and more, until one day Uncle ran out of needles and didn't have money for new ones. Not a single gramophone was sold, he piled up all the merchandise on some horse cart, and it disappeared who knows where. As far as I remember, his only real financial coup was the purchase of a large quantity of blankets from some military auction. In the dyeing process some mistake had been made and instead of being barracks-type brown, they were a rather dirty violet color with pink spots, but Uncle sold them at an extremely low price. Not too long afterward, and not without the participation of the Mode Parisienne tailoring atelier in Kolodetz by Drogobych, everyone was wearing the same wool suits or caftans of a dirty violet color, with pink spots. I don't believe this business deal moved my uncle even an inch toward the cherished borders of the United States of America. So, regardless of the financial coup with the blankets, Uncle was soon left without a penny in his pockets, but with a head full of ideas that sometimes brought him some bank note or other with a horribly small number of zeros. In those days, when some naive person in the café would ask to borrow some money, Uncle Chaimle would always reply, "Sure, when I come back from Paris." "What?" said the other one, surprised. "You're going to Paris?" And then followed Uncle's answer: "I don't dare even think about it."

Then the ticket inspector passed by and announced that the train was about to arrive in Vienna—the capital of our motherland.

FIVE

What can I tell you, my dear brother, about this sublime city; what can I compare it to? I've seen other cities, I've even been to Truskavetz, Strij, and Drogobych, but that would be like comparing our policeman Pan Voitek with His Majesty Charles the First or with our late, great Kaiser Franz-Joseph! Or if you know the one about Aaron, who was so absentminded he entered the synagogue without a hat, and the rabbi scolded him and told him to leave the holy temple at once. Because, he said, entering the temple with your head uncovered is a sin comparable only to that of sleeping with your best friend's wife. "Oho, Rabbi," said Aaron, "I've tried that one too. What a difference!" So's the difference, roughly, between Truskavetz and Vienna.

We walked around Vienna. I was carrying Uncle's small suitcase, and stopped frequently to gape at the houses, the double-decker buses, the trams, the shining carriages, and Uncle would grab my elbow, reminding me that we had to keep going. I'd been thinking, to tell you the truth, that Vienna would look like any city up to its ears in military troubles. Not that you didn't feel the war at all—there were a lot of officers in the streets and the cafés, sometimes a military patrol would pass by or a truck loaded with soldiers, but the city seemed to me carefree and even joyfully frivolous, something like Uncle Chaimle—though a lot richer.

Finally we stopped in front of a hotel: "Astoria" was its name if I remember correctly. This wasn't a building, but a castle, with mythical creatures holding up the balconies and bay windows, a pink marble staircase, and a revolving door of crystal panes rimmed with shining brass. Inside, there glowed—perhaps it was only illusory reflections in the glass—a million lights. Two people in blue and gold uniforms and snow-white gloves, dignified enough for marshals or crown princes, were standing outside, elegantly greeting and seeing off the guests. Two boys also wearing blue and gold, with something like blue pots on their heads, were lifting up and taking down suitcases from the cars, and if I tell you any more, my eyes will start filling with tears of emotion.

I stood there openmouthed, until Uncle Chaimle gently pushed me. "Come on, go in."

"Here?!" I asked, astounded.

"Well, where else? Isn't this where we're going to stay?"

I couldn't believe my eyes and ears. Completely dumbfounded, hanging onto the suitcase, I followed Uncle. The marshals and the crown princes looked at us, but didn't pay any special attention to us—let me add that I was dressed a little provincially but still quite neatly, don't forget who my father Aaron Blumenfeld was, and that he, according to his own words, had even tailored a red uniform for a dragoon from His Majesty's Lifeguards.

Inside things looked even more astounding, with palm trees under the crystal chandeliers, people coming down the broad staircase, which was carpeted in a tender blue, the ladies with tight dresses reaching a little above their knees, smoking cigarettes in long cigarette holders, and the men in tails, exactly like the ones we had in our windows in Kolodetz. Elegant one-armed officers were coming down the stairs, with deep scars across their faces and an empty sleeve tucked under their belts, and monocles. They looked like Germans, and they were floating around proudly like maharajahs on white elephants; it seems that being one-armed with a scar on your cheek was fashionable then. One of those boys with the blue-gold pots on their heads was ringing a bell, and it clanged gently, so as not to startle anyone, and on the small black slate he was carrying around there was a sign written in chalk: "Mister Olaf Svenson." I think it wasn't the boy who was Olaf Svenson, but that they were looking for such a person or something like that.

It would be an understatement if I told you that I was dazed. My throat was dry, it seemed to me at any moment the police would barge in, arrest us, me and Uncle Chaimle, like intruders in a foreign film, or crooks from Kolodetz by Drogobych who had sneaked with sinister intentions into this pink, bluish-golden, aromatic, and exotic world.

Speaking of crooks, as I looked toward the marble tables at which ladies were drinking coffee with cream and elegantly biting a piece of warm strudel, or important gentlemen were reading newspapers, spread out on thin bamboo holders—I mean the newspapers, not the gentlemen—and next to the tables, on gracefully curved Viennese hangers, hung majestic coats that we had never seen in Kolodetz, I remembered a story that must've come from a similar place:

"Excuse me, are you Moishe Rabinovitch?"

"No."

"The question is about the fact that Moishe Rabinovitch is myself, and right now you are putting on my coat!"

But I didn't feel like jokes from Kolodetz, and even less like putting on someone else's coat. At this moment Uncle Chaimle approached an important-looking personage in uniform. Here I couldn't immediately orient myself as to who were the masters and who were the servants, because this one, for example, who looked as if he were the owner of a stable of five hundred horses, peered at my uncle from on high, then bowed a little and turned his ear toward him. It seemed that Uncle was talking softly because of uneasiness and had to repeat his question to the ear bent further still. The stable owner raised his eyebrows in surprise, Uncle reached with two fingers in his vest pocket for a tip, but apparently thought twice and with anxious politeness offered him a cigarette. The man looked at the cigarettes with still greater surprise and shook his head in disgust—he was either a nonsmoker or Uncle's cheap carriage-driver's smokes completely disgusted him, and I think the second hypothesis more probable.

All this lasted no longer than my uncle's two poetic minutes, but to me it really seemed an eternity, until this important fellow gestured with his white-gloved hand somewhere toward the back of the hall. With a triumphant look, Uncle signaled for me to follow him and off we went.

We passed by windows with perfumes and various unfamiliar kinds of lady's paraphernalia, and by a glowing glass advertisement, with a mountain view, which invited us to spend the summer in the Tyrol Alps, thank you very much, but I could hardly accept, since a week later I was due to appear Under the Flags.

Through a revolving door, we made our way into a corridor, in which there were no longer any women with long cigarette-holders and men in tails, but rather, surrounding us everywhere, rushing waiters with trays of coffee and pastry. Beyond them we arrived at an iron door with the sign "Emergency Exit," and Uncle bravely stepped through. We started climbing down the cement stairway, our footsteps echoing from whitewashed bricks through this empty shaft, down and down to the bottom itself. There was another iron door there, which Uncle cautiously opened, and from there we were met by a blast of heat, the rumbling of pumps, and the hissing of steam. As you may have guessed, this was the boiler room. We walked along pipes and tanks, crossed here and there the puddles of water on the cement floor, until opposite us, all of a sudden, there stood a giant, black from coal and grease, and large as life. He glanced at us, and a moment after the white rose of his mouth dissolved in a joyful smile:

"Chaimle, brother!"

Uncle Chaimle gave him a gingerly hug, being especially cautious with his bright-colored, large-checked jacket, then looked at the palms of his hands and said, "This is my nephew Isaac, he's going to war. And this, Itzik, is my good friend Miklos, a Hungarian and a boiler-room stoker by profession."

Chokolom or something like that, said the Hungarian, giving me his big black hand.

Then we climbed up the little iron staircase, following him, and he ushered us into his room—two beds, gas stove, cast-iron sink.

We sat by the small table. Mr. Miklos, who was beaming at my uncle, suggested, "You'll sleep here. How about a beer? The road must've made you thirsty."

"I could go for a beer," responded my uncle.

The conversation was taking place in that strange language that was coined in our beloved Austria-Hungary, and which was used only in interethnic communication, so to speak—a federal Esperanto. Its foundation, or rather its skeleton, was German, but it was invaded impudently by language immigrants of Slavic origin, Hungarian, Hebrew, and even Turkish-Bosnian, who mistreated cases and genders, declensions and participles in a most hooligan-like manner. Yet every ethnic component of the great empire was using its own language, which was visited, of course, by all kinds of other distinguished linguistic guests. Even the Austrians among themselves used a language that they quite frivolously declared to be German, but if poor Goethe could hear them speak, he would hang himself on the first gas lamppost. Quite sometime later, when life put me in closer contact with the indigenous population of this Alpine country, it would've been easier for me to pay the tax on a dentist's practice than to explain to the relevant tax official that I wasn't a dentist. In the same way, when they asked Abramovich if he'd had any difficulties in Paris with his French, he replied: "I personally didn't have any difficulties, but the French people I was talking to—enormous difficulties."

While the Hungarian was fussing with glasses, bottles, and so on, my uncle patted me on the hand. "Have anything to say, soldier?"

"Gotta pee," I said in desperation.

Those were my first words since we had come into the marble world of Astoria. I said them in pure Yiddish, if the term "purity" can be used in regard to this amalgam of German, Slavic, and Assyrio-Babylonian.

SIX

What happened next is really not proper to tell, so let's hope Mama never finds out about it. We were in some kind of pub, Uncle and the Hungarian were quite drunk, and there were three women too. One of them, I have to admit, a very pretty girl, strong and white—she looked to me like a Hungarian peasant—kept pouring this Viennese *heurige* in my glass, young wine that takes the wrong road—not to your stomach, but straight to your head, and I was drinking and drinking it like the last fool. On the small stage a performance was taking place, girls were singing ditties that were not quite decent, lifting up their skirts and showing that thing at the front, and then that thing at the back. And the whole pub was singing, and people were embracing each other, and swaying back and forth to the rhythm of the song—just the way it's done all over our great empire. There were a lot of soldiers and I was feeling sick from the heavy stink of cigars and wine. After all, you know how it is at home in Kolodetz—the Poles were the ones who drank a bit more, whereas Dad would open a bottle of wine for Pesach and what was left of it he'd carefully cork up until Hanukkah.

Uncle hugged me and kissed me tenderly on the cheek. Then he announced to everyone: "My nephew's a soldier! My dear boy's going to war and he'll have his baptism by fire. A consecration! A second bar mitzvah!"

Bar mitzvah, as I told you, marks one's religious coming-of-age. I don't know who invented it—Moses, or King Solomon, or King David, but if you ask me, I don't think thirteen-year-old boys are mature. Anyway, my second bar mitzvah was supposed to make me ultimately mature, I guessed—I'm no fool. Miklos said something in Hungarian to my companion, she grabbed my hand, and dragged me after her, laughing.

"Where are we going?" I asked in confusion, even though, as I said, I could guess, it's just that I was shy in front of Uncle Chaimle.

"Go on, go on, my boy," he said.

The Hungarian woman sneaked me in somewhere behind the stage into a small room crammed with furniture, a mirror, wigs, and all kinds of theatrical stuff. She locked the door and sank into the sofa, giggling. It smelled of paint, glue, and perfume.

"It's warm," she said. Flushed and stimulated by the alcohol, she unbuttoned her velvet shirt as if her breasts had been waiting just for that.

She caught my eyes staring at those white, luscious peasant boobs, took my hand, and put it right there. I was drowning in sweat, and drunk, and my breathing was heavy. Everything in my sight was going double—the girl, the dim lamp at the mirror. I closed my eyes, hugged her, and said, "I love you, Sarah."

"I'm not Sarah, I'm Ilona," she corrected me.

I looked at her, laughed foolishly, and then the smile left my face. Closing my eyes again and relaxing, I saw Sarah, the greenish-gray sparkle of her eyes, Sarah behind a veil, unless it was the smoke of cigars. She was looking at me reproachfully.

"Hey, are you feeling sick?" said the Hungarian woman, pushing me slightly.

I opened my eyes again, they were full of tears, which must have been from the drinking. During the course of my life I've noticed that every time I get drunk, I tend to cry.

"What's the matter with you?" asked the girl, and slipped her hand down my trousers. She said: "You're not here, are you?"

I smiled guiltily, and shrugged my shoulders. By now I really wasn't there. My soul was away with Sarah.

SEVEN

On May 12 of the same year, we were standing in serried ranks, still in civilian clothes, suitcases at our feet, in the well-trodden yard of the barracks. We were not the same any more—familiar and unfamiliar boys from the towns and villages of our dear Galicia, Poles, Ukrainians, Jews, and God knows what else, we were the Reinforcements that His Majesty had summoned Under the Flags. At the end of the line, and a little bit to the side, stood the mobilized clergy. As you're familiar with the religious hodgepodge of our empire, you'll believe me when I tell you that in my opinion we were missing only a Tibetan lama.

To the sound of a brass band, a lieutenant mounted a small wooden platform, appropriately decked with banners and green branches; later we learned that this was Lieutenant Alfred Schauer, or Freddie, as we called him. He had sideburns and a mustache, just like Franz-Joseph. All career officers were trying to look like the father-emperor; there was something quite touching in this. He was, of course, a complete blockhead, I mean not Franz-Joseph but the lieutenant, but this is natural. If he hadn't been born like that he would've become not a lieutenant but a doctor, a seller of frankfurters, or at least he would've been grazing cows by the edge of our creek.

"Boys!" Lieutenant Schauer cried out. "Soon your dream will come true—to lay down your bones in ferocious battle for the glory of our emperor and the might of our dear motherland. Hurrah!"

To tell you the truth, I've never dreamed of laying down my bones for anyone, but the sergeant major—whom one of us soon nicknamed "Zuckerl," because he was fond of pinching our cheeks in a certain way that left a blue mark just as he would say, with passionate malice, "*Bist du, aber, süss,*" which meant he had come to really hate you—so this one sergeant major was staring so hard down the lines to see if we were all shouting "Hurrah!" that the lieutenant, I think, was able to see the uvulas in our throats.

Freddie Schauer then confided to us that things at the front line were going from better to best, victory had never been so near, and it was our high honor to bring it in on the tips of our bayonets. I don't know much about military strategy, but still it wasn't quite clear how we could bring it in on the tips of our bayonets—victory, that is, since before it could happen, we were, according to the dream, supposed to lay down our bones in ferocious battle, and so on and so forth. But this apparently was an example of patriotic poetry per se, as my dear uncle would have put it. I'm not sure if I was thinking all that at the time or if these are thoughts from nowadays. Let's not pretend I was a very bright young man, because it was only later, during this and that war, that I ate enough herring heads, so that these things about the patriotic slogans became clear to me. Do you know that one, about the herrings? Well then, a Pole and a Jew are on this train. The Pole opens his basket and starts eating a fat hen, while the Jew, dirt poor, is eating some bread with the cheapest thing in the world—the heads of salty herrings. The Polish guy asks: "Now, why do you Jews eat so many of these herring heads?" Says the Jew, "They make you really smart." "Is that so," said the Pole. "Why don't you sell me some?" "All right," says the Jew. "Five heads for five rubles." The Jew sells the heads, the other one eats them. Sometime later the Pole says: "Why did you charge me one ruble per head when a kilo of herring costs half a ruble?" "Don't you see," says the Jew, "how you're already getting smarter?"

So my point is that wisdom comes with experience, in other words, with the quantity of herring heads eaten, if you know what I mean.

Time went by. We were learning combat-by-bayonet—rip-rip, hit the ground, splash in the mud. Halt! Hit the ground! Halt! I'm ashamed to tell you how many times Sergeant Major Zuckerl would come up to me, straight up to me, this mustached turkey had eyes on his ass too, and pinch me so hard my cheek was blue and say, "You are so sweet! Let's try it now on our own. Hit the ground! Halt! Hit the ground! Halt!"

And so on.

So, there we were, sitting on the little patch of grass. Some soldiers were washing themselves at the sinks, tin soup bowls were clattering all around, the sunset was beautiful, quiet, and red.

"It's all stupidity," said Rabbi Shmuel, "the biggest stupidity and only stupidity. Why am I here, I'm asking you? To guide you and take care of your souls, so that when you die, you'll go all clean to our God Yahweh, eternal be His glory. The same is supposed to be done by my colleagues—Catholics, Adventists, Protestants, Orthodox, Sabbatarians, and Muslims—to honor the emperor and for the glory of their own God. And what's the point, I'm asking you? When I know that on the other side of the front line there's a fellow rabbi who's guiding our boys—who can tell me now if they're ours or not ours?—to fight against you, to kill you for the honor of their own emperor and for God, eternal be His glory. And then the war will end, and when the plows begin plowing all through Europe, and your bones come up shining white in the fields, ours and not-ours, all intertwined, then nobody will know for what God and which emperor you died. They say that up to this moment our dear motherland Austria-Hungary has given up more or less one and a half million dead. These are one and a half million boys who will not go back home, one and a half million mothers who will not meet them at the door and one and a half million brides who will not lie happily under them to get pregnant and give birth in peace and kindness. Well, I'm asking you, is the Lord not seeing all this? Or is He drowsing and picking his nose? Or is God too, glory to His name for the eternity of time, a senile old man, who is flattered by the fact that people are dying in His name? I don't know, my dear brothers, I cannot give you an answer. In any case, I'm thinking: If the Lord had windows, they would long ago have smashed His panes!"

The rabbi snapped shut the open prayer book and added, "This ends the Friday reading of the Chumash, a chapter from the Pentateuch, amen and *Gut Shabbos* to all."

It seemed to me, honestly, that his eyes were full of tears. Never in our shul in Kolodetz had he ever given a sermon with such feeling.

EIGHT

And so the days flowed by, and we diligently prepared, under the sharp eye of Sergeant Major Zuckerl and the wise leadership of Lieutenant Alfred Schauer, who would appear only rarely, for that great moment when, directed to the front line and screaming a powerful "Hoorah!" we would stab the chest of our cruel enemy with the bayonets of our guns, and those of us who wouldn't lay down their bones would bring victory to our grateful motherland at the point of their bayonets and so forth.

But as it is everywhere, all barracks are actually two barracks; one doesn't in any way resemble the other. In the first one you stomp your feet all day, military commands are shouted out, you sit under your gun, you clean the barrels of your gun with cleaning rods, soup barrels with fat and tasteless goulash are dragged around, soldiers' trousers, torn by pointless squatting, are mended. The second barracks is the kingdom of tenderness, where letters are read or written, photographs of Mama or the sweetheart are shown, dreams about home are dreamed with open eyes staring at the ceiling, dreams about the cows or the little brother, and most of all—I feel embarrassed to tell you something like this about such a fearless outfit as ours—the most frequent dream is about the end of the war, which for us hadn't even begun yet.

But the pinnacle of this kingdom of tenderness, its culmination, or better let's say its throne, was the latrine. This was a long whitewashed shack at one end of the barracks. High above the squatting place there were small windows kind of like vents —and if you stepped on the horizontal plank, you could look outside. And outside, on the sidewalk directly opposite, gathered young mothers and brides, news was shouted back and forth, best regards from Joshka, he said you should write, what else do you need, and other such tidings, seemingly unimportant, but dear to the soldier's heart. Outside, if you lifted your eyes from the sidewalk to the latrine, you could see the soldiers' faces, moved and even weeping, eyes full of love or concern, lips sending soundless kisses to those standing below, and other similarly touching portraits within the square frames of the windows. But if you looked from within, from the side of the latrine, you would see a different truth that was in the form of a line of bare soldiers' behinds, with their underpants pulled down. This was, so to speak, a military alert in case the observant Sergeant Major Zuckerl peeped inside. For this reason, and in order to prevent a sudden enemy attack at the rear, we would put one person on duty at the door. All it took was for him to cry out in alarm, "Zuckerl!" and only a second later we were peacefully squatting, the way it's expected from a military unit disciplined in every respect.

The sergeant major would poke his head in, look over the lines and invariably say, "And quick now, this is not a sanatorium!"

In this way Sarah and I managed to see each other. She was standing across with her brother, Rabbi Shmuel Ben-David, who had some sort of special military status and was able to go outside. As we gazed at each other, Sarah seemed to me divinely beautiful, with these huge, slightly willful almond-shaped eyes with a grayish-green sparkle, and her black curly hair, ending in a heavy braid. Such must have been in those ancient times of Galilee the daughters of Israel, who would comb their hair by the edge of the lake of Genezareth, from the depths of whose lunar waters the silvery little waves reflected the Eye of God, moved to tenderness.

"How are you?" asked Sarah.

"Fine," I said. "And you?"

She smiled and silently shrugged her shoulders.

The conversation, of course, wasn't going well. I'm not one of those who know at any moment what to say to a girl. But the rabbi had a clue and said, "I'll go to the pub for some cigarettes."

We were left alone, if "alone" means a whole line of mothers, grandfathers, or sisters, under the gallery of soldiers' portraits at the small windows, and everyone shouting, everyone wanting to know if the cow had calved. But still we were alone, we could hear only ourselves.

"Take care of yourself," she said.

"I will," I said.

"I hope it'll all be over soon and that you'll come home," she said.

"I hope so too," I said.

"I'll be waiting for you," she said after a long silence.

"All right," I said.

And those who understand will realize that in these words and in the pauses between them was hidden all the tenderness of Solomon's "Shir Hashirim," in other words, the Song of Songs, all the lyricism of the world, all the music, all the artful techniques, invented through the millennia, to express the little word "love." But not to soften your heart too much and God forbid to make you cry, I'll let you take a look inside the latrine, where you'll see me with my bare behind and pulled-down pants and then all the songs of Solomon will fly out of your head.

NINE

We were again standing in lines and we didn't look at all like the motley crew from the beginning. We were Brave Forces, and Lieutenant Schauer, who looked at us with pleasure, was strolling around with his arms behind his back, saying that the motherland was expecting great deeds from us. He also said that tomorrow was our big moment, when they would send us to the front. He said he could already see our heads crowned with laurel wreaths of triumph. I've always liked playing the fool, and so I patted my head. There was no such thing as a laurel wreath there. Sergeant Major Zuckerl quietly hissed: "Private Blumenfeld!"

"Yes, sir," I replied, and stood at attention.

In the morning the bugle was blowing. As of today we were going to listen only to military bugles, and maybe, with God's help, to trumpets of victory. In full military attire, with our packs, helmets, gas masks, folded tents, and aluminum canteens, we were sitting on the dusty cobblestone plaza, next to the gun pyramids, drinking tea for the last time.

Our rabbi Shmuel Ben-David was sitting next to me.

"You look pale," he said.

"I'm scared," I said.

"Come on, you're a man," he said. "Shame on you."

"Belly aches," I said.

"It's from fear. Go do your business, it'll make you feel better."

I got up, looked around and saw Zuckerl. "Sergeant Major, sir, reporting, my stomach hurts, may I be excused?"

"Go to it then and no fooling around, this is not a sanatorium!"

I ran toward the whitewashed shack, and while I was undoing my pants, heard someone shouting out from the other side of the street:

"Hey, is there a soldier in there? Hey, do you hear me? Is anyone there?"

I stood up on the plank, and looked outside: an elderly gentleman was standing there with a bowler and an umbrella.

"What is it?" I asked.

"The war is over. We lost," said the gentleman, with a Hungarian accent, and he didn't seem to be too disappointed about it either. "They just announced that a peace agreement has been signed."

At that moment the bugle started blowing, the soldiers were scrambling into lines, turmoil, commands, first company fall in, second, third, and so on.

And in this, so to say, sublime moment for any army, I was running toward the plaza, holding my pants up.

"The war is o-ver!" I shouted out, lifting my arms, even as my pants fell down.

Right in front of me, ominous as a stormy cloud, the sergeant major was coming.

"Private Blumenfeld, attention!" It isn't easy to stand at attention, salute and hold your pants up. "What are you jabbering about?"

"The war is over, Sergeant Major, sir! They've just announced it."

The thought was slowly penetrating the mysterious and unexplored chasms of his brain: "Is it for certain?"

"Affirmative, Sergeant Major, sir."

He was suddenly beaming: "So we won?"

I beamed. "No, Sergeant Major, sir. We lost."

He thought for awhile again, then pinched my cheek with his deadly pinch. "You're just so sweet! I love the Jews, and some day I'll do something big for them!"

He proved to be on the up-and-up, and kept his word: years later I met him again in the Flossenbürg Oberpfalz camp, where he was a Stürmführer.

ISAAC'S SECOND BOOK

The End of My War, or How I Became a Pole

ONE

I used to think that the end of a war would be something like the end of school—you get your diploma and whoopee, you toss your hat in the air, get drunk as a Cossack with your classmates, and, after you throw up in the toilet, hurl yourself into the waves of life. This is what I imagined. It turned out that the reality was only partially similar: you turn your back on one war, usually with low grades in history and geography, and it becomes your duty to raise them during the next war, and that one's already peeping just around the corner. The armistice you were expecting turns out not at all to be the beginning of the dreamed-of lasting peace; oh no, it's just a vacation between two courses of practical exercises, full of joyous emotions, of sticking the enemy's belly with a bayonet, digging trenches, blowing up things and people, attacks and counterattacks, burning other people's villages and hanging spies and deserters, while your enemy from the rival class does the same but in the opposite direction.

We waited and waited for demobilization, but all in vain. It just didn't come, and our life in the barracks didn't get any better at all, just the reverse. The rains started pouring down, the barracks yard turned into a pool of mud, and Sergeant Major

Zuckerl turned vicious. He would get us up to practice gas mask alerts in the middle of the night, and make us run and lie down in the mud with those disgusting and already redundant gas masks, which stank like a chemistry lesson and made us look like breathless frogs, and on top of that he was always screaming that for him the war wasn't over yet, and that the Jews, the Bolsheviks, and those macaroni-eaters, the Italians, were out to get something for nothing. And other patriotic speeches in front of the boys, all lined up in company formation, muddy up to the roots of their hair, their eyelashes sticky with sleep. What's more, as dessert to the main course, we would learn that the French are complete shitheads, the English, fags, and the Russians, dumb peasants who, whenever they get drunk, make a revolution. And since I hadn't been lucky enough to turn up at the front line itself, for reasons you already know, I couldn't quite understand how it was possible that we and our German allies—civilized, disciplined, and perfectly armed, equipped with gas masks and national doctrines polished to a sparkle, led by military geniuses like Hindenburg and Götzendorf—could lose the war against the shitheads, the fags, and the dumb peasants. Zuckerl would give his explanation—maybe a little debatable but still worth thinking about: it's the Jews' fault and only the Jews' fault—this I was also reading in some little newspaper or another and it was repeated so often that it was becoming self-evident and didn't even need any proof. There was this story about one great headquarters strategist, who was analyzing in Berlin the reasons for the catastrophic military defeat and formulated them clearly, but strayed a little from the scheme—it's the fault of the Jews and the bicycle riders. A shy voice breaks the contemplative silence that has seized the hall: And why the bicycle riders too, Mister General?

But let's go back to our barracks; military strategies are not a job for the mind of the simple soldier. Since I'm telling you about our sergeant major Zuckerl, who had now become really full of hate, and the midnight exercises under conditions of fake gasification in the surrounding area with the French gas "Iprite," I should add that to me personally the sergeant major had a, so to speak, individual approach—as if I personally had signed, and in Yiddish at that, the capitulation in that idiotic railway coach in the forest of Compiègne, to which the Germans would go back for a makeup exam years later. The sergeant major punished me for anything and everything by making me stand motionless and in full army gear under the pouring rain, and in vain were the efforts of my tzaddik—I told you this means a wise man or a spiritual guide—the rabbi Ben-David, to save me from these undeservedly heavy reparations for the lost war. On the other hand, I treated the poor martyr Zuckerl with deep understanding: the meaning of his life, full of jolly blaring trumpets and national aspirations, had collapsed in front of his eyes, and crumbling down was the temple with that one single icon—the radiant image of our emperor, may he rest in peace—Franz-Joseph, with a soldiers' choir of mobilized angels, and the chiming of the soldiers' soup tins, the clicking of the rifle bolts, and the clang of hobnailed boots. A great empire was sinking, somewhere into nothingness; more precisely, into a black or even a red uncertainty, and cheerful and lighthearted Vienna was slowly disappearing, along with that Danube, which Zuckerl, like most Austrians, still believed was blue. And in its somber grandeur, the ancient tragedy of the sergeant major's ideals was expressed in four words: "The war is over," and these words, I feel bashful about reminding you, had been pronounced by no one else but me. After all, I was that messenger who brought him news of defeat, and it is a well-known fact that in olden times the generous and wise kings and sultans would behead like nothing the bearers of bad news. Compared with those bloody medieval times, my stay under the rain in full military getup was just a tender stroke of destiny and a jest of generous benevolence on the part of Zuckerl. In other words, I was a complete fool, who, led by spontaneous and unaccountable joy, did not announce that tragic news more carefully and delicately, with deep empathy for the common misfortune that had befallen us, the way it's expected from a faithful subject, diligently trained in patriotic spirit, and a soldier of His Majesty. Like the fool Mendel, who was assigned the delicate mission of announcing to the wife that her husband, Shlomo Rubenstein, had had a heart attack while he was playing cards.

"I've just come from the café," he told her carefully.

"And Shlomo, my husband, he's probably there?"

"Yes, he is."

"And he's playing poker, probably?"

"Yes."

"And probably he's losing?"

"Yes, he is."

"To hell with him!"

"That's just where he's gone."

So what I mean is that at such a peak—or as the authors put it, at such a sublime moment in the tragic fate of an empire—I should have been more tactful.

But it was not just the sergeant major who was suffering because of the defeat—more and more frequently Lieutenant Schauer was turning up dead drunk in front of our victorious ranks. He was trying to deliver speeches to the effect that the great cause was as immortal as the empire itself and a day would come . . . and on and on with incomprehensible mumblings, yet already missing there were our bones, laid at the altar of our motherland, missing were our heads crowned with laurel wreaths of victory. As people say, history had introduced its light editorial corrections. And when he was sober, or pardon my rude expression, relatively less soused, he and the sergeant major would whisper something, then he would allow two suspicious-looking gentlemen in a carriage to enter into the courtyard of the barracks, and the four of them would lock themselves in the administrative buildings. After such closed-door plenary sessions, our observant eye could hardly fail to miss either the secret disappearance of blankets, boots, and other military stuff from the barracks, or the fact that our soup was supplying Ben-David with the metaphysical connection between the visits of the gentlemen in the carriage and the dramatically declining graph of the protein in the soldier's portions, about which he contemplatively remarked:

"They are stealing, my boy, stealing. After every collapse of ideals comes a widespread decline of morals. After the burning of the Temple and the destruction of Jerusalem by the Romans, the Jews also went looting. This is a most simple, and to a certain extent revolutionary redistribution of property. Whose are the blankets, I'm asking you? Don't believe that they belonged to the people, these are fables. They belonged to the empire. Is there an empire now? Seems there isn't. So?"

I was genuinely indignant: "And you're saying this with indifference—you, the rabbi! But theft is a violation of one of the Ten Commandments!"

"It's okay, there are nine left," Ben-David comforted me, but his mind was obviously somewhere else. He looked as if he wasn't really there. His spirit was far away.

It was a while ago that I'd noticed that some bug had entered the head of my future—with God's blessing—brother-in-law. He'd become pensive or, more precisely, focused on something, on some impermissible and forbidden thought, which was eating him inside. Just like the time when the policeman asked Saul Kogan from Berdichev if he didn't have thoughts on the political situation, and he said: "Of course, I have, but I don't agree with them." Apparently Ben-David didn't agree with his either. I even asked the rabbi one time about this strange encounter I had witnessed through the latrine window. I had pulled down my pants and as usual stepped on the plank and was looking through the square window to see if there was anyone who might share the latest gossip, when I caught a glimpse of the two of them—the rabbi and Esther Katz—talking to each other, and then they went off to the nearby pub. So, as I said, I asked him about it in all innocence and with no wicked intent.

"Ask less. These days that's the healthy way," he snapped.

And I stopped asking about just what it was that Esther Katz, on the pavement across the way, opposite the soldiers' latrine, was there for. I vaguely knew this beautiful and fragile woman, with a man's haircut, who seemed always to be smoking, even in her sleep. She would appear infrequently around our part of Galicia; they said she was some kind of a lawyer. In David Leibovich's café she would chat with our people about this and that in Yiddish, with the rabbi she spoke perfect German, and with my teacher Eliezer Pinkus, may he rest in peace, perfect Russian. Floating after her, just like the transparent scarf she was always wrapping casually around her delicate neck, was the rumor that she was, at one time, a French, and at another time, a Russian spy, but she wasn't. In other years and amid events to which you will be a witness, it turned out that some Jewish Mata Hari she wasn't, but simply a Bolshevik activist from Warsaw—one of the most faithful and most uncompromising ones, whom the Bolsheviks shot down with the strongest passion—sometimes as Trotskyists, other times as Japanese agents. But this happened much later; you'll learn about it when the time comes.

As I've already told you, I don't consider myself very smart, but neither am I such a fool as not to figure out the connection between the appearance of Esther Katz and the small printed pieces of paper that spread among the soldiers. To be honest, they contained definitions that were quite disturbing and offensive to our great empire: the holy war, under whose banners we were gathered, was defined as imperialistic, and we, the soldiers of His Majesty, as mere cannon-fodder; and they spoke about the nations that were moaning under the boot of that European gendarme Austria-Hungary and its bloody emperor (I pictured him, that gendarme, as something in between Sergeant Major Zuckerl and the Polish policeman Pan Voitek, and, of course, with the sideburns of Franz-Joseph). And joking aside, the text of these leaflets seemed to me to a certain extent fair, but bombastic and difficult to understand, and some statements downright exaggerated. Not that we lived a rich life and everything was butter and honey; it was just the other way around. Most of us lived modest existences on the verge of poverty, but I don't remember anyone in our land moaning under anyone's boots, even less so under the boot of His Majesty—this was pure slander, because he hadn't even set foot in Kolodetz by Drogobych. Uncle Chaimle on this occasion would have said that this was just a sample of political propaganda per se.

I asked Rabbi Ben-David to elucidate for me the origin and purpose of the leaflets, and he replied again, "Think with your head and not with your mouth."

I thought with my head and finally I came up with the conclusion that we were standing on the verge of great changes, which would turn our life inside out the way my father used to turn the old caftans inside out, so that they could look—with a little imagination and good will—like new. Flying all the way up here were rumors about the events occurring in Russia, and about a similar mess that was perhaps brewing in our lands too, and in Germany. Sometime before that, like a distant echo from lightning that had struck somewhere beyond the mountains, rumors had reached as far as Kolodetz about some revolt of our sailors from the Austro-Hungarian fleet in Kotor Bay, or as they call it there, in the distant Adriatic shore of Montenegro—Boka Kotorska. But, as I've already told you, I wasn't very interested in politics, while politics itself was showing a growing interest in me. Maybe this was the reason why the people from the military police who came to rummage around under the straw mattresses, through the soldiers' wooden footlockers and in the pockets of their overcoats, took only me out in front of the line of soldiers stretched out along the iron beds and dug not only in that intimate place of mine to my rear. I was standing there naked and disgraced, I had taken off even the underwear my mother made for me, some soldiers tried to giggle, but their laughter froze in the air like an icicle under the fierce look of Sergeant Major Zuckerl.

"What have you read recently?" asked some important military police hotshot with thick glasses through which his eyes unnaturally protruded.

I gave him a look of childlike innocence. "The Bible."

"Show it to me."

Oops, what was I going to do now, since I had no such thing? But Rabbi Ben-David, who was sitting at the end, together with the other field chaplains, saved the situation: "It's with me—in storage, dear gentleman. I interpret the different chapters for him, because he's a little slow."

"This is good. This is very good," said the military police boss, blessing the endeavor without clarifying what was good—that I was a dimwit, or that I had to have the Bible explained to me. "And what else have you read recently? Some small pieces of paper, leaflets, petitions?"

To pretend to be a fool, in order to survive, is an old Jewish art, comparable only to ancient Greek architecture, more precisely the Parthenon. I said, "We read, as a group, Mister Boss, only the field newspaper. It has everything that a soldier and a patriot needs!"

The boss looked at me through his thick lenses. "Are you a Jew?"

"Yes, sir!"

Apparently he did not believe me, because he lifted up with the tip of his cane that certain little thingy of mine that hangs down under the belly button, and fixed his myopic eyes on it.

His amazement gradually developed into explicit astonishment; he was silent for a while, looked around, thought for a minute, and finally slapped me with satisfaction on the bare shoulder. "All right, get dressed!"

With a triumphant look I searched out the eyes of Zuckerl, but they were forecasting a long and heavy stay with my gun—in the rain. Apparently the sergeant major was disappointed that they did not find *Das Kapital* under my armpits, or at least a photograph of Lenin or Leo Trotsky with banners flying in the background.

With a look of regret and a little bit of guilt, Rabbi Shmuel Ben-David cast a glance at me and slightly shrugged his shoulders. He had his arms crossed on his chest, in a God-fearing and humble manner, like the other shamans next to him—God's folks, above suspicion.

TWO

Just in case, Zuckerl hardened the regime and put an end to any sort of city leaves and other caprices, such as visits to the military infirmary, situated in the requisitioned brothel in the small town, in which anyway there were neither whores nor doctors anymore and only our poor doctor's assistant, who prescribed a dose of salts and disinfection of the bed with carbolic acid for every single thing—from sprained ankle to duodenal ulcer. And just at this moment in my biography, when almost all of our glorious military unit was hit by a, so to speak, epic diarrhea, caused probably by spoiled horsemeat that was quite artlessly imitating veal, and half of our personnel was almost constantly to be found in the latrine—right at this moment I received a letter from Sarah. The envelope had already been opened and then glued back again with brown shoemaker's glue. I feel shy about telling you, but truth stands above all: I opened the letter and read it over and over again, squatting in the latrine, with tears running abundantly down my cheeks. Here is the moving letter, I don't want to hide anything:

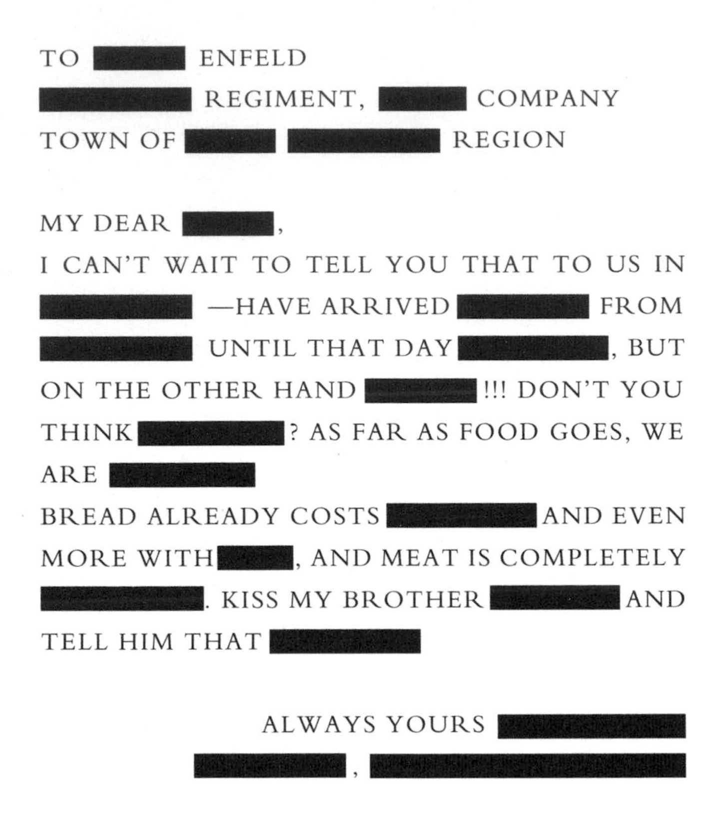
TO ▇▇▇ ENFELD
▇▇▇ REGIMENT, ▇▇▇ COMPANY
TOWN OF ▇▇▇ ▇▇▇ REGION

MY DEAR ▇▇▇,
I CAN'T WAIT TO TELL YOU THAT TO US IN ▇▇▇ —HAVE ARRIVED ▇▇▇ FROM ▇▇▇ UNTIL THAT DAY ▇▇▇, BUT ON THE OTHER HAND ▇▇▇!!! DON'T YOU THINK ▇▇▇? AS FAR AS FOOD GOES, WE ARE ▇▇▇
BREAD ALREADY COSTS ▇▇▇ AND EVEN MORE WITH ▇▇▇, AND MEAT IS COMPLETELY ▇▇▇. KISS MY BROTHER ▇▇▇ AND TELL HIM THAT ▇▇▇

ALWAYS YOURS ▇▇▇
▇▇▇, ▇▇▇

I was reading the letter squatting, as I already mentioned, under the small windows through which for a long time now you couldn't see either those folks with the pregnant cow or the relatives of Joshka, and I was crying with deep emotion—not so much because of what was written or scratched in black ink, but because of the unwritten white lines, in which, I had no doubt, she was telling me how much she was waiting for me and how much she missed me, and how nice and mild the fall was in Kolodetz, and how she was dreaming of us sitting in the ravine above the river, and other tender things, which no censor was able to read, much less scratch out.

I showed the letter to Rabbi Ben-David. He carefully looked at it and said, "The political development is good, there's a lot of scratching out. And the more censored lines there are, the better it will be."

"I don't get it," I said.

"Just before dawn, my brother, the night is darkest. When the censorship gets so thick-witted with panic and fear that it tries to scratch out even the song of nightingales, it means the end is near. Do you get it now?"

"I like this," I said emotionally, "about the song of the nightingales."

Moved to the bottom of my heart, I hugged the rabbi, and touched my lips to his graying beard.

"I'm sorry," he said, "that I called you in public 'a little slow'!"

"Oh, my God, I'd already forgotten it."

"Don't forget it, it's the truth itself. That business about the nightingales is metaphoric, I didn't mean it for my sister, and even less so for you. The nightingales sing before dawn, and to try to scratch out such prophecies is a sure sign that the end is near. And now, run to the can, I feel your end is near too."

But still, I was left with the impression that the business about the nightingales was exactly how I'd understood it, but the rabbi didn't like to have his sentiments caught in their underwear.

Once again it was Shabbos evening, quiet and, as if by a miracle, with no rain. Gone was the little grass corner next to the barbed wire that had been playing the role, so to say, of a military *beys keneses*, a place for ritual prayers. Everything had long ago turned into soggy mud, which malignantly squelched under the boots. That is why we, the group of Jewish boys from our company, were sitting on the chopped wood next to the kitchen, and our rabbi was holding open the scrolls of a small *sefer Torah*, and according to the prescribed custom he was supposed to read the *Derasha,* a certain passage from the *Tanakh.* But this time, apparently, Ben-David did not intend to interpret the stories, very instructive in every respect (though we were really fed up with them), of the seven skinny cows that gobbled up the seven fat ones but still remained skinny, because he went straight to the Shabbos sermon:

"There's news, so don't notice that I'm pretending to be reading from the Law, and don't jump up. There is no Austria-Hungary anymore, if you know what I mean. This fall our teachers will not be telling in a smooth singsong about our great empire, but will be stuttering when they have to show the children where exactly the borders of Hungary or Czechoslovakia are, and explain to them the hidden meaning, and whether in general there *is* any meaning in the fact that Slovenia, Bosnia, Herzegovina, and Montenegro have gone from the rotten empire of the Habsburgs to another—that of the Karageorgievs. The Russian geography teachers will have to give up the habit of calling Poland our western provinces; in the Baltics, they will take down the Russian flag from the flagstaffs; moreover the Russians themselves will for a long time argue, quite loudly, what color their flag should be—tricolored or red. The old teachers will scratch their behinds when asked about the national affiliation of South Tyrol, Dobrudja, Zibenburgen, or Galicia and whose subjects are the Moldavians or the Finns. History, friends, like a deft card dealer, has shuffled the deck and dealt them again—everything from the beginning again, the game starts anew, the bets have been made and we have yet to see who's stuck an ace up his sleeve, who'll get four spades, and who a lonely seven of clubs. This is the law of nature—the strong devour the weak, but their appetite is too big for their digestive system, and because of that they get the runs and acid, which are cured with revolutions. The latter, in their turn, create chaos, and chaos begets new worlds and you hope the world tomorrow will be less shitty than the one today. And so on—till the next deck of cards is dealt, that is—till the next war. It won't be late—the dragon teeth of revenge are sown in the fertile soil of Europe and will give a rich crop, believe me. *Gut Shabbos*, boys, and go home in peace!"

All this mess with the promotion of the empire to a skinned cow in a slaughterhouse ended for us on October 28, 1918, with the creation of the so-called "Liquidation Commission" in Krakow, and on November 14 of the same year. . . .

THREE

. . . Well, that was the day my next historic dream came true, so to speak—one more line from my personal national doctrine and I became a subject of Poland. You'll die laughing, but I went to war as an Austro-Hungarian, and came home a Pole. Not that I emigrated to another country or, say, ran away to distant lands. No, I came back to my dear old Kolodetz by Drogobych, with that spoiled coquette—the little river in the valley, with the same little Catholic church on this side, and the Christian Orthodox temple on the other side of the river, with the same little white synagogue, which looked like anything but a shrine of Yahweh, and even with the same café of David Leibovich, where once upon a time Liova Weissmann used to show his exciting bits of films. But now this was within the borders of the United, Indivisible, and Sacred Land of Poland, the Inalienable, Ancestral Motherland. Sorry about overdoing the capital letters, I know it's just the same as overdoing black pepper in borscht, but I've got no other means of expressing the historic pathos of the moment when the Germans delivered to us the duly certified new boss of Poland, Joseph Pilsudski, may Adonai put him up there on His right knee.

And here, my dear brother, begin my real troubles with this chronicle, which will lose its native vignettes, pizzicatos, and caprioles and start moving, just like the dusty and monotonous roads of our Carpathian foothills, a little bit upward, a little bit downward, up again, down again, and so on all the way to the horizon, with neither abysses nor dizzying peaks. Which reminds me of the rabbi Ben Zvi, who rented a carriage to take him to the next shtetl. So the rabbi and the driver made a deal and took off. At the first little hill, the driver asked the rabbi to get off and push because the horse was skinny and feeble. So Ben Zvi got down and pushed up to the top. Then the driver asked him to pull the carriage down, and so it went, hill after hill, Ben Zvi was either pushing or pulling, till they reached their destination. In front of the synagogue the rabbi paid the driver and said: "I understand, my dear, why I came here—I have a sermon to give at the synagogue. I also understand why you came here—you have to earn your bread, after all. The only thing I don't understand is why we took with us this poor horse!"

With this I don't mean to say that you, my dear reader, are the poor horse, whom I have to pointlessly drag up and down the hilly monotony of life, but if we look at it objectively—well, my apologies, but this is how it seems. Moreover, in the beginning I promised you I would step on two whales, just as the ancients did, one being the First World War, and the other, naturally, the Second. And what do you think is there between those two, I mean not between the two wars, but between the two whales? Water. It's as clear as day.

On the other hand, though, if you were to take a look at even one little drop of this water through the microscope of my favorite teacher, Eliezer Pinkus, may he rest in peace, you would see that there is only seeming emptiness and that there, in the water drop, it is bursting with such life as you couldn't find even in the center of Lemberg, which is now Lvov. Amoebas and other one-celled creatures are living their regular but quite intense routines. They get together and reproduce, they look for something or someone to eat up, and there probably are dramatic separations—especially when one paramecium splits up and its two halves will never meet again in life. You can also see even with your naked eye little fish who, seemingly surprised, as if they'd just run into an old acquaintance, are just about to say "Oh!" when in fact they're devouring a whole company of plankton together with its sergeant major. But don't start crying with astonishment at the great mystery of Nature; this is the only thing I remember from my biology lessons and in this particular case I'm using it as a metaphor.

Because of the aforementioned reason, I don't want to bother you with petty details from our life of amoebas and occasionally of fish who seem about to say "Oh!" but just devour you like nothing, if you know what I mean. This is of no interest to anyone and it's doubtful whether it will wet God's eye with the moisture of compassion. In this sense I understand and modestly share the outlook of our great teachers and prophets from biblical times, who composed line after line, and manuscript after manuscript, The Book of Books, in our language the Law, or the Torah. They knew where their story should run slowly and widely like a river at high water, and where events, like a wild waterfall, should rush down right before your eyes with astounding velocity. At such places in the Bible, where you don't even have the time to stop and look around at the surrounding area, my ancient teachers of composition and the description of things take full liberty to walk the road they want, with the big strides of a hundred Roman *stadii* each. For example: "Adam knew his wife again (you know what they mean, it's not about a regular acquaintance) and she gave birth to a son and gave him the name of Seth. The days of Adam after he begat Seth were another eight hundred years and he begat sons and daughters. And all the days of Seth were a hundred and twelve years, and all the days of Enoch were a hundred and five years, and all the days of Mahalalel were eight hundred and ninety-five years. . . ." And so on, my dear reader, let me not burden your mind with more examples. I am talking about this big stride of my writing ancestors and prophets, may their memory live eternally and unto the end of time, because they left us writing that is being read over and over again, and everyone interprets it his own way and reads it over again, and like this—one thousand, then two thousand, then three thousand years, not like a newspaper that if it's yesterday's, it doesn't serve any other purpose but to wrap salty fish in it. And please don't dare, and if you do may God forgive you, cast a shadow of doubt over the truthfulness of this writing, because it contains a lot of wisdom and it's flowing like the springs of David in the Judaic desert and offers you knowledge for all situations in life. And they're not shamming, the prophets, seized by God's inspiration or by the desire to impress you when they're speaking of people who lived eight hundred or even nine hundred years. If you look at it formally, and from the low point of view of a coldblooded frog, this definitely contradicts science, but I think that in those mighty times of Genesis, thick and strong like a heavy Easter wine, every full moon marked a yearly circle in the life of the oaks and the people, and our human time is measurable with the biblical as the river paramecium with the diamond or the sparrow with the eagle.

But I got carried away and now with God's help I will try to turn and go back to the main path, from which I strayed like old man Noah, who fell asleep Between the Rivers and when he woke up, found he'd landed at the top of Ararat.

And so, let's come down from that distant peak of the Ark and go to our Kolodetz by Drogobych, where I'm standing, with a shy half-smile, the wooden footlocker at my feet.

My mother broke into tears and did not stop covering my now manly face with kisses, my father was more severe and composed, and gave me a rather rough pat on the shoulder, but I noticed the moisture in his eyes.

My mother said, "My dear boy! I can imagine what you've gone through, down there in the trenches. Such horrible things they say about the Senegalese!"

"What Senegalese?" I asked.

"The French, the black ones. They ate up the prisoners of war alive!"

"Yes, sometimes . . . ," I mumbled. Not that it was vanity that prevented me from telling the whole, so to say, gray and prosaic truth; moreover, apart from me, our rabbi Ben-David was also familiar with it, but I just didn't want to destroy, in the eyes of my dear parents, the invisible but heroic monument they'd erected for me.

While Mama was bustling around preparing the food—doubtlessly a festive dinner with our famous stuffed, or *gefilte*, fish, which I have detested since childhood, though I was obliged to partake of this common, and, as they claim, world-famous glory or even triumph of Judaism—Uncle Chaimle and I went over to David Leibovich's café. There my uncle bought for everyone who had the luck to share this historic moment a glass of marvelous wheat vodka and he did it with such a flourish it was as if we'd won the war, and won it mostly owing to my heroic deeds. They started asking me about one thing and another and I was ready to answer—including about the Senegalese! —but just then our rabbi entered the café and I instantly deflated like a French reconnaissance balloon shot down by a German Fokker. The interest of the Kolodetz military analysts, led by the postman Avramchik, who, if you haven't forgotten, participated in the Russo-Turkish war as a signalman, was immediately transferred to the rabbi and he was literally bombarded with questions.

I don't want to say anything bad about the Jews, God forbid—you know I am one—but you've probably noticed that unusual passion, I would say obsession, with which they ask questions and are in no way, no way at all, interested in the answer, because they know it in advance or so it seems to them. And if your answer isn't what they'd expected, hard luck for you: then they tumble you up and down inside an avalanche of arguments, smash you down under an iceberg of proof, and at the end finish you off by sticking you up against the wall like you were wallpaper, with a quote from either the Bible or Karl Marx. For a similar case in life I can give you the following advice: if Jews bombard you with questions, listen to them calmly and go smoke a cigarette in the room next door. They won't notice your absence at all but will start arguing among themselves. There's another way out: instantly, at that very moment, agree with them and in no way take up the catastrophic initiative of disagreeing with them. This option, by the way, is probably even wiser. Like this rabbi of whom they asked: "Rabbi, what in your opinion is the shape of the Earth?" "Round," said the rabbi. "Why round? Can you prove it?" "Well, then, let it be a square, am I going to argue?"

In our case, however, Rabbi Ben-David did something, to tell you the truth, a little mean: he calmly listened to the questions, accompanied by comments, references to historic sources and their respective quotes, and he neither answered nor agreed nor disagreed, but generously pointed to me with his hand: "Why are you asking me—a, so to say, rearguard rat—something like a mess supplier or a shopkeeper of God's Word, who hasn't even touched a weapon? Here, ask *him*—he's the fighter, he'll tell you how he protected the motherland with full army equipment, with a bayonet stuck on his gun and a gas mask gassed by the French in the pouring rain!"

All faces, just as if obeying a command, turned to me, and in them I read admiration and respect, and if I am not exaggerating, even adoration. Thank God, at this hour in the café of David Leibovich there were only Jews and, as I told you, no one was interested in the answers to their questions.

Please don't think that I'm deliberately delaying my meeting with Sarah by using trite literary techniques to create suspense—suspense itself exists in the natural order of things. My soul was flying to Sarah, longing for her, I was telling her a hundred times in my thoughts everything that had built up in my heart. "My dear," I would say, "my one and only little bird! Dream of my dreams and blooming peony, my quiet Saturday joy! Your two little bubbies—" Wait, this bit about the little bubbies is from King Solomon and does not refer to Sarah! I'm taking it out but I won't start all over again, because no matter how I approach it, I'll still slide down the ancient track and fall into the arms of Shulamit. And it wasn't her that I loved, but Sarah, may the author of the Songs of Songs forgive me.

Sarah and I met as soon as the next morning. I pretended to be strolling just by chance with Ben-David to the synagogue—or was it the other way around?—the rabbi pretended to invite me just by chance to walk with him. Then he casually suggested, "Why don't you come in and have a glass of tea?"

And I casually shrugged my shoulders in agreement and then I saw her: she was carrying a basket of laundry on her hip, her sleeves rolled up, bare feet in slippers, her wet shirt open and revealing a tiny part of what wouldn't have escaped the eye of King Solomon either.

We stared at each other like complete fools, and the rabbi, so it seemed to me, was enjoying our embarrassment. Eventually she said, first wiping her hand on her skirt and then shaking my hand, "How are you?"

"Fine," I said. "And you?"

"I'm fine, too. Please, come in."

"All right," I said.

I had forgotten all about the little birds, and the blooming peonies, and my quiet Saturday joys. I don't know why people are so shy about expressing openly in front of the world their longing for each other, the most powerful and tender natural attraction, but they pretend to be proud or indifferent and they don't consider, especially if they're young, that the sands of our life have been measured by God unto the last grain and that every carelessly wasted second of love sinks irreversibly into eternity. And the young, don't they figure out that in this voice of the heart is hidden all the strength of humankind, all the divine meaning of its existence, with all its pyramids, Homers and Shakespeares, Ninth Symphonies and Rhapsodies in Blue, all the admirable beauty of the verse for Shulamits and Juliets, and the different Nefertitis, Mona Lisas, and Madonnas?!

But one way or the other, we were sitting by the table in the little parlor of Ben-David; Sarah and I didn't dare look at each other and now, while the dear rabbi is pouring the tea, I'll show you by example how long a biblical phase is: exactly nine months and ten days from the moment I sank my spoon in the tea cup, the mohel was circumcising our little boy, to whom we proudly gave the name of my grandfather—may he rest in peace—Elia, Ilyusha for short. Or as they say: "A boy was born and God's blessing came upon the earth."

All night I was playing, or if you'd rather call it, screeching on the violin, good Jewish men and women with heavy shoes were dancing and singing old songs, clapping hands to the rhythm, while I myself, my father and mama, then Uncle Chaimle and the already-graying Ben-David were dancing the Ukrainian *gopak*. Sarah was still exhausted from the delivery but boundlessly happy, and Mama wasn't letting her do a drop of work—not even pour vodka for the guests. Pan Voitek came, he wasn't a policeman anymore but the mayor of Kolodetz, and he brought a huge white round loaf of bread, covered with a white linen cloth. And other neighbors too—Polish and Ukrainian—came along to raise a glass to the health of little Ilyusha. The only people who didn't come were the local Catholic priest, who was in any case a pure anti-Semite, and the Christian Orthodox priest Theodore, who kept to himself because of that old reason, which you already know, related to the misunderstanding that changed the faith of humankind, specifically that it wasn't Christ who kissed Judas on the forehead, which is what I think happened, but the other way around. This is a separate story, it has nothing to do with anti-Semitism, and it's purely our own internal issue whom we should crucify and whom we shouldn't, as far as Yeshua is concerned; in other words, Christ and Judas are our own Jews, not from Kolodetz, of course, but this doesn't change anything. Anyway, the priest didn't come.

So all through that wonderful day and during the following long night after the Eighth Day, when our rabbi Shmuel Ben-David laid on a pillow of purple velvet his little crying nephew by the name of Elia Blumenfeld, whom the mohel then carefully circumcised to bring him into the bosom of Abraham, and when neighbors were coming in one after the other, like the wise men to the Virgin at the cave outside Bet Lehem, or Bethlehem as you call it, then I, happily embracing Sarah, deeply understood that all people—it doesn't matter who—the Jews, the Poles, or even if you take the Bushmen from the Kalahari desert—are created by God, glory to His name, to love each other, and not to wage war against each other. This was the real end of my war and the beginning of the profound peace that I concluded in my soul with all human beings, may they be blessed by His generosity with goodness and wisdom!

There is one more circumcision coming up—my second son Joshua seems to have been hiding behind the door and came up right after his brother. I already told you that Joshua, or Yeshua, means Jesus (it's the Greeks' fault because they couldn't pronounce a bunch of sounds and in this way misled humanity) but this is a different issue too. I don't mean to offend anyone, I'm just reminding you that the Christian Son of God Yeshua was also circumcised on a purple velvet pillow and I'll just use the occasion to be a nuisance to you with my old joke about Mordechai, who couldn't figure out why his Polish neighbor would send his boy to a seminary:

"Because," said the neighbor, "he can become a priest."

"So what?" asked Mordechai, surprised.

"Then he can become a cardinal!"

"And, so?"

"And one day he can even become pope!"

"So?"

The neighbor got upset. "What do you mean 'so'? A pope! What do you want him to become—God?"

"Why," said Mordechai, "one of our boys did, didn't he?"

Sarah and the children and I had a little house with a little vegetable garden, not far from my father's workshop, you remember, Mode Parisienne. I was of course working there, not as an apprentice anymore but as an equal, so to say, associate, and from the thought of hitting me with a wooden yardstick on the head, my father was very far. On the one hand, my heroic past from the war had changed his attitude toward me, and on the other, I was now really far from being that silly boy who would lose his mind over fiacres and ladies in pink.

FOUR

And so my life went on as a subject of the *Zhech Pospolita*, in other words, a Polish citizen—up and down, and up and down again along the gray, as I've already put it, hills of everyday life—turning old caftans inside out, and, with the craftsmanship of the Jewish tailor, from a piece of cloth barely enough even for one suit cutting not only the suit but an additional vest, with an occasional symbolic slap for Ilyusha, and also for Yeshu, whom everyone called "Schura"—the Russian nickname for cut-up—because the two of them literally, as we say, "crushed the onions in the garden," in other words, were always up to some mischief or other, for which I in my turn would get a soft, mildly reproachful look from their mother, Sarah. Oh, Lord God, Sarah, how I loved her! How she filled my life to overflowing—it takes my breath away—the kind, the good, the silent, the faithful. And now, in my old age, when I'm writing these lines and she is long gone, my eyes fill up with bitter tears of remorse, because I never told her this, never—not even when she left for the mineral baths with the children. . . . No, this will come later, it is still early for the mineral baths and everything that followed! And as the stallions of my story impatiently and wildly gallop through time, I've almost missed that point in Sarah's and my life—or if you'd rather call it, that milestone—behind which peeps a sweet face with freckles and reddish blond hair like mine, and grayish green eyes like Sarah's: our child Susannah, our third in order of appearance.

The family had gotten bigger. From the carpenter Goldstein we had to order a new, bigger table, because at the Shabbos dinner we were a bit too many—my father and my mother, and Uncle Chaimle, who never got married, Sarah and me, the children, and not too rarely—when he wasn't engaged in his strange and somewhat secretive affairs—our dear rabbi Shmuel Ben-David. Sometimes my sister and her husband, the assistant pharmacist Shabtsi Krantz, from Lvov, would stop by. I mentioned the carpenter Goldstein, and don't be surprised that in our modest, and sometimes even poor part of the world, there were mountains of Goldbergs,* and there were zillions of Goldsteins and the Zilbersteins, not to mention veins of more precious stones like rubies. And all this wealth was spread out in the lavish flower gardens of Rosenbaums, Blums, Krantzes, Lilienthals, and, excuse me, Blumenfelds. There was also one iceberg, Isidor Eisberg, but I swear, he had nothing to do with the fatal end of the *Titanic.* And maybe the poorest resident of Kolodetz was the widow Golda Zilber, this was her name—gold and silver—who for pennies at the market would sell roasted pumpkin seeds. Don't think, please, that this time again, following an old Jewish habit, I'm making a detour from the story, taking a short cut through Odessa to Berdichev, but I was talking about our new Shabbos table. And on these Friday nights, after dinner and everything else that was due by ritual, people

* Goldberg—"Golden Mountain," Zilberstein—"Silver Stone," etc. [Mr. Blumenfeld's note]

ate seeds—pumpkin seeds, not sunflower. Sunflower seeds were a specialty of the Ukrainian women, leaning over their fences, crunching seeds with fantastic speed, performing all sorts of technological operations with the tongue alone, and when spitting seeds, capable of hitting you with them on the forehead from a distance of two Russian versts. No, the Jews, sitting around the table, are eating pumpkin seeds on Shabbos evening—eating them slowly, with dignity, and intently talking about life. It's hard for me to calculate the amount of information that was exchanged on one Shabbos night in Kolodetz around the festive tables, to the crunching of pumpkin seeds, with the rare seconds of silence filled by the quiet and pensive cracking of seeds between the teeth, like logs quietly crackling in the fireplace. Some call it the "Jewish newspaper," but this, in my opinion, is simply a poor description, because the amount of news, rumor, gossip, and data of all sorts—starting with political news about Soviet Russia all the way to the comet, which, according to some clairvoyant, was rushing with insane speed toward Earth, and would supposedly lead to an inevitable catastrophe—they couldn't fit into any one newspaper on the whole planet. And to this if you add the ever-present stories for boosting self-esteem that are as a rule decorated with fantastic and simply incredible details, fruit of the rich Kolodetz imagination, about the banker Rothschild and Lord Disraeli, and about Leon Blum also being a Jew, and then the reverse, for suppressing our growing pride—about that anti-Semite, equal to Nebuchadnezzar and all our ill-wishers put together, who seems to be about to grab power in Germany, even though he is an Austrian sergeant major or something—Adolf Schicklgruber—you'll understand that I do not exaggerate when I compare this Shabbos exchange of thoughts and knowledge accompanied by the crunching of pumpkin seeds to the library of Alexandria, with all its papyruses, parchment scrolls, and cuneiform clay tablets. And a tragedy not less than the end of this library of Alexandria took place that Friday, when at the market some Polish *pan* from Tarnov kicked old Golda Zilber's basket because she happened to be standing in his way, and the seeds spilled out all over the mud. This was the death, right in front of the eyes of the astonished residents of Kolodetz by Drogobych, of hundreds of papyruses with news, gossip, and knowledge, thousands of rolls of parchment and handmade Arabian paper, tons of clay tablets with wise saws and jokes, kilometers of telegraph tickertape with reports from Soviet Russia, and news about the comet that keeps dashing toward Earth and Baron Rothschild and that evil fiend and philistine Adolf Schicklgruber —all of these, hidden in those seemingly miserable baked pumpkin seeds, so contemptuously called the "Jewish newspaper," were now rolling in the mud in front of the weeping and desperate Golda.

It isn't good to brag about charity—it's something spiritual and discreet—but let me tell you anyway that we collected money and paid for Golda's pumpkin seeds, and even the mayor Pan Voitek produced a passionate curse in Russian, addressed to that idiot from Tarnov, and gave his share. By the way, I don't know why, but all of us—Jews, and Ukrainians, and Russians—all cursed in Russian. Much, much later, after that other war, when I visited the country of Israel—both for work and just simply to see the land of my ancestors—I noticed again that phenomenon: Babylon is just a chirping kindergarten, compared to this Tower of Babel in that new country of ours, may Yahweh bless it with peace. Everyone there speaks the language he brought with his luggage, and everyone has his own specific opinion on all issues of politics, war, and existence, but once you get to swearing, there suddenly arises a national monolithic unity—everybody swears in Russian. Why this should be so, I can't say. Maybe some linguist will decode this phenomenon, so unique in its glamour and richness of expression.

I still went through Odessa to reach Berdichev, but tell me, brother, can you change what is given to one by God and is, so to speak, in one's blood? Can you make the tiger eat grass or the fish build itself a nest in that poplar over there, let alone keep a Jew from going off the straight path of his story, here and there—once to pick a little yellow flower, another time just to look around, breathe in the fresh air, share with you how beautiful God's wide world is, and tell you in relation to this or that either a joke or a *khokhma*?! Or a Jew stops to watch a herd of cows and to give valuable advice to the herder, even though he hasn't milked even a single cow in his entire life. He likes to give advice, he's crazy about it, this is also in his blood, and in this regard the ancient Talmudists from the Babylonian Sanhedrin have an interpretation of the mystery of why God only at the end, on the sixth day, created man and woman. The answer of the wise men couldn't be clearer: had Adam and Eve, who were Jews, been created in the beginning, they would've driven the Creator insane with all their advice. It's even said, I don't know if it's true, that during the Sinai operation, in front of every Israeli soldier in the trenches, there was a sign saying: "During attacks, it is strictly forbidden for soldiers to give advice to the ranking officers!"

So I was talking about the new table of the carpenter Goldstein. Well, one Shabbos night we were all gathered around that same table and the candles were lit. My father hadn't yet read the festive *brokhe*, when my brother-in-law showed up, Sarah's brother Rabbi Ben-David. But he didn't come alone; with him was—guess who?—Esther Katz, the lawyer from Warsaw, who, once, a very long time ago, had brought into the barracks the inflammatory leaflets, because of which I had to stand stark naked and miserable in front of our lined-up company. Throughout the whole evening she was reserved and silent—I told you that she spoke all languages, as if she had invented them herself, so she didn't have any problems with Yiddish, but she would respond briefly and politely, constantly casting glances at the rabbi. There was some tension about her, and I was left with the impression that this fragile and valiant woman was in fact quite a shy person, committed entirely to a cause that I didn't really comprehend well. When we moved to the pumpkin seeds and exhausted the topic of the comet, Uncle Chaimle, who was a little bit informed about everything, directly addressed her, to my disbelief, as "Comrade Katz," even though in my opinion neither at that time nor later had he anything to do with all that business, and was only showing off how up he was on everything. Anyway, he addressed her with the usual questions about the situation in Soviet Russia. She answered reluctantly and briefly, said only that great deeds were being done there, that the newspapers in aristocratic Poland were lying, cast a glance at Rabbi Ben-David again and became silent.

Then Ben-David carefully started: "Could Esther stay with you tonight? You understand that with me, in the synagogue, it's inconvenient. Moreover, I'm an old bachelor . . ."

He laughed a little dryly and artificially, my mother and father shared a brief worried look, then my father said brightly, "Of course, Itzik's room,"—he meant me—"is free. Of course!"

"Not that there's anything . . . ," the rabbi started casually again, "but there's no reason to make noise about her spending a night here. You know what I mean?"

My father and Uncle Chaimle nodded conspiratorially, even though they hardly knew what it was all about.

In the morning when I went to work at the shop, the guest had already left and my father said that Shmuel Ben-David had come when it was still dark and taken her away.

Much later, when I had already eaten enough herring heads, if you know what I mean, it occurred to me that on that night she had either come illegally from Russia or was going to Russia. But this thought, I repeat, came to my mind much later, when the Bolsheviks shot Esther Katz.

Another old acquaintance of ours stopped by at Kolodetz —Liova Weissmann, you remember, the one whose unconquerable Austro-Hungarian army was always irresistibly advancing. He was discreetly whispering to people that he was holding a meeting for Jews only, with a very important agenda, at the coffee shop of David Leibovitch, but I hope you won't be surprised if I tell you that only seven people showed up, including myself and the rabbi Ben-David. The others had either caught a whiff of politics, or at just that moment the damn tooth had started to ache, or the cow was calving, or the roof tiles had cracked, or rain was coming, or there was simply no one to mind the little dairy store. I don't think the ones who didn't turn up missed very much, because Liova Weissmann announced what all of us already knew, namely, that the storm clouds over Europe were getting darker, that in Germany the harassment of our Jewish brothers had intensified and that Hitler, that same Schicklgruber, had announced in Linz the annexation of our former motherland Austria to the thousand year Third Reich and other things like that. He spoke about the necessity of unifying the Jewish social democrats, and the rabbi nervously objected to such Zionist leanings, as he called them, that we should not separate the Jewish proletariat from their brothers in fate, and so on. I don't know who was right—maybe both, and maybe neither. You know that story about the rabbi who was sought by Mendel and Berkovitch to settle their dispute. The rabbi listened to Mendel and said: "You're right!" Then he listened to Berkovitch and said: "You're right, too!" His wife cried out from the kitchen: "It can't be that one is right and the other right, too!" And the rabbi replied: "And you're right, too!"

In any case, the dispute that was threatening to deepen the separation among us seven people did not flare up, because the mayor Pan Voitek entered the coffee shop. He politely said hello, sat down, and ordered a glass of tea with three spoonfuls of sugar.

Then he said, "You haven't shown films for a long while, Pan Weissmann. It's a useful entertainment and in every respect worthy of support, while for political meetings permission is first to be requested from the mayor's office. Not that I have anything against your Jewish organizations, Pan Weissmann, but laws are to be kept and respected."

Clearly the government was not particularly worried about such social democratic unifying or separating initiatives, they were scared of others, but it's not my job to meddle in politics. All of us sneaked out one after the other, only Rabbi Ben-David stayed behind and also ordered tea with three spoonfuls of sugar.

Because of the above-mentioned reasons, the social democratic union of the Jews from Kolodetz by Drogobych didn't happen, but this didn't affect in any way the development of events in the world.

FIVE

And in the meantime events in the world were flowing and rumors were getting more and more confusing and alarming. We already knew by heart where Teruel was and what had happened at Khalkin Gol between Soviet and Japanese military units, and what the problem with Alsace and Lotharingia was, and we also knew that the Mannerheim Line was hardly just an ordinary line on the map. Just at that time a German family came to Kolodetz out of the blue, Fritz and Else Schneider. The last name sounded quite Jewish, but they were not one of ours, just the opposite, they were pure Aryans. They didn't talk much, moreover they couldn't even say their names in any one of the Slavic languages, but with us they somehow found understanding, because as I've already told you, our Yiddish is a precious mixture of different languages with a predominant presence of German scraps. The Schneiders had nothing to do with tailoring, it was just their family name that meant "tailor," and they opened a small shop for the repair of bicycles and all kinds of motors. A little later, when our good neighborly relations grew stronger and they were even paid a visit by the rabbi, with whom they chatted in a friendly manner and in the purest German, it became clear that they'd fled to our part of the world because of their insurmountable dislike of the Führer, with whom they had some kind of disagreement on basic matters of existence.

Our rabbi adored them and insisted that the Brown Shirts would manage to survive only another couple of months or so, because they were a pack of barbarians who'd encountered united resistance from the German people, who'd given the world this thing and that person. Just how far from the truth my brother-in-law was there's no need for me to explain. I suppose you've got insights of your own into Human History as not just the cherished memory of great men; you've also got some ideas about nations that have given the world this and that, but are capable of pulling such mean tricks on you that you'd probably curse even your mother's milk. I remembered Nahum Weiss, the plumber from Dresden, who was still managing to keep his head above water, but was expecting at any moment to be sent away with five pounds of personal belongings as a person of non-Aryan, that is, Jewish origin. When his still undisconnected phone rang up and a rude voice asked: "Am I speaking with Obergruppensturmfürhrer Otto Shultz?" poor Nahum Weiss sadly replied, "Oh, my dear sir, have you ever got the wrong number!" In the same way our otherwise deeply learned rabbi, who could follow the path not only through the labyrinths of Hasidism and its first great elder, the Baal Shem Tov, but also Karl Marx, was also wrong about the number in connection with the impending collapse of Hitler, as unfortunately we could never even imagine at that time.

I don't want to tell you a long story about the events that followed. You can simply take a look in any booklet to learn about the rapid speed of that festering boil again swelling in the womb of Europe, which could not help bursting at even the lightest prick of the thorns of the slightest conflict between countries. This time it wasn't at all about a banana peel in Stockholm, neither was it about the murder of some archduke, because, I repeat, when a war has to explode, it explodes, and what triggers it loses any meaning whatsoever. In this case I think it was about the Germans who were requesting something from Poland and the allies of Poland didn't want to give it, after they had already given Austria, and the Sudetenland, and whatever else had been requested of them—both in front and behind—and after that idiot Chamberlain was pledging in Germany eternal friendship with the Nazis, and Molotov and Ribbentrop were kissing each other like two old feygelahs. Please don't think that these are reflections of mine from that time, I was too ignorant to have them then, but time imposes its transparent layers one after the other, bringing closer or taking further away the events as if seen through binoculars—first from one side, then from the other—and then things that used to be unclear to you in the past are covered with thoughts of today or, if you'd rather call them, delusions of today.

So the whole affair ended up—or better to say, started again—with the quite aged military analyst from the Russian-Turkish war, the postman Avramchik, who again brought me a yellow piece of paper with more or less the same text, something like "Within seven days of receipt of this . . ." and so on, as you've guessed by now. And so, my dear mother Poland, holy land of the ancestors and so on, was summoning me Under the Flags.

This time a lot of us were called up—Jews, and Ukrainians, and Poles. It's neither a literary caprice nor some amazing set of circumstances, but summoned again was my brother-in-law, the wise rabbi Shmuel Ben-David. I won't tell you how

Sarah cried and how I stroked her hair, explaining that this time the war would be brief, without even suspecting how close I was to the truth. And so, on the next day we were supposed to leave for the West, to the German border, where the fearsome war had already flared up.

On September 17, 1939, already outfitted by my unit in Drogobych with a complete set of military gear, at seven o'clock sharp in the morning, I showed up at the small square next to the bazaar—the same place where Golda Zilber met the demise of the Alexandrian library and where those mobilized from Kolodetz were assembling. This time the spiritual rank of Rabbi Ben-David was not, God knows why, taken into consideration by the military field officers and he looked a little strange, even funny—his face shaven and his hair cut short—in soldiers' clothes. The women were gathering at the side, some were crying; Sarah was quietly weeping too. She'd come with the children, and my mother and father were there as well. There was no military music, but to make up for it Pan Voitek, the mayor, came to see us off personally, full of epic sentiments and completely aware of the historic moment that our motherland was experiencing.

And now, hold tight to your chair so you don't fall off: despite the overall pathos of the moment, I was not destined to bring victory at the point of my bayonet, or at least to lay my bones in the Pantheon of the motherland, because for me personally, as well as for my dear brother-in-law Rabbi Ben-David, and also, by the way, for all the men who were gathering at the little square in Kolodetz, once again the war was over before it started.

The whole point is that Sarah and the children and I, Rabbi Shmuel Ben-David, Mama and Dad, and also all of my dear neighbors—Pan Voitek, the Poles, Ukrainians, Jews, and even the German family Fritz and Else Schneider—all of us, including the Roman Catholic priest and the Orthodox priest, saw the realization of our next national ideal that exact same morning. Or, as the political commissar Nikanor Skidanenko announced from the top of the T-34 Russian tank, we were released from the yoke of feudal-aristocratic Poland and annexed to our workers-and-peasants' fatherland, the great Soviet Union.

And so, my dear brother, the dream, which I never imagined having, came true, as they say in the labor union reports, 100 percent, and I was already a conscious citizen, living in the Soviet *miastechko* of Kolodetz, the once-upon-a-time Austrian-Hungarian province of Lemberg, the former Polish *voevodstvo* of Lvov, and now, suddenly, an outpost of the world revolution.

ISAAC'S THIRD BOOK

The Red Front, or the Five-Year Plan Speeded-Up

ONE

Excuse me, please, for starting with a khokhma, you know, an Hasidic fable that's not even funny—but maybe with some effort you'll figure out the moral. It's about the blind man Yossel, whom even the children, otherwise capable of making fun of any unfortunate soul, respectfully help across the street. So one time this Yossel goes to the rabbi, feeling the way with his cane, and asks him, "Rabbi, what are you doing now?"

"I'm drinking milk."

"What does milk look like, Rabbi?"

"Well, it's a kind of white liquid."

"What does 'white' mean?"

"Well . . . white like a swan."

"And what does 'swan' mean?"

"This kind of bird with a curved neck."

"What does 'curved' mean, Rabbi?"

The rabbi bent his arm at the elbow. "Touch here and you will know what 'curved' means."

The blind Yossel carefully felt the arm and eventually said, gratefully, "Thank you, Rabbi. Now I know what milk looks like."

In the same way, my dear and patient reader, don't be fooled by either the curve of my arm, which is writing these lines, or by my modest attempts to explain things to you. Don't be fooled into thinking that you'll understand, just like the blind man Yossel, what milk looks like or, for instance, my new motherland the U.S.S.R., for I never learned whether what was happening in Kolodetz by Drogobych looked like what was happening, say, in Tambov or Novosibirsk, and if the term "Soviet" had the same meaning here, there, or for the Yurts somewhere in the Kara Kum desert. That is why to this day I get irritated when some little journalist from abroad passes through Moscow for three days and then, according to his political affiliation, starts explaining, with an expert's tone, to the ignorant and blind world what milk looks like, without realizing that he's only felt the curved arm of Moscow and that the seemingly good and the just can be fake, and the seemingly bad, which we are in a big rush to get rid of, could be a misunderstood or unappreciated good. Especially if you think about the immense size of this newly acquired motherland of mine—so immense that there are places from which it's closer to go over to Japan and buy half a kilo of meat than to reach the next Soviet town. Let alone that problems with meat aren't only related to the close proximity of Japan, since it was exactly from those distant Siberian lands that there came to us all the way down to Kolodetz the case of the citizen who entered a Soviet butcher shop and asked: "Could you weigh half a kilo of meat for me?" He got a polite answer: "Sure, bring it in."

Because of the above reason, don't expect from me head-spinning generalizations, because, on the one hand, I'm not the kind of person who thinks that way—you remember the rabbi once described me as a little slow—and on the other hand, because I simply didn't understand many things, which even to this day, in my old age, have still got me scratching my head. Don't expect either, that following the fashion, I will jump and start spitting on this third motherland of mine, because, if you've noticed, I may have unconsciously made a harsh or critical comment about the first two, for which I apologize, but I never allowed myself to talk against them, or to speak of them with disrespect. So don't think that now, in my capacity as a Soviet citizen, and hence a fighter in the avant-garde of progressive mankind, I have suddenly changed so much that you won't recognize me. Don't be like that fool Mendel who saw someone in the street and exclaimed, "How different you are, Moishe, without a beard and mustache!"

"I'm not Moishe," said the other one, "but Aaron."

"Look at you! Even your name is different."

My name remained unchanged, but in Russian fashion I am now citizen Isaac Yakobovich Blumenfeld—a fact that, I swear to God, in no way makes me different.

Otherwise things in general changed quite substantially. To put it in other words, our transition from Austria-Hungary to Poland was somehow easier and smoother, with no major calamities, just David Leibovitch taking down the portrait of Franz-Joseph in his café and sometime later, when the situation got clearer, putting up Pilsudski in his place, and Pan Voitek going from policeman to mayor. For greater vividness and clarity we could say that my father, Aaron Blumenfeld, had stuck his needle in one side of the caftan as an Austro-Hungarian, and pulled out the thread on the other side as a Pole. Well, there were some minor mishaps, like the assassination of President Narutovich, or, say, the Krakow uprising, but that one didn't knock us out and passed like a spring cold. Whereas things were now changing radically, we could even say at a revolutionary pace, otherwise there wouldn't be any sense in any of this shot-swapping October 1917, and Lenin could have quite calmly ridden in the first class compartment of the Berlin-Petrograd train, and not, as they say, in a sealed freight car, and then he could quite as easily have gotten a cab, instead of climbing onto an armored personnel carrier. I would give you as an example of such a radical, or if you prefer, revolutionary change, the taking down of the Mode Parisienne sign. This French fashion seemed to the new bosses, who had come either from the inner part of the country, or from the Polish prisons, quite decadent and incompatible with workers-and-peasants' fashion trends, and we—that is my father and I—became simple workers at Artel #6 of the Headindprodunit. Don't be amazed at this difficult-to-pronounce abbreviation; I don't remember if it sounded this way or something like it, but it's just a kid's toy in comparison to some other considerably more complicated and more revolutionary blends of nine or even twenty-three words, that after you try to pronounce them, it takes you half an hour to untangle the sailor's knots your tongue's been twisted into. What is inexplicable in this case is that sometimes a similar Soviet abbreviation is longer than the word that it's made out of—a phenomenon that was researched by the Institute on Paranormal Physical Phenomena in Leningrad. A similar phenomenon was discovered by Shimon Finkelstein, who claims he saw a snake one meter and twenty centimeters long from head to tail, and two meters long from tail to head. To the objection of Mendel that such a phenomenon is impossible, Finkelstein replied: "Well, how then in your opinion is it possible that from Monday to Wednesday there are two days, and from Wednesday to Monday, five?"

The change in name and status of our atelier also brought about as a natural consequence the taking down from the window, which, if you remember, was at the level of the sidewalk, of the by now quite weathered ladies in pink and gentlemen in tuxedos, and their replacement with the slogan "THE FIVE-YEAR PLAN SPEEDED UP!" And in that case, as with the ladies and gentlemen from the damned bourgeois past, something enduring and eternal was put up—and thank God for that, because there was no indication of which five years it was all about, or in what way my father and I had to implement it.

Of course, it would be naive of you to think that this was the only change that the new Soviet reality lavished on the modest life of our forgotten little province. It might seem a little exaggerated, but even though our life from one point of view became harder, especially with regard to provisions, from another our confidence grew, and we were filled with the sense that we were part—a small, perhaps, but important screw—in a great, not quite completely incomprehensible mechanism, something like a time machine, and I do mean future time, with its own place or role in the gigantic historic khokhma that was playing on the world stage. Believe me, it's true, and most people believed in the Soviet power or wanted to believe in it, even when it dawned on them that it was an illusion and they realized they were being plain lied to. Only if you're religious will you understand what I mean, because the Holy God, glory to His name, has more than once deluded you and promised things that He might have intended to fulfill, but was then distracted by other things and forgot. But you haven't even for a second come to doubt His glory, you've searched for extenuating reasons or consolations of the God-delays-but-doesn't-forget or God's-mills-grind-slow variety. Or don't you think so?

And while we're on the subject of God, I can solemnly announce to you that the unreasonable action of the Polish military authorities, who cut the hair and shaved the beard of the wise Shmuel Ben-David, speeded up the process of his final choice: he became chairman of the Club of Militant Atheists, which was situated in a corner of the Culture House "October Fireworks." If you're wondering from where these fireworks popped up in our Kolodetz, I'll give you a simple answer: this was the former café of David Leibovitch, who was appointed culture commissar with a fixed Soviet salary. Pan Voitek, or more precisely Comrade Voitek, was arrested and questioned for only two hours in his capacity as former mayor, but the loyal citizens of Kolodetz gave favorable references for him and he was appointed the Director of ZAGS, which was the Office of Citizen Registration. He noted down in the Kolodetz council records the weddings and the divorces, the newly born and the deceased, may their souls rest in peace—the deceased, that is.

Don't ask me about the other common acquaintances of ours—every one took surprisingly fast to his frontline post in the generally clumsy, forgive the expression, system of Soviet bureaucracy, but still we have to spare some time for Comrade Lev Sabetaevich—you remember Liova Weissmann with the films?—because he became the editor in chief of the *Red Galicia* newspaper and his case turned out to be not so simple. Because, if you remember, he wanted to unite the Jewish social democrats, and this last word, especially in combination with the last but one, enraged the Bolsheviks like the red bullfighter's cape enrages the bull. Poor Liova Weissmann, at a meeting in front of the comrades, including the representative of the Center, Comrade Esther Katz, had to criticize himself elaborately and honestly. If you're wondering what "the Center" might mean, I'll give you a hint that this was a very foggy Soviet definition, which was simply intended to create respect and it could mean anything, from the local committee in neighboring Truskovetz to the higher institutions of the endless party or state ladder from Lvov, Minsk, and Kiev to distant Moscow. I hope you know what self-criticism means: it means butchering yourself with your own hands, skinning yourself and presenting your skin stretched on a rack, or to put it in biblical terms, covering your head with ashes, tearing your shirt, and only then will the convened panel make a great effort to prevent you from plucking out all your hair. I would give you a piece of advice for a similar case in life: in no way try to prolong and take the guilt as a bitter medicine, spoon by spoon, but jump courageously into the ocean of regret and confess at once all your sins and mistakes since the time of the First and the Second International till the present day, and if in the silence you hear the tapping of a pencil on the table, and the Russian "*malo, malo*" ("insufficient, insufficient"), just go straight ahead and without any petty bourgeois run-around, place upon the scales of compassion also your personal guilt for the death of Herculaneum and Pompei. Then you'll be saved, and your career for the next two or three five-year plans secured, because the Russian as a rule has a sensitive and emotional nature and if he's touched by the sincerity of your repentance, he may even invite you to his house for tea, though you'll hardly get any, because this is the code name for a different beverage, and after one bottle of this stuff, he'll kiss you on the forehead and announce that he not only loves you but also respects you.

I wasn't present at the rehabilitation, because I'm neither a party man nor an activist like my brother-in-law Ben-David, but he told me that Esther Katz was silent most of the time, because she could hardly stand the fools, and she meant not the poor well-intended Liova Weissmann but the comrades, who came from the Center to investigate him.

In general, our transition from petty bourgeois, class-unconscious slaves of Capital, I mean that capital in the safe of Rothschild and not *Das Kapital* of Karl Marx, to the avant-garde of workers from all over the world, happened without special histrionics. With one exception that I don't understand to this day and whose logic I continue to search for without success: the German family Fritz and Else Schneider was most politely asked by the Soviet authorities to pack their bags, and, as we learned later, accompanied to the border and handed over, against a written receipt, to Hitler's authorities. This was done, they say, according to some Soviet-German agreement but—forgive my rude expression—I piss on an agreement that renders back the refugees of one regime into the hands of that same regime, so that they could be sent to camps and maybe even executed. As my parents used to say: "God's deeds have neither length nor depth, neither is it given to us to comprehend them."

Even Esther Katz shrugged her shoulders helplessly. "I don't know . . . maybe they're agents from Hitler?"

"And so they return defective merchandise to the producer?" asked Rabbi Ben-David skeptically.

Esther Katz swallowed her ready answer, which, as it seemed, wasn't convincing even to herself.

TWO

One magnificent silvery lock of hair mischievously curled itself, just like our Kolodetz river, through the raven black Galilean locks of my Sarah, who continued to look at me with love and faithfulness in her big gray-green eyes and despite my irritation kept on stubbornly putting the best piece of meat in my bowl of borscht, though it was due, according to Jewish patriarchal tradition, to my father. Our eldest son, Ilyusha, was studying law in Kiev and this also was part—together with music and medicine—of the Jewish tradition, and please don't believe the myth that commerce is the Jews' element. Maybe once upon a time in Phoenician antiquity it might've been true, but today any average Armenian, Syrian, or Greek will three times over buy and sell the Jewish merchant, who won't even have a clue. If it were any other way, then Kolodetz would have been a center of world trade, though even you could have made the counterargument from the doubtless fact that we were not exactly brimming over with David Oistrakhs or Doctor Wassermanns! Our younger son Yeshua seemed as if he'd been rocked to sleep with the "Internationale" since he was in his cradle, because he was entirely dedicated to his membership in the Komsomol, including in DOSAAF—a society for the support of the army, air force, and navy, and he was crazy about—imagine that!—flying gliders. Both Sarah and my mother—old Rebekha—were terrified by these doings, until I forbade them to meddle in the young people's lives, and in this plural number I include his sister Susannah too, who, in her turn, deluded by her brother, was jumping with parachutes and even won some kind of a sports medal.

My father was already quite aged and couldn't see well, which not only prevented him from gloriously continuing his tailor's artful craft of turning old caftans inside out, but even kept him from knowing where he had stuck his needle. Despite my insisting that he take more time to rest, he continued to come early to the atelier and to leave it when we were locking up, perhaps by habit, or in full belief that he maybe needed to give me a piece of professional advice. Moreover, some of the old men naturally withdrew from "October Fireworks," that is, the former café of David Leibovitch, and gradually moved over to our place, in this way creating a second Jewish cultural sanctuary. There they weren't involved with discussing the role of the Jewish proletariat in the global revolutionary process but mainly with the family of Baron Rothschild and their not insignificant problems, and also with forecasts about the coming defeat of Hitler and what Churchill said about that—an area in which the main expert was the postman Avramchik, already retired and proudly wearing the honorary badge of the Commissariat of the Post and Communications. The old men loved Churchill and the English, some unexplainable magnetism drew their thoughts all the time in that direction; and at the same time, because of a quite understandable reaction, inherent to the Jews since the times of the Spanish Isabella and the Great Inquisitor Torquemada, they delicately avoided making any comments on the economic situation of the

Soviet Union or, say, the most recent interview of Stalin with a *Times* reporter, regarding Soviet-German relations. Such interviews and all kinds of announcements by TASS or articles in *Pravda*, diligently reprinted by Liova Weissmann in *Red Galicia*, monotonously repeated the same thing over and over again, namely that our relations with the Krauts are getting better and better, and there's no massing of troops at any borders, which the wise old men of Kolodetz allowed to pass with no comment, closing the issue with an exchange of glances and a quick transition to the always relevant topic of Baron Rothschild.

Believe me, the attractive power of that baron and his relatively important place in the life of Kolodetz was not an accident. He provided hope and faith, and strengthened the invincible Jewish optimism and belief in the fully realistic chance of getting rich and becoming a millionaire—a belief comparable to the unquestionable fact that any vendor of popcorn in the United States has a chance of becoming president. Kolodetz by Drogobych, naturally, was quite a way from America and such expectations could have hardly referred, for example, to Golda Zilber, the vendor of pumpkin seeds, not only because women cannot become president of the USA, but because of many other reasons too, including the skill of the old men of Kolodetz in distinguishing the probable and the possible from the improbable and the impossible, and not getting carried away with fantasies. Just like one time Kaplan said excitedly to Mendel: "Do you know who I saw yesterday in the subway in Berdichev? You won't believe it: Karl Marx himself!" To which Mendel, skeptical in principle of any kind of fantasy, replied: "You're talking nonsense, there's no subway in Berdichev!"

On Fridays before dusk the workshop would suddenly become deserted and everyone would hurry home, because the

Soviet authorities at least so far were being tolerant of local traditions and the labor unions were not preventing the Jews from celebrating Shabbos the way it should be. Then Mama and Sarah would lay a white tablecloth on the table once made by the carpenter Goldstein, and my mother would light the candles with a trembling hand, getting at the wicks with difficulty, then say the prayer in Hebrew like a mechanical riddle. My two newly hatched Komsomol activists, with hands tangled in prayer fashion, would try to snicker and wink, but having encountered the stern look of their mother Sarah, they would stifle their atheist inclinations.

To you it might seem strange—this mix of Soviet power with Hasidism, but I don't exclude the possibility that Karl Marx himself, whom Kaplan saw in Berdichev, used to light up a menorah when on Friday nights he had dinner with Jenny. The faint religious-mystical mist surrounding this night, sacred to the Jews, has long ago been blown away and it's become a popular ritual, something like the Easter painting of eggs in the dynastic communist families who have serious doubts on the topic of the Resurrection, or, say, the enormous drinking-to-unconsciousness on May 1, another Soviet tradition, also exciting, that has long lost any trace of the religious.

Every Shabbos night we were visited—sometimes with a package of meat, sometimes with a huge carp of unknown origins, or even with a bag of Georgian mandarin oranges, rare for our part of the world—by my dear brother-in-law Shmuel Ben-David, now registered, who knows why, as Samuel Davidovich Zvassmann—maybe because of that heroic endeavor of prisoners, exiled in Siberia from the times of the czar, to make their names sound less Jewish and if possible more Russian revolutionary, an endeavor that renamed Leib Bronstein as Leo Trotsky. And maybe it was all done because of conspiracy reasons, which hardly explains the transformation of my brother-in-law from Ben-David to Davidovich, or Weiss to Belov, or Zilberstein to Serebrov, or Moishe Perlmann to Ivan Ivanich. Apparently there's some other reason here, but it's not my business to decipher it. And if you weren't constantly diverting me from the path of my story, I'd add that the former rabbi visited quite often accompanied by Comrade Esther Katz, who was always shyly apologizing for her unannounced appearance. I would tenderly look at them—these two not-so-young-anymore people, who had dedicated to others the best years of their lives and the most valuable part of themselves, who with a messianic passion had scattered their youth in roaming around the vast earthly and heavenly chasms, looking for the big truths, while they, the truths, so often turn out to be, unfortunately, illusory and deceiving shimmers of water in the desert or fake golden coins that rust after the first humid winter. And maybe in this there's also some kind of meaning from God—in the searching and not in the finding, and maybe their youth was not all wasted in vain, but generously planted in the field of the future for distant rich harvests. I don't know. I would observe them and it seemed to me that these two truth-diggers, she dedicated completely to a new religion, he trying painfully to marry an old one to *Das Kapital*, had finally lit upon happiness—if not the communal one, at least the small, personal one. They were not indifferent to each other and maybe had something even bigger than that. But the two converging directions of their souls were not meant to come together and become one; you'll get a report on this a little later.

The Shabbos candles were burning. We were sitting around the table and enjoying the peace that was resting over Soviet

Kolodetz as a blessing from God, and somewhere in the distance a record player was flooding the area with the song of the three tank crewmen—three joyful comrades in the war machine. This was at the time a very popular song, because things with the Japanese in the Far East were not going well, and the song was telling how the samurai crossed the border at the river and how we smashed their faces. This, by the way, is an important thread in my story and I will go back to it a little later, when my Soviet motherland summons me Under the Flags and sends me into holy battle with the above-mentioned Japanese samurai.

On my right side was sitting as always my dear Uncle Chaimle, who as the director of the public "Refuse Disposal" department was concluding the last years of his life before retirement and was responsible for the only horse cart that gathered the town waste, with its driver and simultaneously chief garbage man, Avrom Morgenrot—the not-completely-normal albino.

Uncle Chaimle said, "I heard a new joke. Someone asks banker Nahum why he's not playing poker with Count Galitzki anymore, and he says: 'Would you play poker with an outright thief?' 'Never!' the other one says. 'Well, Count Galitzki doesn't want to either!'"

We laughed, even though it wasn't a new joke, but nothing can prevent a Jew from having a bit of a laugh. Only our former rabbi didn't laugh. He was somewhat pensive and anxious, his spirit far away from where we were.

And Uncle Chaimle went on: "By the way, Shmuel, it's Shabbos now, isn't it?"

The former rabbi woke up; his spirit came back to where it belonged. "I think so. Why? Oh, yes, I know what you mean. Tell me to whom should I give the keys and I'll hand them over."

"Which keys?" asked my mother.

"The keys to the shul," angrily explained Uncle Chaimle. "He closed it up and on top of that put a lock on it too!"

"There are silver objects inside, Chaim," said Ben-David in self-justification.

"It's not about the silver objects, but about your golden lips, Shmuel," my father calmly interjected. Apparently this topic had been discussed before and we were involuntarily becoming witnesses to a coup that was intended to bring back our former rabbi to the kingdom of God. "We need to know right now: Who will read the prayer in shul tomorrow?"

Our former rabbi was silent for a long time, cast a confused look at Comrade Esther Katz and finally said quietly, but firmly, "Not me. Whoever wants to can do it, but not me. I can't be your rabbi, it's not fair!"

"Well, well now," Uncle Chaimle said sarcastically. "You can be chairman of the Atheists' Club and that's fair, isn't it? What would it cost you to combine that function, speaking in the Soviet way, with the position of rabbi? What's stopping you, I ask you?"

"I have reasons of a moral nature. Find yourself somebody else," insisted Shmuel Ben-David.

"And who'll lead our tribe through the desert?" Uncle Chaimle asked somberly and the desert *khamsin* blew out of his words, and my teeth ground the dust of the sand.

"Our people don't want just anyone," my father said, "just you, Shmuel Ben-David! You and nobody else, if you understand what I'm telling you."

Ben-David apparently understood, because he was being spoken to in Yiddish, but he quietly cursed in Russian, and then immediately, like a stray sheep that has found its sheepfold, went back to his mother tongue. "What are you all jumping on me for? And you, Chaim, since when did you become such a Hasid, when the last time you went to shul was the day of your circumcision? The desert! Look at him now—some anti-Soviet Moses! Why don't you lead them through the desert, and split the Red Sea in two!"

"You're talking nonsense," said Esther Katz flatly.

But our former rabbi was already burning up. "Yes, you go ahead, Chaimle. I'm not going to waste my time because of a handful of religious idiots!"

Esther Katz put her hand on his arm. "It's not good to talk like this!"

I was silent, because, honestly speaking, I wasn't one of those who would get a bellyache if I didn't go to the synagogue on Saturday. But unexpectedly, this quarrel, which I would compare to a theological dispute between hellenized Sadduccees and learned Talmudists, was joined by my son Yeshua. Apparently he already considered himself worthy of participating in such a debate—historic for the Kolodetz Jews—because he'd flown Soviet gliders. He said, "Uncle Shmuel is right a hundred times over! Haven't you ever heard of something like the 'opium of the people'? We must put an end to this medieval Hasidic Jewish stupidity!"

Silence fell, during which Sarah quietly said, "Yeshua, leave the table. . . . Do you hear me? I said leave the table!"

But he didn't get up, stubbornly fixing his eyes on his plate.

"And those who believe in the One Who Is? Eh? And believe seven times, and seven times seven times?" calmly asked my father, and as he gradually raised his voice I could hear in it the distant trumpets of Jericho, and feel the rage and power of our ancient ancestors. "If I, for example, believe in the only and fearful God of the Jews, Adonai, am I an idiot? I'm asking you, Shmuel! Or a medieval Hasidic dumbhead? I'm asking you, Yeshua!"

Biblical lightning didn't strike, nor did a bush burst into flame, but I don't know where this old man's hand found so much strength that when he struck hard, the dish of borsht flew off across the room, broke into pieces against the white wall, down which the red beets poured like blood.

Sarah and I looked at each other, and her eyes seemed sad and somewhat guilty, as if they were apologizing for her brother's words.

Ben-David stood up, and said quietly, "Excuse me. Excuse me, Aaron. All of you. I didn't express myself well, I know. Forgive me. Tomorrow I will come and open the synagogue, and I will say the prayer. And you, Itzik, will read that piece from Book Three of Moses—about the idols. Excuse me."

He bowed respectfully and went out, and Itzik, if you remember, is me. Esther Katz said in confusion, "Don't be angry with him, I beg you. . . ."

THREE

Our people came triumphantly, as if they had won a small war, wearing the obligatory small kipas and the wraparound white ritual tallis shawls, and the Shabbos service took place. The rabbi Ben-David murmured briefly "*Baruch ata Adonai elohenu . . .*" —blessed be He, our one and only God.

I wouldn't say that the synagogue was crowded like it was in pre-Soviet times—mainly missing were the young people, and even the old people did not, as it were, put in an appearance. Some, I think, stayed away because of a loss of faith or because they just didn't feel the spiritual need; I don't exclude pragmatic reasons, such as an upcoming admittance to the Party, or the most commonplace fear, and about this one I've got my own opinion, may the old men devoted to the shul forgive me, because this fear has been speculated on quite a bit in recent times. I wouldn't say that the Soviet authority was fond of churchgoing and religious rituals, just the opposite, but the times when these things were viewed askance and with spiteful iconoclasm had gone by, and anyway in Kolodetz I didn't feel anything of the kind. Maybe in Novosibirsk or Karakoum it might have been different, I wouldn't venture to say, but I know that the refuge of fear is the human soul. That is why I truly despise those who maintain today that they didn't go to meet with God because of fear. If I were God—you understand, I'm just supposing, and have no such aspirations—I'd rather forgive the pagan and bless the one who doesn't hide his disbelief in Me, than the one who hides his faith and is afraid to follow it, and looks around to check if there's another eye, apart from the Eye of God. Or remembers Me from time to time and quickly buys himself off, "just in case"—with either a coin dropped in the cash box in the Christian church, or a small candle, or an absentminded murmur of "Amen" in the synagogue, while secretly looking around and calculating how Menachem Rosenbaum managed to acquire those new shoes, the elite kind produced by the "Red Proletariat" factory for high-ranking party comrades. Forgive my rude expression, but such chicken-livered religious hypocrites I would send to hell, if such an institution exists.

You've probably sensed in these contemplations of mine the influence of, or even direct quotes from, Rabbi Shmuel Ben-David and so you should, he taught me to doubt belief and to believe in doubt. He taught me to look the celestial truths straight in the eye and if God doesn't lower His eyes in confusion, it means that He and I think alike, at least on the issue in question. As far as earthly truths are concerned, the rabbi didn't teach me anything, because he considered himself a novice who was still just beginning to figure out the alphabet of a new and still unwritten Torah, with a new Book of Moses' "Exodus" that would tell the story of how humankind went through the ordeal of the desert of the present day, and finally reached the Promised Land, the blessed Canaan of the future.

I've strayed a little, but if you've forgotten where we were, let me remind you: we were at the synagogue of Kolodetz by

Drogobych, Rabbi Shmuel Ben-David—or if you wish, Citizen Samuel Davidovich Zvassman—had just read, or rather sung and murmured, the prayer and now it was my turn. And so, according to the rabbi's instructions, I started chanting, like a string of pearls, the words from the third book of Moses: "You shall not make idols for yourselves, or set up for yourselves carved images or pillars, or place figured stones in your land to worship upon, for I the LORD am your God." And so on, you know it by heart. I was reading with feeling, but my thoughts were flying somewhere else: Why had the rabbi chosen exactly this chapter? And what was he trying to suggest?

Now, as I write these lines, many, many years after that Saturday in the synagogue of Kolodetz, I think I know: his gods were Truth and Serving People, and he was deeply disturbed and confused by the clarity of this faith, its simple humanity, which blended with the celestial so much that the two became one and only one; but he was disturbed by the graven images about which I was reading from the Torah. To say it more clearly: over our newly annexed Soviet region a torrent of portraits of Stalin and Lenin came raining down, mostly of Stalin, and busts and statues of Stalin and Lenin, and again mostly of Stalin, and posters with slogans, and again busts and casts of leaders full-face and in profile, and were they not those forbidden idols and stones with images to which the Law says we're not supposed to bow? And which were meticulously copying the One, glory to His Name, who claims with quite nebulous arguments that there exists no one but Him? And I'm convinced that Ben-David was ready to renounce all the gods—both earthly and heavenly—to leave his heart free for the Truth and only for the Truth, which is in fact only one and there exists no other but it. And where was the sense in giving up some idols, whom you considered outdated and unjust, in order to bump your nose, as you stared back into the past of the ancestors, on other, newer ones, toward which Ben-David also felt torturous suspicion, because they were letting out into the air a very identifiable smell of sulfur?

When it came time for the Shabbos preaching, the rabbi said, "I searched for God in this home called Heaven and I didn't find Him, so don't you go looking for Him either, because He isn't here. Look into your hearts, brothers, and if you find Him there, let your hearts become your synagogues, your temples, your sacrificial pyres and Tables of the Law. Because if God is love, only in the heart can there be love, and not in stones. What is this building if not stones? And what will become of our hearts if they stop being a sanctuary or, to put it our way, an Ark of love to Man, and by this we do not mean one person, but all people, of all different skin colors, all tribes and tongues, all lands and seas—from the countries of eternal heat to the countries of eternal frost—because only all of them together are God. And there is no other God but this one. My dear brothers, frightful obstacles lie ahead of us that will bestow frightful suffering: take your eyes off the sky and look at your feet so as not to overlook the earthly pains of your fellow men, or sink into the first trap of indifference. The great ancestors left us the priceless spiritual treasures of the Word, the beginning of all beginnings, keep them, respect them, because they are the invisible bond of our dispersed tribe that has survived through the centuries and the millennia, through which other tribes have been created, risen up, and disappeared for ever. Be respectful to other faiths, but do not be obedient and submissive to your own, because this is exactly what you will be asked for by the paid priests of made-up gods, both earthly and heavenly. They will want to turn you into slaves and servants of masters' tables, blind men in the darkness of ignorance and lies, and not free people striding toward the light—the enemy of ignorance. Our great father and prophet Moses brought the Tables from the Sinai mountains. They contain unfathomed depths of wisdom, and that is why they are the Law. Follow it, but with your common sense and not like cattle, in order to avoid falling into the Tables' abyss, and don't be afraid to violate the letter of the book in the name of His spirit. Do not be His obedient tools, but His courageous judges. And if your neighbor possesses castles built with the stolen stones of your huts, then, brothers, wish for the castles of your neighbor, and make of them your common home! And if he has a thousand sheep and a hundred camels and you have none, wish for the sheep and the camels of your neighbor, so that they will become your common herd! And if he seduces your women, do not accept it obediently as slaves, but go and seduce his! Amen and *Gut Shabbos*!"

Indeed, what a pity that Karl Marx couldn't hear this talmudic commentary on the Books of Moses!

FOUR

It may seem strange to you, but the old men didn't become indignant at their rabbi's Shabbos preaching, just the opposite—they went home satisfied that the shul was again a home for the gathering of the good Jews of Kolodetz. Apparently about the meaning of the Law they cared not so much, but, as Uncle Chaimle would say, about the Law as such, and this gives me some explanation of the noisy approval and even adoration with which some people listen to the speeches of the deputies in their own *knessets*, without even paying attention to their meaning. In any case Ben-David, full of compassion for the neighbors, agreed, temporarily, until a new rabbi was found, to fulfill simultaneously the role of tzaddik, or spiritual shepherd, both in the synagogue and the Atheists' Club—in the first case for those who believed in God, and in the second, for those who believed in Marx. And to tell you the truth, he handled wonderfully his complicated mission of helping the spiritually blind and teaching them not to be the stupid servants of slave feasts, and leading them through the mazes of doubt, and he never let them live with the delusion that the curved elbow, especially if it ends with a clenched and ominous fist, either human or divine, is the whole truth about milk.

The November celebrations dedicated to the twenty-third anniversary of the Revolution had passed long ago, and what in the beginning seemed to us new, unusual, or incomprehensible had gradually become Soviet routine, a way of living, and we were adjusting—each one as he could—to its requirements. In connection with the upcoming May 1st holiday, we were given from above—this is the exact phrase, "given from above," a new immediate plan, according to which our workshop at Cartel #6 and so on—let's not twist our tongues with that abbreviation—had to increase its level of "labor productivity" by 4.20 percent. Plans, you should know, used to be "given from above," and there was something grand and mysterious about it. Somewhere on high above the clouds some invisible deity was "giving from above," like the Tables of the Law from Sinai, file folders with percentages, deadlines, and commitments according to abilities whose fulfillment was later adjusted according to needs, just the way it was with the ancient Ten Commandments—in which theft, for example, if in particularly large proportions, could be qualified as an over-fulfillment of the plan for legitimate profits, and murder, if in bigger batches, as the fulfillment of the immediate plan for the defense of national interests. My father and I spent a long time pondering but in the end couldn't come up with any efficiency improvements or changes, apart from the origin of the needles, and so the imported German ones were replaced by the local versions from the tractor factory—a little rough, but, because of that, easily adaptable to defense needs. I don't even know if we managed to increase productivity by 4.20 percent, because we couldn't figure out the baseline prerevolutionary percentage, but we received a triangular flag, which to this day may be hanging there somewhere on the wall, with a golden sign on a red background: "OUTSTANDING WORKER IN THE MAY FIRST COMPETITION." This flag meant that we had participated—my father and I—in the aforementioned competition, even though it wasn't clear with whom exactly we were competing and in what incomprehensible (at least to me) way we had excelled, but in all this, you understand, there was some kind of inclusion of our small atelier into something big, common, and meaningful, while in its old form Mode Parisienne was a lonely speck in the tailoring galaxy, a needle lost in a haystack of caftans, a basement workshop, in which the only larger event that connected it to God's big world was the tailoring of a red uniform for some hussar of His Majesty's Lifeguards—a myth in my father's view comparable to the *Odyssey*, the *Kalevala* or *The Song of the Nibelungs*.

And it was exactly at this, so to say, festive May 1st peak of my story, marked by a red triangular flag, that trouble came: through Kolodetz, like thunder and lightning, the news that early that morning our fellow citizen, veteran of the Russo-Turkish war, and bearer of the honorary badge of Posts and Communications, Abraham Mordekhaevich Apfelbaum, more commonly known as Avramchik, had been arrested by the institution of the NKVD, which stood for the People's Commissariat of Internal Affairs, or, as we put it, the political police. The first, and maybe the only one who beamed at this news, was our Catholic priest, who, as I've already informed you, was a militant anti-Semite, and any trouble that fell upon any Jewish head he viewed as God's punishment and an expression of supreme justice. But just as his beaming smile had reached its apogee, and was approaching its perigee, the priest himself was arrested, it was said, for being an accomplice. An accomplice in what? Nobody knew.

And even as early as the next morning Pan Voitek was arrested, our former police chief, former mayor, and also already former head of the ZAGS—the department for the registration of citizens and so on. In this case, the situation was a little clearer, the case, so to say, spread in whispers and went from one ear to another. That is, the case was a half-liter bottle of vodka, which Citizen Voitek had brought secretly in his pocket into the club "October Fireworks," which unlike the petty bourgeois ways of the times when this club was David Leibovitch's café, now prohibited the consumption of alcohol, so our Voitek was secretly pouring from the bottle into his glass, pretending it was drinking water. But it is not what the NKVD would arrest you for—they too were full of bearers of the shield and sword of revolution who would pour down their throats the same liquid in the same water glasses. They did it mostly in secrecy and behind closed doors and maybe this is why they were called "fighters at the quiet front." No, not for this, but because after two and a half glasses, which exactly meets the Soviet standard for a half-liter bottle of vodka, Citizen Voitek announced that Stalin was a piece of shit and that he had sold Poland to the German shitheads in return for half the amount from the deal. From the law's point of view, with this he was on the one hand undermining the prestige of an authority figure, and Comrade Stalin was without doubt exactly this type of figure, and on the other he was heaping an insult on a neighboring country, with which the USSR was having diplomatic and, we could even say, friendly relations. This meant, according to the Kolodetz legal experts, no less than a public reprimand, and if the authorities wanted to be strict about it, a fine of up to five rubles. But what this failure of Voitek's could have had to do with the arrest of Avramchik and the Roman Catholic priest, for the time being no one could say. We could only gather our patience and wait till the next day, when Citizen Voitek would no doubt get out of detention, after he had been reprimanded or had paid the five rubles for his reckless, drunken chatter. Then he would probably be able to explain to us what the connection might be between a drunken Pole, an old Jew, and a Catholic priest, apart from the one that all three were loyal Soviet citizens, residents of the little town of Kolodetz by Drogobych. Some other unknown person spread another rumor, specifically that Avramchik, at the time when he was still a postal officer, had received and illegally appropriated a check for a hundred thousand dollars, sent by Baron Rothschild to his compatriots in Kolodetz, and together with the priest and the head of the ZAGS, Citizen Voitek, had secretly drunk away the money at the local railway station bars. But hardly anyone believed this version, composed apparently by extreme admirers of the baron, who were mixing up their pure dreams with the rough, so to say, Soviet reality. This rumor about the railway station bars was even more unbelievable because of the fact that in our region, all the way up to Truskavetz, any bar tab exceeding two rubles, with the only exception being three rubles fifty kopecks on the eve of May 1st of the October Revolution, paid in one evening by the same fellow, caused well-founded suspicions of shady deals, illegal income, or that the payer of the above-mentioned tab was a cashier, and maybe even a spy, with one foot in jail.

One way or another, we didn't know what violations it was all about, but the authorities apparently had a swift and determined grip, no doubt about it. They even tell this story in Berdichev, when Mendel called from a pay phone:

"Hello, is this the NKVD?"

They replied on the other side: "Yes, this is NKVD. Go ahead."

"You're doing a bad job!" said Mendel and put down the receiver.

A minute later he called from another pay phone. "Hello, is this the NKVD?"

Someone patted him on the back and said, "That's right, Citizen Mendel, NKVD. We do our best."

The next morning, however, to everyone's amazement, Voitek was neither released nor did we hear anything about the five-ruble fine, which, according to the know-it-alls at the workshop, he inevitably had to pay. Deeply confused, I ran to the synagogue in whose yard, if you remember, was situated the little house of our rabbi.

"Don't ask me, I don't know a thing!" Ben-David raised his hand somberly before I even asked him.

"All right," I said. "I won't ask you. But why have they arrested Avramchik? He's eighty years old!"

"First, you went ahead and asked me. And second, if someone is arrested, it's for some criminal act, not for his age."

"You believe Avaramchik is capable of such an act?"

"I said 'someone,' not Avramchik. And if you please, try to understand what you're being told: I don't know anything! Don't ask me, I'm in a lousy mood anyway!"

We were silent for a while. The rabbi pushed the sugar bowl toward me and poured some tea. In the silence our teaspoons rang against the porcelain cups like little bells.

At one point my tea went down the wrong way, I choked and, coughing, raised my teary eyes to the rabbi. "Just incredible, to get himself into such a mess! He's just an old man. . . ."

"Eighty years old," the rabbi helped me.

"In my opinion this is some outrageous blunder, there's no other explanation. But on the other hand, they arrested three separate people."

"Well then, three outrageous blunders," said the rabbi dryly. "This morning Esther took the fast train to Lvov. She will clarify the case, if they themselves don't have a plague of outrageous blunders over there."

At the time I didn't understand him, but when our comrade from the Center, Esther Katz, came back from Lvov, she was even more confused than I was.

"Is such a plot possible?" she asked. "It's terrible—they've started mass arrests in Lvov, the arrested have already started making confessions. You won't believe it, but do you know whom they've arrested?"

"I know," said the rabbi. "Liova Weissmann. Did I guess right?"

She wasn't even surprised by Ben-David's insight, but took it as something natural. She, no less than the rabbi, knew well what that last word—"arrested"—meant in the eyes of the orthodox Bolshevik, if you know what I mean, in combination with the last but one—"they"—regardless of the self-criticism and the skin stretched on a rack. As far as "they" were concerned, certain political inclinations, even if they happened in the early and innocent years of your youth, were looked upon as a virus that for a long time might seem innocuous or even dead, but given the right environment and the necessary temperature, lifts one eyelid, most frequently the right one, looks around, and then in no time at all an epidemic breaks out.

"A big Trotsky-Zinoviev subversive conspiracy has been uncovered. They were organizing destructive acts during the harvest. The traces lead to a foreign country," she reported matter-of-factly.

"Oh, my God!" I exclaimed. "Avramchik and the harvest! Avramchik and a Trotsky-Zinoviev terrorist group! . . . The priest and Pan Voitek—well, now I understand . . ."

"Why 'well'? And what do you understand now?" the rabbi asked dryly, looking at me with astonishment.

"I meant to say," I mumbled, "that after all, the two of them, the priest and Voitek, are Poles. A foreign body, so to say . . ."

"Really?" said the rabbi. "So they are a foreign body. Foreign to whom, if I may ask? Because Avramchik is a Jew, for someone he could also be a foreign body! Ay-ay, Itzik, I'm ashamed!"

To tell you the truth, I felt ashamed, too.

FIVE

My children—that glider enthusiast Yeshua and the parachute jumper Susannah—accepted without reservation the Soviet regime, and gave it their firm Komsomol support for the complete eradication of . . . and so on, let me not bother you with stupidities. My mother and father were silent and would only turn their heads every now and then from each other to one of the people speaking around the table that Goldstein, the carpenter, once made, because the old were about as familiar with politics as King Solomon was with the moral norms of sexual life. Uncle Chaimle was fully on the side of the authorities or at least this is what he would say—don't forget he was a Soviet employee with a short time left before his pension, and Sarah was silent and when she would lift them toward me, her greenish-gray eyes radiated sorrow and a feeling of anxiety.

You'd probably be surprised if I told you that the only people who didn't believe a word, and I mean not even a comma of what was being said or written in the newspapers, were the old men, who continued to gather in the workshop. These wise naifs were, so to say, completely out of it, and thus as completely foreign to all this mythology as, for instance, a true-believing son of Israel on whom you try to foist the story of that Yeshu, who seemed to have resurrected himself, lifted the stone off his grave and taken off for heaven. Of course, they were cautious enough not to utter a single word of comment, but an apparent hint of their appraisal of events was in their shared glances and the speed with which they jumped, like hungry wolves, on poor Rothschild.

Of course, Pan Voitek was released neither the next day, nor the next month, but thank God, he saved himself the five rubles, because he was sentenced to fifteen years of exile in Siberia with the corresponding expropriation of his citizen's rights. Avramchik and the priest, as simple accomplices—unknown to whom or for what—got off the hook easier, with five years each. About poor Liova Weissmann we never heard anything again. He just annihilated himself, disappeared into thin air like morning mist and was gone.

To this day, I'm still full of regret that at that time I unknowingly let myself become a servant at a foreign master's table, as our rabbi Ben-David used to say, that I, through the mere fact of accepting the possibility of guilt on the part of the arrested Poles, had followed the malevolent will-o'-the-wisp of my unenlightened soul that led to the warm and comfortable abode of complicity. And this complicity or unconscious participation always begins with the conviction that those closest to you, the people you know best, are innocent and that everything around them is a consequence of some misunderstanding or malicious slander, while the others. . . . Well, as far as the others and particularly the most distant and the least known to us are concerned, they're probably the true destroyers and agents of foreign powers and no matter what you're telling me, there's no smoke without fire. . . . And don't you realize, you fool, that this one, who's closest to you, whose innocence you're ready to swear by, is for the other people the unknown one and for them, in particular, the true harmful agent? . . . Don't you realize, you fool, that this is how that mechanism is wound up, to make you full of suspicion toward others, and of others toward you?

At that time, and during the next wave of accusations and trials, I couldn't comprehend then, I didn't comprehend even later, and I will never comprehend the hidden meaning, the secret and cherished purpose of this unreal, insane—I would even say mystical—passion for collective self-destruction, this all-devouring and blood-thirsty Moloch, into whose flaming and insatiable throat obedient crowds would go, sometimes as if they'd been put under a spell by the smoke of secret shaman herbs, entering in disciplined lines, here and there even singing psalms of praise, wave after wave, large helpings of tens of thousands of people, and each one of them individually a sacrificial lamb on the altar of the future.

There were of course many who resisted, who didn't pronounce themselves guilty, who swore and cursed, or whimpered in fear, or wanted to write and let Stalin, who suspected nothing, or so they thought, know all about it and tell him what was being done behind his back, but the line behind them was pushing them at a steady rate toward the flaming throat. And those whose mission it was to push them forward knew in advance, with the doom and obsession of medieval flagellants—those Catholic fanatics who, possessed by evil spirits, whip themselves bloody—that they themselves in their turn would be pushed by the ones coming behind them. And maybe in each of them there was a tiny spark of hope that precisely he would be the one to escape the bitter cup of poison. Maybe, I don't know.

I'm reminding you that a lot of these feelings and thoughts of mine came to me quite a bit later, when I'd lived through and learned about things that then I'd neither seen yet nor could have known about, but let me repeat to you that the transparent layers of time lie one on top of the other and through this magnifying glass you can see better the truth about old delusions, or, I repeat again, accumulate fresh ones.

The newspapers and radio were emitting new waves of uncovered plots, full and sincere confessions, trials, rallies, and incantations, which were gradually weaving us into a sticky and venomous spider web. I said "radio" by habit—such a device the people in Kolodetz didn't possess, we had "reproductors"—a truncated cone of black cardboard, hanging somewhere on the wall, from the bottom of which would spring news, music, speeches, articles, and commentaries. You could neither escape nor switch to another station—just the opposite, this single one would latch on to you as its prey and follow you around, biting your behind, no matter where you put yourself in hiding—in the bedroom and under the bed, in the kitchen and even in the street, where the same cones, only now metallic, were hanging from posts, above entrances, and on roofs. As far as I remember, only the public lavatories didn't have these black funnels. We used to recognize them, and there's a grain of truth in this, that as a big cultural and moreover free acquisition—considerably bigger than the record players of Uncle Chaimle—out of them, I mean the funnels, would pour and flood upon us not just Tchaikovsky and Prokofiev, and not only Chekhov's *Three Sisters* or the poems of Mayakovski, which I don't underestimate at all, but also information about what was being uncovered, about the rallies and revolutions, the trials and sentences, and sincere confessions and repentances related to the above-mentioned

Trotsky-Zinoviev monsters and all kinds of other destructive-subversive groups. Unceasing resolutions from labor collectives and military units to Comrade Stalin were read, which expressed the unfaltering will of all the Soviet people, I emphasize *all the people*, which includes logically my will and that of my family, even my mother Rebekha and my father Aaron Blumenfeld, to break the spine of the imperialist plotters. Shall I also mention those foreign writers and journalists, some of them really big names deserving of respect, who were invited to the trials, running up a Soviet tab at the Metropol Hotel and devouring black Astrakhan caviar, and then writing—and some of them may have been sincerely misled—about the brilliant prosecutor Andrei Vishinksi and the genuine confessions of the prosecuted? Let me not mention as an example and proof any names, so as to avoid condemning them or their descendants and admirers to the same repentance and shame that to this day do not give peace to my lonely nights.

And now I ask, since I don't have an answer to the question: What in fact was the goal, the hidden meaning, or, if you like, the simple benefit of all this? Was it a gigantic experiment of the One Who Is, with us, the ants, inhabiting the earth and naively considering ourselves the masters of our life and destiny? And is it given to the ant to penetrate the meaning and purpose of God's experiments, even though, to tell you the truth, if He got a kick out of all this, I would personally participate in the breaking of His Window Panes!

But you'd be wrong with the answer to my question if you were to rush to generalizations, or if you haven't noticed, or you haven't wished to notice, that right next to this world of fear, lawlessness, and dark insecurity there existed another, parallel world and it's this one that confuses me and maybe confused those others, the foreign writers and journalists from the Metropol Hotel: in that second world dedicated and selflessly great scientists were working on earth-shattering discoveries, children were going to school and youths to the universities, excellent books were being written and sincere songs were being sung, world class mathematicians and poets were being born; the depths of the universe were being penetrated and the depths of the atom nucleus; there was a Moscow Art Theater in it and the Bolshoi, and Galina Ulanova; for concert tickets people stood in lines five blocks long, there was the Hermitage, Sholokhov, unvanquishable chess players, Papanin stepping onto the North Pole, Chkalov flying over the ocean, Eisenstein opening a new era in cinema, and the USSR as the most literate and youthful country in the world. Some of it might have been accomplished through violence, I don't deny it, but the main, the great part, required a free spirit—after all, could slaves have achieved it? And you would again be making a big mistake if you believed the anti-Soviet press of that time that the people were collectively cursing Stalin: in those days and the years that would soon follow, people were throwing themselves into battle and dying with his name on their lips, and let it, his name, be seven times damned and seven times seven. Even the ones who were going to be shot by his own order gave out their last cry in his praise. Whether this was collective madness I don't know, but this is how it was. I, Isaac Jacob Blumenfeld, the future ZEK 003-476 from the concentration camp in Kolyma, Northeast Siberia, hereby state that this is how it was, and if you've got an answer to this riddle of riddles, which, believe me, will tear at human consciousness another hundred and two years, and if you know what milk looks like in fact, please, write to me, I'd be grateful!

SIX

The knot of doubt about the justice or injustice of what was happening around us and what was torturing me with unanswerable questions was split by one single stroke: early in the morning the rabbi Ben-David descended the three steps of the atelier. Pale as half-baked unleavened bread, his lips trembling, he fell into the chair, but couldn't say a word for a long while.

I asked quietly, "Esther, too?"

He nodded.

"And now?"

He shrugged his shoulders.

My father lifted his eyes from the Soviet picture magazine *Ogoniok*, which he was only leafing through because he couldn't read Russian very well, even though, like most people in our region, he managed to speak it somehow, and looked over his thick glasses: "What is it, Shmuel?"

"Nothing, nothing," said the rabbi.

My father's hearing was weak, but he understood that the question didn't concern him and plunged back into the magazine pictures.

"And now?" I repeated.

"I don't know."

"So," I said, "everything's a big delusion. Chasing the wind, nothing, and the shadow of nothing."

The rabbi looked at me with heavy eyes red with fatigue. "'I saw everything done under the sun, and here—everything is vanity and chasing the wind. . . . And I set my heart to know wisdom, and to know madness and folly, but I learnt that this too was chasing the wind. . . .' If this is what you mean, Itzik, then before you another Jew has said it, I'm sorry, but he's ahead of you by several thousand years. But he also said: 'He who stares at the wind will not sow, and he who gazes at the clouds will not reap.'"

"And you, despite all this, still believe it was good, what Comrade Katz was sowing? After you know what she's reaping now?"

I give you my word, believe me, that for the first time in front of him I called Esther Katz "comrade" without sarcasm. It happened spontaneously, like a cry of despair. Or else by this I wanted to associate myself with my good rabbi, to suggest to him that I wasn't a stranger to his suffering, or maybe it was to express my sympathy and closeness to that small, gentle woman, with a man's haircut, so completely dedicated to a mission and full of faith in the country that became our motherland and was now paying her back so unfairly.

"I don't believe in violence—even when it's in the name of a good purpose. The way I don't believe that the cuckoo's egg, laid in another nest, will hatch anything different from a cuckoo. Violence hatches the violent. Dictatorship, even if it's in a revolutionary nest, hatches dictators. That's what I think, let that bearded fellow who believed that dictatorship in the name of justice and brotherhood will bear justice and brotherhood, forgive me."

This is what Rabbi Ben-David said, not answering my question.

That same evening the rabbi cancelled the discussion at the Atheists' Club on the topic of "Religion and Darwin's Theory" and went to the synagogue, where they didn't even expect him. There he preached his sermon:

"During the Exodus, when our great patriarch Moses led our tribe out of the slave land of the pharaohs, deceived were those brothers of ours who expected that beyond the expanse of the sea that engulfed the enemy chariots in pursuit were the green meadows of Canaan, its crystal creeks and vineyards heavy with grapes. They were crazy, because they believed that crossing the sea would be the end of their suffering. And it was only the beginning! They were crazy, because they didn't understand that the Promised Land means not the bestowed-as-a-gift, but the deserved-in-the-future land and that they will reach it only after a long, long, in fact endlessly long journey through the desert, after pain and hardship, wandering and suffering. You know, brothers, from the great books of Moses, how those weak in spirit and greedy for quick and easy fruit in their desperation and anger abandoned their God and leader through the desert, and went back again to the faith of the infidel pagans, and again started to bow down to the Golden Calves of their past enslavement. Let us understand them without cursing and scorning them, let us leave a free place at our table and some bread and wine for them, because it is not given for us to judge.

"The way, my brothers, is hard, and it will take neither a year or two, nor a generation or two; unfair and even monstrous will be the hardships of this road. Because our slave souls are not yet ready and free from the captivity of pharaoh-delusions, and we have not accepted the truth of the way that is in and of itself both a goal and faith in the goal! And those who have lost this faith, who have spilled it as easily as a broken string of fine Baghdad beads, will lose the strength and the will to go forward. And soon, left without direction and goal, and tired of meaningless wandering, they will spread their black Bedouin tents and remain forever hostages of the desert—between the past and the future. And the dry Sinai winds will blow sand into their souls, and whiten the bones of their dead ideals.

"Canaan, brothers, is far, very far and let us pray for those who are not with us now and who endure hardships along their arduous way. Let us give them handfuls of hope, like spring water. Let them drink, and let us caress their tortured faces with our wet palms, and touch our lips to their foreheads—as a blessing, a sign of loyalty and shared pain. Let them, like us, brothers, not lose hope that Canaan is there and that there is a Canaan!

"Go home in peace and *Gut Shabbos* to all. Amen!"

I think that no one but me understood that this sermon was also a prayer for Esther Katz. And maybe a great self-delusion, a mirage in the desert, I don't know.

SEVEN

It was the middle of June, a dry and hot summer. The wheat around Kolodetz was swelling with gold and rocked by the breeze in heavy waves. Sarah had some back pain and this was not the first time, either; her kidneys were not quite well and I was categorical, even obnoxious, and stood up against her submissive readiness to endure her suffering in silence just so there'd be someone to look after the old people, cook for the children, and water the dahlias in the garden.

In the regional hospital of Drogobych they wrote that Citizen Sarah Davidovna Blumenfeld needed sanatorium treatment and gave her a card for some mineral baths in the north, toward Rovno. She didn't want to go, discomfited maybe by the fact that she had rarely left Kolodetz. Her heart sank with heavy, evil premonitions. But I, the fool, got upset and insisted. Eventually Sarah agreed halfheartedly because the children offered to accompany her. It was, as I said, the middle of June, and in our region summer vacation started early—because of the harvest and such reasons—so Schura and Susannah went about getting her settled in the sanatorium. You'd be wrong if you thought they were doing it most altruistically; though they loved their mother, their scheme still included a visit on the way back to their aunt Klara and her husband Shabtsi Krantz, to get a taste of big city life in Lvov, with its theaters and concert halls. You remember, I believe, that my brother-in-law was an assistant pharmacist and as such he was an indisputable family authority on all issues concerning human health and medicine, just like the renowned and expensive Jewish doctors, who if they are in Austria prescribe medication for which you have to mortgage the inherited real estate of your grandmother, including her engagement ring, and if they're in Russia, recommend to you an infusion of Irish moss, a remedy that, after you've been to all the pharmacies in the region, you learn was last imported during the time of Nicholas II and is nothing more than a sentimental memory of bygone times. So, like them, I mean, our family pharmacist Shabtsi Krantz most heatedly agitated on behalf of a substitute for the mineral baths and other grannies' foolishness in the form of fresh lemon juice, which we hadn't seen for a long time in Kolodetz, mixed with pure Greek olive oil. The only ingredient available to us for this doubtlessly miraculous medication was the Soviet geography atlas with the most precise location of Greece. This fact to a large degree tipped the scales of hesitation on the side of the sanatorium mineral water treatment.

At the railway station Sarah's eyes filled with tears and our two Komsomol activists, pressing their heads to hers at the window of the car, were gently, but with the unconcealed self-confidence of the young guards of the working masses, caressing her and explaining to her that a human being would soon land on the Moon, while Rovno was a good deal closer. I, standing on the platform, trying to lighten the atmosphere, told a catastrophically old joke about Rosa Schwartz, who was leaving with her children for the mineral baths when her husband, Solomon Schwartz, who was seeing them off at the railway station, said, "If it starts raining, come back. Come back immediately!"

"Why should we come back?" said Rosa Schwartz. "If it comes down there, it will come down here too."

"Yes, but here rain is cheaper."

The children looked at each other, Sarah smiled lightly; apparently my joke had breezed by their ears and splashed on the wall on the other side of the compartment.

The three minutes passed—this is the length of the stop of the fast train to Lvov—and the train took off silently. I waved, they waved, I met Sarah's grayish green eyes and in them I read deep apprehension, which nothing could explain.

EIGHT

This was, I repeat, toward the middle of June, and several days later twenty-three men from Kolodetz received summonses to appear Under the Flags. I showed mine to the rabbi, he in turn showed his to me and smiled sourly, because the Austro-Hungarian and the Polish stories were repeating themselves, we were tied to each other by fortune. The rabbi, of course, was not mobilized either as a rabbi, or even as the chair of the Atheists' Club, but as a regular Soviet private from the infantry, which is, as you know, the queen of battles. And where exactly her majesty was going to be sent and to fight whom was explained to me by none other than the experienced-in-solving-similar-military-and-other-riddles-of-the-universe rabbi Ben-David:

"Without doubt from Lvov we'll be sent to the Far East. The sly Japanese have started sneaking up again along our border."

"And where, more precisely, so I can write Sarah?" I asked most idiotically.

"Have you ever heard the waltz 'The Hills of Manchuria'?" the rabbi said somberly. "Somewhere around there. There's a record player, you can send it to my sister."

It may seem strange to you, but I felt excitement, I could even say deep elation: oh my God, Manchuria, on the other side of the world! My ears rang with the battle trumpets and drums of the epoch, joined by the powerful bass-baritone of a Cossack orthodox choir that was performing a church interpretation of the "Internationale"—my country's anthem at that time.

Of course, I didn't send Sarah my exact address, or exactly which Manchurian hill we were talking about, because on the one hand this was not officially announced to us, and on the other, because I wasn't born yesterday, through my head, if you remember, had passed not one or two military ordeals and I knew very well what a military secret meant. To Sarah I wrote only that these would probably be routine maneuvers or in the worst case insignificant border incidents, about which it's common knowledge how they end—with the smashing of the Japanese with one slap, like a Siberian mosquito that's landed on your neck. This at least is how things looked in the movies. I also wrote to her not to worry and to drink her mineral water calmly, because it was possible that before her prescribed three weeks were over, we would be back already in Kolodetz, decorated with Samurai trophies and garlands of Manchurian flowers. In my letter I did not exclude the possibility of the Japanese proletariat voluntarily joining our side, refusing to fight against the worker-peasant USSR. Then probably some of them would wish to come with us and settle forever in Kolodetz next to their Jewish brothers in class. The latter, of course, was an attempt at a joke; I hope you remember how I, since my youth, had loved to pretend to be a dummy, and this had always amused Sarah, who at similar clown performances of mine would always smile gently and lovingly, pointing her finger at her temples.

On June 22, 1941, at 6:05 A.M., we were standing at the railway station, waiting for the passenger train for Lvov. "Railway station," to tell you the truth, is kind of pretentious as a definition for this little house with the sign "Kolodetz Station" surrounded by golden swaying wheat, and the dark strip of willows marking the capricious course of our little Kolodetz river. A dusty cart road went through the fields and the orchards and from there in the distance you could just see the pointed bell tower of the Catholic church. If you've got any questions regarding the situation of Kolodetz in world railway traffic, I will tell you that our little native town wasn't Paris and as a rule trains took off from it before they even arrived. And still we would outsmart them by throwing our luggage, and ourselves after it, through the windows, and before the locomotive engineer knew that this was Kolodetz, the most dexterous among us, sitting comfortably in the compartment, had already opened a bottle of home-brewed wheat vodka.

And so, the passenger train, which was of that type about which they say that it stops at every roof tile for three seconds, was lazily rattling along in the silent sunny morning amid the wheat, with the bright red islands of blooming poppies scattered here and there. The conductor passed by the twenty-three heroic fighters against Japanese militarism, who, having attacked and conquered the train in zero time, didn't have tickets, and were casually showing their summonses with the proud, unconcealed confidence of those called up Under the Flags. These small mobilization slips served us as tickets with their printed text and with the dots, filled in by hand in violet ink, which apart from indicating our Lvov destination, also instructed us to carry a second set of underwear, socks, toothbrush, and other everyday details for an apparently short but victorious war, usually designated in the communiqués as a border incident. And so, first Lvov, and then a long, free-of-charge—and most important—pleasant trip. This reminded me of Mendel, who also decided to travel around a bit and visit people in Odessa for Rosh Hashanah, this holiday we have. And because, unlike us, he didn't have the right to a free trip, he stood in line at the ticket office of the Berdichev railway station. When his turn came, he was most politely informed by the girl comrade how much was the price of a ticket to Odessa, second class: "Seventeen rubles."

Then Mendel thrust his head in the arched window at the counter and discreetly asked, "How about twelve rubles?"

The other one got upset. "This is not the place for Jewish bargaining. Seventeen rubles and not a kopek less. Piss off, there are people waiting in line behind you!"

Mendel with a casual whistle went up and stood at the end of the line, and when finally his turn came, he again thrust his head in the window at the counter. "Fifteen rubles final, comrade?"

The ticketseller seriously lost her temper. "Get out now, do you hear me?!"

He again stood in line, but at that moment the train for Odessa whistled and took off.

Then Mendel lowered his head at the window and said with deadly sarcasm, "And now, comrade, who lost fifteen rubles?"

It was probably eight before noon when the train was invaded by a merry new crowd of mobilized guys from the surrounding villages, traveling to different units, but with the final destination of faraway Manchuria or somewhere around there, and with them a new stream of information poured in about events at those places. Let me tell you right now, that unlike other times, our rabbi was sad and closed up in himself, his cheerful friendliness and readiness to participate in any conversation—a quality so Jewish, like the readiness to give advice on any question, about which I've already told you—had evaporated, he was silently looking out and I knew that his soul wasn't there, but following Esther Katz in her lonely and terrible journey through the Desert. And the newcomers were energetically telling stories about the battles at Khalkin Gol and Khasan Lake, about how we'd simply plucked all the feathers off the Samurai and the whole job was done by our fearful T-34 tanks, and that if it wasn't for the treachery of marshals Tukhachevski and Blücher, we would've long ago been drying our socks under the blooming cherry trees of Fujiyama.

And it's exactly here at this place in my story that I'll remind you of Mohammed, who, since he didn't go to Fujiyama, Fujiyama came to him, maybe it wasn't like this in the original but you get what I mean. Because suddenly, with a deafening roar low above us, a bunch of airplanes flew in and a second later a carpet of bombs came pouring down. The train stopped, the wheat around went up in flames, and someone was shouting in a loud voice:

"Get off the train and go lie in the ditches! God damn you, jump through the windows fast!"

Thank God, we had long ago learned the typically Russian art of using train windows as entrance–exit arteries, because a minute after that, with the second wave of airplanes, several boxcars exploded into bits and pieces. It was simply unbelievable that the Japanese had reached all the way to Drogobych so fast, on the other side of our immense country, without us hearing a single thing about it! Now I know that part of the responsibility for that slightly delayed information was carried by those black cones, called "reproductors," which quite often reproduced world news with delays of some hours, and sometimes several days or months, if they reproduced them at all.

Now, what shall I tell you, brother, you're a smart person, and long before me understood what it was all about and what had come down upon our heads. You know, that at exactly that time when our train cars, blown into spare parts, were flying in the air, Molotov was announcing on the radio the atrocious invasion of the German-Fascists' troops and calling the Soviet people to a holy war. This, of course, we couldn't have known, or heard amid the burning wheat and the heavy clouds of smoke. Only several hours later it became definitely clear to us that the enemy had crossed not the Khalkin Gol river in the Far East, but the river Bug on the other side of geography. For the same reason the "Hills of Manchuria" waltz was apparently being substituted with an invitation to the "Lili Marlene" tango.

NINE

My first thought was Sarah—I had to find some connection to Rovno and help her come back home to Kolodetz. Don't call me, please, a fool—not that I'll deny it, but I don't know if even in the Kremlin or if Comrade Stalin himself was fully aware at that hour of the apocalypse that was beginning, that's why you'll forgive my naive idea that I could somehow buy myself a train ticket and go and find her. Moreover, I had been summoned Under the Flags, and diversions from this high goal in Soviet country were severely punished. And it was enough to meet the eyes of my rabbi Ben-David, who wasn't expressing anything but desperate acceptance of my bottomless foolish optimism, to understand how wrong our children had been, when they assured their mother that the trip to Rovno would be far easier than the upcoming—according to Komsomol notions about the near future—trip to the moon.

By a miracle this unexpected air attack didn't claim any victims, but passengers and mobilized men alike, going toward their military units, split into groups and dispersed in the panic caused by the next wave of low-flying airplanes, which left in their wake, beyond the forest horizon, a series of subsequent explosions—military ammunition dumps were hit, gasoline storage units or something like that.

To this day I don't know and I probably never will whether those call-up slips, tied only to rumors that were spread around even quite deliberately as misinformation about impending military operations in the Far East, were not simply dust in the blue eyes of the Germans and thus a discreet form of mobilization, in which case Hitler had just seized the day. Were the Soviet authorities really caught with their pants down and completely surprised by the German invasion? Or had they put themselves to sleep with the boisterous declarations of TASS that everything is fine, Madame La Marquise? I don't know, but if the latter is true, and as I remember how the German tanks, airplanes, and storm troopers penetrated the defenseless, unprepared Soviet land like a hot knife in a lump of butter, I ask myself: how did they *not* know in the Kremlin and *not* anticipate what was known or felt by our good old men in Kolodetz, while they were winding and unwinding the ball of yarn of the Rothschild family problems?

I don't rule out the possibility of their knowing it, because, as it became clear much later, they had been warned by our man Sorge in Tokyo, and by our intelligence guys in Berlin, and by a high-ranking Bulgarian general, who was shot because he told them even the exact day and time of the attack. In this case, was Stalin expecting in a most idiotic fashion that up until the very last moment his pal Adolf would have second thoughts and finally fulfill the threat, desired by both Germans and Russians alike, that he would swoop down on England? Exactly the same way, that four years later, this one and the same Adolf expected and believed, as Russian bombs were exploding above his own bunker in Berlin, that the Anglo-Americans would swoop down on

Russia and he'd get off with a mere fine for illegally parking tanks at inappropriate places abroad?

If I'm not mistaken, I've gone slightly off the track, but now I'll go straight back to the burning wheat.

The panic and confusion that seized the whole area were indescribable and my memory has retained just scraps of a nightmare dream, fragments from a picture torn into small pieces, in which you can't tell anymore which is which, or what's up and what's down. Only one thing was clear to us—we had to reach Lvov at any cost and it was thanks only to Rabbi Ben-David, who didn't lose his presence of mind, that we managed to remain uninjured from the fire storm that was wrapping us in black sooty smoke and devouring wheat and villages. In front of us on the dusty torn-up roads the first streams of refugees flowed in, striving eastward and always eastward, while in the opposite direction there were already military columns of infantry, horse carts, and cavalry; endless, endless lines of volunteers—still in civilian clothes and barely equipped, or old beat-up *kolhoz* trucks, packed with badly dressed defenders of the fatherland, often even without a uniform, and only a red band on their sleeves. There was no music, no marching, not even the song of the three tank men—those three jolly fellows; people were going to battle silent, intent, and solemn. From the refugees we would learn of rumors that clashed and contradicted each other: that our boys were heading toward Warsaw, that the Germans were just in front of Kiev, or that whole German divisions had surrendered because of that same old delusion of ours that the proletariat of all nations, which every morning would unite around the headlines of the newspaper *Pravda*, wouldn't raise its hand against the worker-peasant Soviet Union. In any case, the rumors were mostly favorable—you can imagine that at such a moment people are ready to believe in even the most incredible but longed-for lie, rather than the bitter truth.

Our group fell apart once and for all and melted into that chaos. My good rabbi and I spent the night in some deserted hut, probably for the field guard, which was like a quote from another peacetime song, because in the field the pumpkins were still blooming, carefree with their big bright yellow flowers. The night was full of amorous grasshoppers, fireflies that were winking coquettishly, and in the distance, every now and then, the echoes of sharp bursts of machine-gun fire—so far away, as if in the forest a woodpecker were hard at work. The rabbi disappeared and about an hour later came back with a big slice of brown village bread and a chunk of cheese. It seems strange to me now that I didn't even ask him where he got it from; in that nightmarish unreality I wouldn't have been surprised if he had come back on a motorcycle, wearing his rabbinic Passover outfit or, say, the uniform of a red *politcommissar* from the tank divisions. Exhausted, he threw himself on the mat of woven willow shoots, covered pitifully with a torn Ukrainian rug, and silently gave me the food. And I, the fool, hungrily bit into the bread and the cheese, without even asking what bushes, thorns, and barbed wire had torn his clothes and scratched his arms. But even if I'd asked, what would have been the use? This reminds me of Abramovitch, who came back home after a tiresome journey and got upset with his wife, while he was examining the blisters on his feet.

"You didn't even ask how I was!"

"Oh, well," said his wife. "How are you?"

"Oy, oy, don't ask!"

TEN

Sometimes on army transport carts, more rarely on military trucks, and mostly on foot along the dusty roads between villages, exhausted to the very limits of our strength, we finally dragged ourselves to Lvov. It was evening but there were no streetlights, the city was roaring with explosions, in the north the sky was red with fire. Soviet soldiers were running toward some destination, dragging a heavy machine gun, two nurses were bandaging the side of the head of a chap wounded by burning pieces of oil-soaked cloth, which were emitting more smoke than light. Nobody even answered our question about what exactly was happening in the town.

It wasn't necessary to convince ourselves that at this time of night, our only option was to get somehow to my sister and her assistant pharmacist, where maybe Schura and Susannah were still to be found—the naive romantics, who came all the way from Kolodetz to watch *Othello* and listen to Rachmaninov, without even realizing that a slightly different performance would be presented to them.

We passed turned-over and incinerated streetcars, wrapped in their own wires, by the side of a still smoking automobile with its four doors wide open, which turned out to be, who knows how, in the middle of a fountain. And right in the middle of the boulevard we saw, as if ready for a grand concert, a Petrov piano, which people who were running away must have wanted to take with them but along the way had thought twice about. In the high school yard the cement cast of Lenin, with a thumb stuck under his vest, and his other hand pointing toward the bright future, was overturned, and even the hand pointing to the above-mentioned bright future was partially broken and from the inside iron rods quite prosaically peeped out, and from the depths of a rampaged and burnt shoe shop, a crazy telephone was ringing constantly. Such a picture it was, dear brother, of devastation and panicked flight, which—I imagine —was probably described in the TASS communiqués as a "planned and organized evacuation of the population," and by Radio Berlin as an "indescribably enthusiastic welcoming of the liberating German troops."

On a side street close to us again three young soldiers came running up with a machine gun, set it down on the pavement, and hit the ground in anticipation, and I, in a most friendly manner, hailed them in Russian: "Hello, comrades!"

The soldiers didn't even reply, and I was just about to ask them about the situation and this and that, when my rabbi squeezed my arm above the elbow till it hurt and dragged me in the other direction.

"Idiot!" he hissed. "Don't you realize they're Germans?"

How could I have figured it out in the darkness, and moreover, at the movies I had seen mostly what the Japanese samurai looked like, and not German soldiers. We went away fast, but behind our back someone shouted in Russian-German: "Hey, Russki, halt! Stop! Stop!"

Behind us, nailed shoes started heavily stomping, and we stopped, without daring to turn around—in expectation of a shot in the back. It didn't come, though, the sinister shot, and the soldier, who caught up with us running, asked, breathing heavily, "Do you have matches? Matches!"

And for greater clarity he struck the fingers of his hand against the index finger of his other hand.

The rabbi reached into his pocket and handed him a box of matches, and with an almost salon-like politeness, quite uncustomary for our Kolodetz, said, "*Bitte, mein Herr!*"

It seemed to me that his hand was shaking slightly, but the boy turned out to have been well brought up, because he said a kind "*Danke!*" and clumsily ran up to his chaps, who for some unknown reason were lying on the ground, with—keep in mind—dead silence reigning all about them. I don't know exactly, but I think this was the first and last time during the Second World War that a representative of Hitler's victorious Wehrmacht and a rabbi had such a polite and cordial exchange.

We finally reached the old apartment building in which my people were living, and went up the dark stairway with difficulty, as we didn't even have matches anymore to get to the right floor and the right entrance. But one way or another, I managed to feel my way around, since the buzzer, of course, wasn't working—it had gone silent for a long time now and, if I remember correctly, during the whole of the Soviet period of their life, the Krantz family had been waiting for the technician who was supposed to fix it and who was apparently not going to show up until the complete triumph of communism.

We had been knocking on the door for a long time when we were flooded by some kind of yellowish light. The door of the neighboring apartment opened, a man at the threshold lifted, high above his head, a gas lamp that was flashing in his eyes, and only after taking a good look at us did he ask, "Who are you looking for, gentlemen?"

I immediately noticed the word "gentlemen," which was so foreign to Soviet life that it had the effect of a phrase out of a Chekhov play. This is how we learned that Mr. Assistant-Pharmacist Krantz had been mobilized, my sister evacuated with the polyclinic in which she was working as an attendant, and as far as my Komsomol youths were concerned, "the young sir and the young lady," who had been visiting here, they had enlisted, as far as he knew, as volunteers on the very first day of the war.

We stood silent in the corridor in front of the ruins of our last hope of finding a connection with our people, while the neighbor, who again lifted the lamp to take a look at us, asked, "And who are you?"

And there we were, sitting in the big guestroom, the kind with high plaster ceilings, furnished with magnificent antique pieces built during the lavish Austro-Hungarian times. I secretly spotted the Catholic cross in the niche on the wall and the porcelain figure of the Madonna under it.

"You probably come from afar?" asked the host.

It didn't take us long to explain what had happened on our long road to Manchuria, because in the yellow light of the lamp from the big mirror across from us, two disheveled, dusty and quite suspicious characters were staring back at us, while—let me tell you this too—our host, with his checkered dressing gown, smoothly combed silver hair, which had once been bright blond, and high pale forehead, briefly suggested the air of a Polish aristocrat from an old genealogical tree, who had somehow and unknowingly survived under the blows of the revolutionary axes.

"And you must be hungry?" he asked, still so politely.

The rabbi and I looked at each other, I was ready to mumble some lie of the "Thanks, please don't bother" variety, which was written in the unwritten code of good conduct for the residents of Kolodetz by Drogobych, but Rabbi Ben-David nodded with a sincere readiness. "Yes, very. I think we haven't eaten since yesterday."

In this way we got eggs sunnyside up and sausage, while our host observed us with unconcealed curiosity. "You're Jews, right? If the family Krantz are your relatives."

I nodded and after I swallowed my food, I asked in turn, "And you're Polish?"

He smiled. "Is it obvious by my accent? Polish, professor of ophthalmology in the local polyclinic. My wife is also a doctor, now she is at a graduate course in Leningrad and only God knows how and when we'll be together again. . . . And what are your plans? I'm sorry, I don't mean to be excessively curious, but if we judge by the German radio stations, Lvov is already behind the front line and by tomorrow the resistance of your people in the city will be crushed."

My signal system picked up that "your people," which is why I cast a glance at the rabbi, when the host invited us to stay the night with him. I didn't know if it was reckless of my good rabbi, but he quite enthusiastically accepted. And I, admittedly, wasn't sure that this, so to speak, foreign element, wouldn't open the window and call the German soldiers down below—those fellows who owed us a box of matches. Quite soon I had an opportunity to confirm again that Rabbi Ben-David had a healthy instinct about decent people that was seriously different from the class notions of the comrades from the Center, because this pale professor-ophthalmologist turned out to be to an equal degree a decent and noble anti-communist, with a barely perceptible Polish streak of anti-Semitism—something like a good aged wine with a bitter aftertaste.

A big discussion around dinner, which we quickly polished off, didn't happen because we were dead tired and the pan ophthalmologist accommodated us in the servants' long-unused room—a dear memory from different times.

We slept like logs and in the morning, thoroughly washed, clean-shaven and reeking of Soviet "Troinoi" eau de cologne, which we discovered in the bathroom, from our host in his checkered dressing gown we received magnificent tea with toast and butter. He even apologized for not having milk: he had gone out early in the morning, but the milk shop was closed. Can you imagine—our motherland is burning, millions are being displaced here, there and everywhere, and Mr. Doctor is apologizing that the milk shop at the corner is not performing its duties to the community! We were having breakfast in the kitchen, with the copper pans hanging above the stove and the white-blue ceramic tiles, which featured Dutch women with wooden shoes and windmills. The host was again observing us with curiosity, as if he had never seen Galician Jews.

"And you intend to report yourselves to the military unit and to go and defend the Soviet regime?" he asked unexpectedly.

"Yes," said the rabbi mildly.

"What is your profession? Excuse my curiosity."

"Rabbi," said the rabbi mildly.

The professor choked on his tea, and again, but more quietly, asked, "And you intend to fight for the Soviet regime?"

"Yes. And now we intend—if God helps us—to get to our people."

"To your people, yes . . . ," the professor repeated uselessly, and on a sudden interest turned to me: "And you?"

Well, what about me? While the rabbi went out to the balcony for a smoke, upon my weak shoulders fell the effort to explain the whole Jewish puzzle of kinship relations between me and the rabbi, the young man and the young lady who had gone as volunteers to the Red Army, and last but not least, their mother, the rabbi's sister and, as they say in the trade union reports, contemporaneously my wife Sarah, who at this moment was at the mineral baths somewhere in Rovno, because of some kidney trouble. Brief and clear. Not that are absent those types of kinship relations with the Poles, but with the Jews kinship entangles itself in such a pathological knot of umbilical cords, interdependencies, and affinities, that by comparison the Oedipus complex is a hardly noticeable mental quirk—something like a twitch of the eyelid. The case becomes even more complicated by the fact that all Jews, literally all of them—starting with the sunflower seed vendor Golda Zilber all the way to Baron Rothschild, are relatives on their father's side, I mean by that rib of Adam's, which started that whole family scourge.

I remained with the impression that my genealogical vignettes, starting from the next door apartment of the assistant pharmacist Shabtsi Krantz and reaching all the way to the mineral baths by Rovno, the professor let pass by his ears with boredom, because he interrupted me in a businesslike manner: "Did you say Rovno?"

I nodded silently. He looked at me with his transparent blue eyes, kept silent for a while, and only after that said, "Rovno as of yesterday is in the hands of the Germans. I'm sorry."

At that moment the whole carefully constructed kinship pyramid collapsed upon me, the whole world of Adam and Abraham with concern for all relatives collapsed—from Rothschild to Golda Zilber and Albert Einstein. Only Sarah remained, who was silently looking at me with her grayish-green eyes. Sarah, oh, my God, I forced her to go there! I had to reach her, I had to reach that unfamiliar place somewhere around Rovno and take her out of there—despite everything, despite all armies, divisions, and the SS Stormtroopers of Schickelgruber!

Of course, this was my first and immediate aspiration. But it didn't take any special effort on the part of my rabbi to convince me of the hopelessness of the idea of penetrating Nazi-occupied territory in order to discover a sanatorium somewhere around Rovno. My only hope, which the rabbi raised in me, was the possibility that the patients had been evacuated in a timely fashion to the interior of the country. Then the problem was transferred from Sarah to us, who had turned out to be such fools as to mix up the road for the Far East and on our own fallen into the trap of the near West.

Speaking of traps, I remember that the professor brought in from the street a leaflet in three languages—German, Ukrainian, and Polish—in which it was proclaimed that thanks to the victorious German military power, our dream had come true—Lvov and the region had been liberated from Bolshevik oppression and annexed to the Eastern Territories of the Reich. In addition, we were politely informed that during a three-day period all communist functionaries, Jews, and Soviet officers in hiding were supposed to register at command headquarters, or else, according to wartime rules, they were going to be. . . . Well, shall I tell you, or can you guess yourself?

"Lvov and the region!" Did this mean as well our little town of Kolodetz by Drogobych, my old parents and the permanent *sanhedrin* from our workshop, my dear neighbors and acquaintances—Ukrainians, Poles, and Jews, including David Leibovitch's café, with the orphaned Atheists' Club and the once-upon-a-time ardent believers in Jewish social-democracy?

And so, my dear brother and my unknown reader, my motherland was changed for the fourth time and now I was solemnly joined to the big German family, but with one detail, which spoiled the holiday a little: as a person of Jewish origin I was supposed to register myself during a three-day period at command headquarters, and I really doubt that the reason behind it was to create an opportunity for me to be given congratulatory telegrams and flowers.

"I don't know what I can advise you," our professor said, quite concerned. "I deal with myopic eyes and not with myopic social utopias, and that's why I have no sympathy either for the Russians or for their Soviet authority. I have to admit, and please don't be offended, but I don't feel any particular tenderness for the Jews either, especially for all your different Karl Marxes, Rosa Luxemburgs, Leon Trotskys, or *tutti quanti* Kaganoviches, who dead or alive are seriously responsible for our present-day troubles."

Rabbi Ben-David wanted to say something in disagreement, but the professor raised his hand. "Please, I have no desire whatsoever to start a political debate. But since I, as a Pole, can't stand the Germans any more than you can, and especially these present-day ones, I don't see any other way out for you but to sneak somehow east, and go to those whom you call 'yours.'"

"This is what we intend to do," the rabbi said calmly.

The professor was silent for a while, then moved his pensive glance from the rabbi to me and finally said, "I still don't understand, I honestly don't understand what connects you to this idea, when you know what outrages are being committed in Soviet Russia. Or don't you know? Haven't you even heard?"

The rabbi smiled sadly. "A very dear person, maybe the dearest person, a woman, is now in the steel grip of what you call 'outrages.' I don't even know if she's alive or if she'll be alive much longer. And still, I will fight to defend the Soviet country from fascism. This is a different question, it's hard for me even to explain it to you. And you, I dare say, are confusing the idea with the system and this is welcome to the system. It likes to be confused with the idea, and even to be perceived as its only materialized expression, equivalence, and interchangeable equal. How can I make myself clear? As far as I understand, you are a believing Christian, and does the Christian church not want to be identified with Christianity? But the Idea is one thing, and the System that has to materialize it, another. And a day comes when the defense of the Christian ideal of brotherhood, love of one's neighbor, and forgiveness for all, is taken up by the Inquisition, the Crusades, and the technologies for burning witches and chasing the devil. The spiritual glamour of your Christian idea is imperceptibly replaced by the glamour of church ritual, and the asceticism and personal dedication of the early Christians by the gluttony and lechery of abbots and cardinals. Isn't it so? The system has its own survival needs and logic, and if the Idea stands up to them, so much the worse for it—it can be silently buried and replaced by an exact copy or a demonstration model. But you remain true to the original idea, regardless of everything. You can deal with myopic vision, but are powerless in front of color-blindness. And exactly there lies the zone where the Idea and the System blend so tightly that you don't know which one you are serving: the ideas of Christ or the canons of the church."

If the rabbi had finished with an "Amen and *Gut Shabbos*!" this would have been one of his usual Shabbos sermons on questions of life and the universe.

The professor laughed soundlessly. "So you consider me to be politically color-blind?"

"I think you're an honest person, who isn't obliged to carry someone else's cross in the name of someone else's ideas. Everyone crosses his own Desert, in search of his own Canaan! In any case, you said something about the Jews, Marx, and responsibility. Let me remind you that Karl Marx was not a Marxist, nor was Christ a Christian. Ideas are the children of their time and these two, as well as the apostle Paul, Baruch Spinoza, or Sigmund Freud, are to blame neither for the distortion of their ideas nor for the fact that they were born Jewish. By the way, Hitler and Stalin, and the great inquisitor Torquemada, are not Jews, but this doesn't change anything!"

That same evening the professor brought two old Polish identity papers and with shyness admitted that he had stolen them from the clinic's archives. To me fell the identity documents of one Heinrich Bjegalski, known in the clinic as the doorman Pan Heniek, who died of a stroke sometime before the Soviet era, and the rabbi became neither more nor less than the chief—the head intern Karel Miechkowski—who went to his mother's funeral in Gdansk and forgot to come back. I resembled the porter Pan Heniek in the glued photograph as much as poor Avramchik resembled Ramon Navarro and the difference could be noticed even by the blind Yossel. I expressed my concern, but the professor said:

"Don't worry, Mr. Blumenfeld. For the bureaucrat, especially the German bureaucrat, it is important to have a number, a photo, and a stamp. Here is the number, here is the stamp, and do your best to keep them from noticing the difference between the photo and you."

"Your photo, see, was taken before you had typhoid and viral encephalitis!" the rabbi added nervously.

So here we are—two Polish citizens, liberated from the Soviet oppression, who are strolling through the streets of Lvov, looking for some address, which, according to the words of Rabbi Karel Miechkowski, was the former secret meeting place for Esther Katz. There, according to the hopes of the rabbi, we could get in touch and so on.

I tried to walk calmly and nonchalantly, and looked bravely into the eyes of the frequent German patrol pairs with dogs, who, as it seemed to me, regarded us intently and with suspicion. Sometimes I even gave them a friendly nod.

Just like Mendel, who told his friend, "Yesterday the ticket inspector came into the tram, and can you imagine, he looked at me as if I didn't have a ticket."

"And what did you do?"

"I looked at him as if I had a ticket!"

And so, we were walking around, looking at the numbers of the houses, till at one point my rabbi said, "Wait here and don't move."

And he crossed the street and dived into the entrance of a building.

And right at this moment in the narrative, something happened that defined my destiny for years ahead. Or as some authors would say—there was a dramatic turn of events.

This dramatic turn consisted in the sudden appearance, as if from somewhere deep below the ground, of trucks with soldiers. The soldiers jumped out and in no time made a thick circle around us, the peaceful civilians. There was sudden panic, the

German shepherds were barking viciously, tugging on their leather leashes, and the soldiers were pushing us with the butts of their carbines toward the trucks: "Los, los, los . . ."

In confusion, I pulled out the—as it seemed to me—saving identity documents of Pan Heniek, and since, as you know, the German language isn't foreign to me, and I had been all the way to Vienna, I announced to the German officer that people were waiting for me in the ophthalmology office and other such nonsense, and he only pushed me a little more with his butt to make me get on faster.

The last thing I saw when the trucks were pulling away was my rabbi Shmuel Ben-David, who had come out into the street. He was pale as a porcelain figurine of the Madonna, and when the truck passed him by, he lowered his eyelids, perhaps as a sign of courage, or perhaps as a last good-bye.

It turned out that my underground life under someone else's name in Lvov lasted less than the life of a one-day fly, and the man who is destined by Yahweh to have things happen to him—well, he cannot escape them. This is a proven fact.

It was only when they crammed us into the trucks, littered with dirty, stinking straw, that I could hear from the small barred vent the conversation between the invisible engine drivers and understand that our route was through Warsaw for Berlin, can you imagine?

So, this is how, my dear brother, myself and another 399 citizens of Lvov, courteously situated over the straw of ten horse wagons, were sent on a business trip to Berlin, the heart of our new motherland—the German Reich—designated in the schoolbooks, or, according to the historically proven hypothesis, the Third, or Thousand-Year.

ISAAC'S FOURTH BOOK

"To Each His Own," or to the Concentration Camps, with Love

ONE

In our Kolodetz they used to tell this story about three Jews from different parts of Galicia, who by the will of fate, during a certain historic period called "Soviet Power," happened to be together in the same prison cell, before they were sent off to the faraway Siberian camps, each according to his own crime.

"I've been sentenced to fifteen years," said one by way of introduction, "because I was for Moishe Liebermann."

"I too got fifteen years," the second one said, "because I was against Moishe Liebermann."

And the third one said, "They also gave me fifteen years, because I am Moishe Liebermann."

I'm not making a direct comparison, God forbid, but in the horse wagons, on the damp, dirty straw, they had crammed all of us together—the supporters of Soviet power, the opponents of Soviet power, and this same power itself in the persons of the honest Soviet workers from institutions and factories, who happened to be exactly in the wrong place at exactly the wrong time, as you recall. Not one of us could say why we were captured like rabbits in the streets of Lvov, what we were guilty of or whether we were guilty at all, and—most importantly—where they were taking us. The hypotheses of the sharper minds, in whose number I in no way dared to include myself, were quite controversial and in reality unconfirmed, because the war was, so to speak, still quite new and Europe was just beginning to accumulate rich and fruitful experience. According to some we were being packed off so that we could be exchanged for German hostages, which to me seemed not very plausible, because the Germans already had in their possession a much richer assortment for barter in the form of complete military units already taken prisoner, including here and there a supply of nice fat decorated officers. According to others we were traveling to the interior parts of our new motherland in order to replace mobilized specialists from different areas of German life. This was more probable, even though I don't believe that in Berlin, or say Baden-Baden, they had a deficit of tailors skilled in turning old Jewish caftans inside out.

One way or the other, the road turned out to be quite long—I don't remember anymore, five or six days and nights, during which they threw at us only some bread or boiled potatoes in homeopathic rations, which would make even a family of cockroaches have spontaneous dystrophy. And as to certain physiological details, please, spare me the memories!

The train moved slowly. At some places, probably railroad junctions, our boxcars would jolt along back and forth for hours, we could hear railroad mechanics' whistles, cries, the barking of dogs, and at one place we even had music blaring out from a brass band—they were welcoming or seeing someone off, but it was hardly in our honor.

Lying on the straw, I was thinking with concern and tenderness about everyone and everything—about Sarah and the children, so abruptly taken by the whirlwind of war, about my father Aaron and my mother Rebekha, about Uncle Chaimle and the others who remained there, in that outer, and as it seemed—already inaccessible world, to which I was hardly likely to return. And what had happened, I was wondering, to my rabbi, who, pale and frozen on the sidewalk in Lvov, followed with his eyes the movement of the departing truck? And where now were Esther Katz, Liova Weissmann, Avramchik, Pan Voitek, and the Catholic priest? Had the collective calamity that had fallen on our heads spared those whom Ben-David defined as "the System," and had the aforementioned system, before the lethal danger that was threatening it, not let go of its iron grip and spit them out to freedom, after apologizing for the small annoying misunderstanding? Clickety-clack, clickety-clack . . .

It was probably long after midnight when I woke up from the silence that had suddenly fallen. Our train had halted and this wasn't a station, and it wasn't an intermediary stop either, with the familiar asthmatic puffing of locomotives, maneuver-directing whistles, and that secret ritual with the banging of a small hammer on the wagon wheels, which always reminds me of our old railroad worker Shmoile Abramovitch from the railroad junction of Drogobych. Excuse me for straying a little from the road taking us to the heart of the Reich, but let me tell you how good old Shmoile banged most patiently and diligently on the wagon wheels in Austro-Hungarian, Polish, and Soviet times, and when he retired they even awarded him the Medal of the Red Labor Flag. Deeply moved, Shmoile delivered the following speech:

"Dear comrades and fellow railroad workers! Thank you for all the good words that I have heard. Thank you also for the high honor of the medal for my half-century of faithful service at the Drogobych railway station with that small hammer and its long handle. But now, before I retire with my pension, please, dear comrades and colleagues, explain to me why it's actually necessary to bang the wheels of the wagons and what's the good of it?"

So, what I'm saying is we didn't hear any banging or whistles. Around us, for the first time in several days, there was complete silence, as if the locomotive had taken off, leaving the rest of the train in some bottomless tunnel. Only in the morning, when gray light filtered through the vents, did they start noisily opening the sliding wagon doors and ordering us with undeserved rudeness to get out. We were surrounded by pine trees, full of birdsong. The rails ended with two buffers and a barrier of wooden crossbeams, and after the stale air in the wagons, in the first moment it seemed to me that through some misunderstanding we had ended up in German paradise: it smelled like sap and damp soil, and through the branches, high up there in the morning mist, sun rays were streaming in smoky beams, with three million gnats whirling about in a crazy dance. Such a picture would have seemed quite characteristic of peacetime and even a little like a resort if it hadn't been for the soldiers with dogs and the whitewashed wooden planks with directions—all saying quite different things, but with two words repeated in all of them—"*Streng Verboten*," which means "strictly forbidden." The time would come when, having gotten to know my new fellow countrymen the Germans, I would understand how tenderly, one might even say voluptuously, they are devoted to that word *verboten*, and how that also attached *streng* commands respect, like the clicking of a lock or a pair of handcuffs. All signs were stamped with a deadly skull and crossbones, which evoked in me nostalgic memories of my adolescent years, spent with Captain Morgan on the Tortugas Islands. Here, of course it wasn't about pirate flags and yo-ho-ho and a bottle of rum, but about minefields and, in certain strictly defined circumstances, shooting without warning. Our coniferous surroundings consisted of very tall reddish pines, diligently trimmed almost to the tops, where their green hats darkened—as if the forest had gone through special training in the army, because here, unlike the slovenliness and waywardness of the pre-Carpathian forest, all the trees were equally tall, lined up in straight rows, and not even one would take a single step ahead, or stick out its belly or behind. This comforting sense of order was enhanced by the fact that each tree had military stripes cut into the bark in the form of fishbones—something like the stripes on the sleeves of our Soviet officers and political commissars from the time when they hadn't yet restored the royal officers' epaulettes and the "Internationale" hadn't yet been prohibited, but that's a whole other subject. I soon figured out that the small clay bowls at the base of each lieutenant's or even maybe fieldmarshal's stripes on the pine trees were collecting sap, and that we were going to produce from it—I'm trusting you with this secret—turpentine for military purposes. And if you were to look through the pine trees as they stood in ranks for a morning military inspection, you would observe in the distance the chesslike rows of orderly barracks with spots of camouflage on the roofs. You're probably impatient to learn where we were and I'll tell you: this place was somewhere in the Brandenburg forest and had the mysterious name "Special Site A-17."

And here we are, brother—all mussed up and crumpled and unshaven, with bits of straw sticking to our hair, standing in two rows on the vast square plaza bordered by the green barracks. In the small space between them—something more or less like an alleyway, swept clean and marked by large black numbers—you could see the second row of barracks and even the roofs of the third. The rhythmic mechanical din drifted toward us, lathes turned, and something else that hissed somewhere behind the barracks, as if a prehistoric monster were lying around, giving an occasional snore and periodic heavy sighs, and the dusty windows of a long shed now and then gleamed with the blue lightning of welding tools.

The soldiers behind our back—in full military getup, with helmets and submachine guns, holding tight their dogs' leather leashes—had such a militant and edgy look, as if we, the exhausted travelers to the unknown, who had let themselves be captured in the streets of Lvov, were any minute going to jump at them with knives. None of us of course had any such intention, nor did we have any knives, just the opposite—we were a little frightened, but you know yourself, the military and the police like to take situations seriously, it boosts their self-confidence. And if these fellows had had gas masks on their heads, they would have brought to mind those absurd midnight battles with ghosts in the middle of that field supposedly gassed by the French, you remember.

We stood like this for a long time, not daring to make the slightest movement, until there opened a barrack door, above which was written "COMMANDANT," and from the wooden veranda with three steps there rolled out a round creature in an officer's uniform atop polished boots. Swiftly, with a rapid and narrow stride, the creature walked around the square, looking at us carefully, as if he were searching for a particular acquaintance of his. I don't know from racial theories, or from the authentic Aryan shape of the skull, but if it's true about the descendants of Siegfried being manly blue-eyed, blond, six-foot-six knights, then the grandmother of this *nibelung* had had something to do with a Hungarian Gypsy, or God forbid, with the corner grocer, Aaron Rabinovitch.

The nibelung said, "Do you understand German, or do you need a translator?"

An indistinct murmuring ranged up and down the line, covering the whole spectrum of nuances from "yes" and "a little bit" to "no," which completely satisfied the boss, who continued: "I am *Oberlieutenant* Brückner and I am your chief. Keep in mind, this is not a concentration, but a labor camp. And you are not camp prisoners, but workers. After the *blitzkrieg*, which our invincible army is waging from the Atlantic to the Russian steppes and which will finish in a few months, you will go home, having fulfilled your obligation to the Reich. You will be paid for your labor, after the deduction of expenses for delousing, work clothes, food, and lodging. Discipline here is iron, remember this too, and every attempt to deviate from it will be punished as desertion or sabotage. Because it is necessary to observe the strictest military secrecy, correspondence here is forbidden. Am I clear so far?"

So far he was clear; in his intonation one could even detect distant notes of good intentions. I don't know if they were coming down the hereditary line from Siegfried, or from the sinful attraction of his grandmother to Hungarian Gypsies and Jewish grocers, but this is how it was and these good intentions would be confirmed more than once in the playing out of my personal destiny.

The Oberlieutenant rolled over one more time to the motley lined-up crew, which we definitely were at that moment, then stood stock still in the center of the plaza and asked, "Is there someone who speaks good German? Who doesn't stutter it like a Galician Jew, but knows it well, spoken and written, if you understand what I'm talking about. Is there anyone? Let him step forward!"

I was most sincerely offended! Under the circumstances it may seem to you careless on my part, but why in the world would this hog, who was speaking in such a Saxonian dialect that his German was barely comprehensible, think that we stuttered it?! Though for the others, say the Poles and the Ukrainians, this was a language used in moderation every now and then and only in extreme need during Austro-Hungarian times, for us—even somewhat enriched by Russian blessings and, as I already told you, with some Assyrian-Babylonian additions—our Yiddish still remained in the most direct sense of the word first cousin of the German. This offended national pride of mine made me step forward—a linguistic step, so to speak, in defense of the native tongue.

The chief came up to me, looked at me with his arms crossed behind his back and finally asked, "What's your name?"

I almost said "Private Isaac Blumenfeld," but something grabbed at the coattails of my soul and I swallowed the answer, changing it in flight to "Heinrich Bjegalski, Herr Oberlieutenant!"

He eyed me skeptically and I understood him completely: my appearance as a generally shabby wretch, a dark-skinned descendant of the Maccabees, had about as much in common with the presentable blondish Poles as my new commandant Brückner with Tannhäuser. In this respect we were equals, no doubt.

"What was your job in Lvov?" he asked.

"Ophthalmology," I said.

"Doctor?" he asked.

"Doorman," I said.

"Doorman? And you studied German?" He raised his eyebrows.

"Affirmative, sir, I've studied it," I said.

"And who, according to you, is the author of *Faust*?"

"Johann Wolfgang von Goethe, Herr Oberlieutenant. 1749–1832."

Tannhäuser was flabbergasted, and I sent up silent gratitude to my favorite teacher Eliezer Pinkus, may his soul rest in peace.

TWO

Some people think that the study of literature at school has no practical application and that it only fills up empty space between two recesses, which is not true at all. Eliezer Pinkus, in order to cultivate in us the need for basic knowledge about this seemingly useless subject, and also in connection with the abovementioned patriarch of German literature, would tell us the story of Mendel the fool, who visited our capital, at the time Vienna, stopped at the monument of Goethe by the Ring, and said with indignation, "He was neither an emperor, nor a military leader, nor an anything. He only wrote *The Robbers*!"

"*The Robbers* is not by Goethe," someone said to him, "but by Schiller."

"So you see," insisted Mendel, "he didn't even write *The Robbers* and such a monument they've erected for him!"

I wouldn't say that the bits and pieces of schooltime literary reminiscences that had stuck to my memory like the fluff of sheep wool to a thorny bush were particularly helpful during my tailoring days in Kolodetz, but at this moment I really for the first time understood the applicability of literature classes to real life—an indisputable benefit, comparable for example to the knowledge gained from geometry class showing you how to calculate with old man Euclid's help the square centimeters necessary to tailor an additional vest. In this particular case, as a result of my acquaintance with Goethe (1749–1832), I ended up not at hard labor in the camp but in the office, under the direct supervision of Boss Brückner. I don't know if you've ever been in the army, prison or camp, but these are the places where most spontaneously and from the depths of popular creativity are born the nicknames of bosses, and they stick to them eternally, like a mole on the nose. In this case, an anonymous poetic soul stuck the nickname "the Radish" to our boss, thus hitting the nail on the head, because both his reddish face, and the harmonic equivalence of his height and width, brought to mind this magnificent natural product, regardless of the fact that I had never in Kolodetz come across brightly shining bald radishes in boots.

Despite the prohibition against speaking on this topic, it's high time I informed you what exactly was this Special Site A-17 and what in particular was special about it. It produced cartridge cases for artillery shells, shells for our egg-shaped air bombs and land mines, as well as similar half-manufactured products of the first necessity. The fresh smell of pine turpentine borne by the breeze was convincing evidence that the barrels carried out together with the ready-made products up to that silent line in the forest contained a chemical derivative of unknown purpose.

This production from different barracks, documented in the books as workshops with certain numbers and codes, transformed itself into figures, memos, and reports, and my historic mission consisted of the mechanical entering of data in the respective columns and registers, as well as the sorting of documents arriving from the kitchen department on expended quantities of potatoes, turnips, beets, and oat flour for the feeding of about two thousand people. I told you already that neither at that time nor later could I understand why this "special site" didn't belong, in spite of its mitigated regime, to the category simply of concentration camp, seeing as I do in my mind's eye the pitiful shadows of predominantly Polish origin, who were lined up as early as dawn in their gray duck clothes under the clanking sounds struck on the hanging piece of rail, after which for sixteen hours a day they scratched with files, hammered, pushed wagons, carried casts for iron-casting, and did all kinds of other things till the next clanking of the rail at nine in the evening, under the sharp eye of the German machine workers. The latter were living separately and had a permit to visit the town, so they could drink beer, and I wouldn't say that they acted rudely toward that evolutionary facsimile of the Egyptian slaves, they just treated them with the conscientious indifference with which the master treats the pliers, the plane, or the rasp—without compassion or tenderness, but also without malice, which as a rule the inanimate object cannot evoke.

In the beginning I slept together with everybody else, in the sleeping barracks with two rows of wooden bunk beds, but with the development of the activity about which you'll now learn, the commandant grew fond of me, and I was transferred to the office, where there was an iron bed to which destiny had given a modest role during the Second World War. I can't say that I was enthusiastic about the Radish's order to leave the common quarters, despite the indisputable comforts of a more privileged situation, because in the first several days this raised everybody's hackles against me and filled them with suspicion regarding my readiness to commit national treason. This is how it usually is in the army, camp, or prison—people don't like the privileged ones, and are predisposed to consider them *a priori* stoolpigeons and agents provocateurs, which explains the black eye I got by accident in the dark. I was genuinely suffering from the inability to explain to my comrades in fortune that I belonged to the tribe of Israel and could therefore hardly be persuaded to become a secret spy for the Nazis, even though history has noted such cases, shameful in every respect. It wasn't easy for me either to wriggle out of that Saturday evening ritual, when my comrades in fortune had the right to wash themselves in the low brick building, conditionally called the "Bathhouse" and consisting of two parallel water pipes rigged with shower heads, from which there spouted either boiling water, capable of skinning a rhinoceros in two seconds, or ice cold double pneumonia. My excuses about unfinished office work, so I could get out of such collective hygiene activities, were related, you remember, to that little thing of mine hanging down under my belly button, and which, if you recall, had once upon a time made even the police chief lift it up with his cane and fix the thick lenses of his spectacles upon it. Because you can hide your faith or origin, but how can you hide the great deed of that servant of Yahweh's, who had circumcised me in order to gather me into the bosom of Abraham?

The Radish, by the way, didn't even try to ask for spying services from me, because he turned out to be a sentimental Nazi, needing like any human being warmth and affection. This was expressed by the necessity, during the late night hours, of having to listen to his essays on loneliness and love, which soon made me reach the conclusion that Oberlieutenant Immanuel-Johannes Brückner, head of Special Site A-17, also known as the Radish—I mean the oberlieutenant, not the site—was suffering and was head over heels in love. With whom and how, I would find out later.

The aforementioned essays would unfold in width and depth mostly after the drinking of a bottle of "Corn"—corn meaning grain, of which they made a final product, called by the same name, or, as we would term it, ordinary wheat vodka. You know that I'm not much of a drinker, but he would order me to follow him on his journey through the wet wheat, and I, despite faking that I drank more than I could in reality, would usually get drunk ahead of the boss and the two of us would weep together—each of us about something of his own. Of course, the situation was not always so romantic; the oberlieutenant would sometimes get into sudden fits of violent rage, threatening to hang all the Poles from the site as outright saboteurs and enemies of the Führer, and for punishment would leave the whole camp, including me, for two days without food. This happened mostly when the client factories would send a written complaint about cracks and bubbles in the casts, about our careless attitude toward strict standards or about ordinary sand in the residue of that derivative in the barrels, in which turpentine, produced by us, played a major role. I don't think that all these faults undermining the prestige of Special Site A-17 and its good name were by chance, but if this was conscious sabotage, it was done so skillfully that its main author could never be discovered. These cracks and bubbles multiplied drastically at just that time when, with the next human transports, they started bringing in people from the occupied Soviet territories, but it's not my job to comment on the problem, because this may have been on account of the low level of technological culture in Soviet Russia, as a result of which sand was found not only in the barrels but also in the lubricating oil of the machines, lathes, and cutters.

During one such understandable fit of rage on the part of my boss and benefactor, when he tried to distract himself with a game of chess, I in a most ungrateful manner checkmated him with black pieces as early as the ninth step, which caused my fully deserved incarceration for three days. It seems that the Radish experienced my exile more painfully than myself, who was simply lying around in the dark, damp cell, built as an addition next to the bath and performing the function of a punitive institution, because as early as midnight on the second day I was taken out by the guards and delivered under the gun to the office, where the bottle of Corn was already uncorked. Following that late night of mutual contrition, I learned to lose chess games skillfully and believably and a second incarceration became unnecessary.

My description of the camp environment would be incomplete if I didn't tell you about senior-master Stakhovich, a latheworker from Lodz, dragged down to these Brandenburg woods not like us, a ragged bunch captured during a blind and accidental raid, but after a targeted search for masters in the trade. He was an expert in everything, a so-to-speak universal technical genius, who fixed the machines, electrical appliances, and motorcycles of the guards, and one time even the boss's radio receiver. This Stakhovich, who walked with a marked limp in his left foot—a result of childhood paralysis—in his capacity as senior master had liberty of movement within the boundaries of the camp, and it is he who brought me all kinds of reports from the workshops to put in the corresponding account books.

One time, when the boss had gone off and disappeared somewhere in Brandenburg, from whence he would return probably late at night and even more probably drunk, Stakhovich brought the documents and I invited him to sit down and treated him to a cigarette filched from the Radish. In our business relations we spoke German, he had a more or less good command of it. The

Pole inhaled the smoke deeply and hungrily—cigarettes at the time were rare and expensive and the small kiosk, serving mostly German personnel, sold them individually, under the table—and I looked at his rough hands, their cracked skin covered by a thin web of unwashable grime. I was gazing at them with respect and jealousy, because those hands could do everything that I couldn't, when suddenly he said in Polish:

"You're not Polish and you're not from Lvov."

"That's to say—what do you mean?" I tried to feign astonishment.

"What I mean is, you're a Jew, I discovered it a long time ago by some words which no kraut would use. You're from somewhere in southern Galicia, aren't you?"

I was bowled over by his fine ethno-phonetic sense and after some hesitation, gave in: "It's true."

"Don't worry, no one will find out."

In a certain sense I was relieved, because at least in this private instance I felt I was being spared the suspicion of collaborating with the Nazis. Stakhovich looked at me intently, thought about something, and then asked, "Do you want to do me a big favor?"

"Namely?"

"You're able to go out to the loading ramp; I'm not allowed. While you're writing down the numbers of the crates and things like that, can you send my regards to the locomotive machinist? He's German but speak to him in Polish. Tell him: 'Best regards from Stakhovich.' And if he gives you a package, can you bring it to me without being noticed? I warn you, it's dangerous. Very dangerous. You can refuse if you want to."

My heart leaped into my mouth. "And what's in the package?" I asked quietly.

To my generally polite question he answered quite rudely, "It would be healthier for you if you didn't know. Do it if you want, if you don't—forget about it, period."

I did it. Stakhovich neither thanked me nor in any way hinted at it afterward. But in my soul I conducted quiet evening discussions with my rabbi, for it seemed to me that I felt his presence, somewhere close to me, even that I saw him in the darkness—pale and with that glaring look of a madman or someone possessed with which he delivered the Shabbos sermon.

"You did well," said the rabbi, "but don't think you're a hero, because anyone in your place would've done it. Your children and my nephew Schura and niece Susannah are fighting somewhere a life-and-death battle, and do you know where my sister and your wife Sarah are, and your other son Elia, and your father Aaron, and your mother Rebekha and Chaimle and all the rest?"

"What about Esther Katz?" I asked, not without a certain malice.

"Esther Katz too—wherever she is, whatever happened to her, in her soul she's with those people who are stopping the German tanks with their chests! Get it?"

"Got it," I said.

"And what were you thinking—that you'll play chess with the black pieces and pretend to be losing the game till the end of the war, while others are dying? And that the bitter cup of hardship will pass by you, because you're the pet and the bosom buddy of the head of a Nazi camp? Shall I remind you of Joseph, from the tribe of Israel and the son of Jacob, who was brought to Egypt as a slave, became the favorite of the pharaoh, but didn't forget his brothers? And aren't you a slave, who became the pet of his master? True, Itzik, you're not a wise prophet like Joseph but a complete fool; on the other hand, your Radish is not Amenhotep either! Remember your brothers, remember them. I've already told you who they are: all people, of all skin colors, all tongues and tribes, all lands and seas, because a mortal danger is encroaching on all of them and the seventh year of disaster is coming, and its name is fascism. Remember your brothers and be a Joseph!"

"I understand you, I'll remember it," I said, "but what was in the package?"

"How should I know," said the rabbi, "if you don't know? Because you're dreaming of me, not me of you!"

I was awakened by a powerful roar, thick and dense as a carpet that covered the top of the clouds. The Anglo-American air fortresses were flying over again. . . .

THREE

They, the fortresses, had recently been flying over us almost every cloudy night. Then the bright spots of the searchlights crawled through the clouds, meeting each other, overlapping each other and crossing each other, drifting apart, while beyond the forest, over in Brandenburg, began the sewing machine clatter of antiaircraft fire. The lit-up shells stitched the sky with wide seams, but the invincible airplanes passed through the skies like cows pregnant with bombs, which some pitiful mosquitoes were trying to divert from the goal. The cows gave birth somewhere far away, then, relieved, came back by the same route and again with the searchlights and the sewing machines and the glowing seams that stitched the clouds and the sky, until a full and tired silence settled in.

During such cloudy nights, long before the airplanes buzzed in the dark, somewhere far away, anxious sirens would begin to howl and minutes after that the lights in the camp would go out. Then would occur the wondrous transformation of Oberlieutenant Immanuel-Johannes Brückner from commandant of Special Site A-17 into tender lover, I would even say a priest in the temple of Eros. At such times, he would sit on his bicycle, his electric headlight dutifully dimmed according to orders, with just a thin bright thread of light that reminded one of the eye of a winking Chinese and that, with its trembling beam, marked out the route to the gate and from there to the woods. Beyond the forest, somewhere in the plain, was the village, which I never got to see, temporarily inhabited by his Berlin lady love. And I, camp inmate Heinrich Bjegalski, former doorman at the Lvov ophthalmology clinic and currently manager of the private office of the oberlieutenant, was using a roll of black paper to darken the windows and switching on the gas lamps in order to read another chapter from some novel, with which the aforementioned private office was well equipped. Such an act of solidarity with my boss was my strict post at the telephone so that if someone from the city management called, for whatever reason, for example to check on our military preparedness, I would politely inform him of my name and position, and also that Herr Oberlieutenant was somewhere in the camp surveying the premises, can I take a message, sir, and other similar maneuvers for deceiving the enemy. The Radish would come back before dawn puffing like crazy from the arduous effort of biking up the hill, but happy and exhausted, and for my nocturnal vigilance would give me one *reichsmark*. And one reichsmark was something significant for a camp inmate, who was going to be paid after the end of the war, after expenses were deducted for delousing and so on, and with it you could still buy from the kiosk a lot of things produced in the most ingenious ways just from soybeans—salami, coffee, chocolate, or, for example, onion bread, with just the onions being authentic.

And so life flowed along with the alternation of clear moonlit nights, which condemned me to days without soy salami and onion bread, and the darkness of winter clouds hanging over my hours of vigilance by the phone, while the Anglo-Americans and the oberlieutenant tended to business.

Everything would have gone on like this, if life, in principle prone to surprising vignettes and caprioles, hadn't decided otherwise: one night, in the silence between two cannonades, when the airplanes had passed by and hadn't yet returned, and I was reading by the rickety light of the gas lamp something from the Dresden Indian Karl May, the door opened and a raging blonde valkyrie, of the plumper kind, stormed into the office.

"Where is he?!" angrily asked this, let's call her Brunhilde for now, waving her hand behind her back at the post guard, who had brought her and obediently closed the door and remained outside—a fact that partially demystified the identity of the lady.

I dutifully stood up, the way a gentleman does in front of a lady, even more so when the gentleman is a camp inmate, and the lady German. "Whom do you mean, dear madam?" I asked.

"Don't act dumb! I'm asking about Oberlieutenant Brückner!"

"He," I mumbled, "I mean Oberlieutenenant Brückner, at the moment, as you see . . . is somewhere around the site, so to say."

"Listen, are you a fool, or are you making a fool out of me? He's in the village with his mistress, and you're covering for him! I know everything, everything's been reported to me!"

"I'm sorry, but with what right—" I began heroically, but she interrupted me nervously: "With the right of a lawful wife!"

Uh-oh, what now—when I hadn't even been warned about this kind of situation?

She sat down and started drumming with her long polished nails on the table. "Her address!" she ordered unexpectedly.

"Her exact address in the village, or I will tear your head off! I will send you to Buchenwald, if you know what that means!"

I knew what it meant; the glory of that picturesque little place near Weimar had reached us here too. I must have been very sincere when I told her I didn't know the address, dear Frau Brückner, nor did I know the aforementioned lady from the village, nor anything about this matter, because she believed me for the first time, and asked for a cigarette. I always had cigarettes, stolen from the boss, even though I wasn't a smoker—there was always some inmate who would beg for a smoke.

"I'll wait for him here," she said decisively, elegantly lighting up her cigarette and waving the smoke away with her hand as if she were the number-one competitor of Marlene Dietrich. The nicotine apparently lowered the adrenaline in her blood; she calmed down and looked at me with curiosity, while I stood straight, as was due. "What's your name?" she asked.

"Bjegalski. Heinrich Bjegalski, madam."

She looked at me from feet to head, in which I read a slight contempt. "The Poles," she said, "usually are handsome men."

I shrugged my shoulders apologetically: "There are occasional exceptions."

She again started drumming with her nails on the table, then unexpectedly asked, "Where's the schnapps?"

"What do you mean, dear madam?"

"Listen, I told you, don't play the fool! Or do you think I don't know how you guzzle it down every night with that randy mongrel, my husband. So, where is it?"

I was resolved to die on the scaffold if I had to, but not to betray my benefactor—a heroic but futile decision, because the valkyrie caught my unintentional look and opened the cupboard under the files, where sitting unawares there were three bottles—

one already opened, the others untouched and virgin—and our two small glasses, respectively, engraved with such dear memories.

The lady silently filled up the glasses, drank one bottoms up, and then in a commanding fashion pointed with her exquisite finger to the other one. "You drink too!"

I drank, I had no other choice—I was a prisoner, and she was a German. Then she poured again and I drank again. I've already told you that I'm easy prey to King Alcohol, that's a novel in itself, and, in no time, my eyes were shining bright and I felt a strange and luscious weakness. The woman stood up and briefly, for no reason at all, laughed a throaty laugh, in which there sounded notes whose millions-of-years-old sacred and encoded meaning could only be misunderstood by a real idiot.

"Come!" she commanded, with an almost tender insistence.

I didn't dare obey until I had looked behind my back, in order to make sure that the order was not meant for someone else. But there was nothing behind me, except for the portrait of the Führer and in this specific historic moment, he was hardly the one destined to become the instrument of female revenge.

O Lord God, life surprises you with all kinds of strangeness! I was faithful to Sarah, I swear, but if I have to be honest, I will add that I had probably been faithful because of the lack of an occasion, which would confirm or deny the abovementioned claim. For such situations in life, I would advise you not to believe the one who swears that he would never in the world touch lobster with tartar sauce, if you're not convinced in advance that such a thing had even been offered to him.

I knew that what was about to happen and what was as unavoidable as the Law of Gravity was impermissible and sinful, and that I was pushed to it by dark satanic forces, but I hope you'll be forbearing toward a generally normal man, even from a certain point of view a virtuous nebbish, who hadn't seen a woman's skirt since biblical times. You'll understand him and forgive his original sin!

In short, I myself didn't realize how I found myself with the blonde valkyrie on top of that iron bed, which was the greatest generosity I ever received from Lieutenant Brückner. Now that I'd also been awarded the privilege of consoling his wife, I was obediently grateful for the honor.

I am by nature a shy person, so let's skip the details, in order to come to the moment when Brunhilde put herself together, restored the thick layer of lipstick to her lips, and while smoking her second cigarette, looked at me intently again.

"Strange," she said. "For me the Poles are really handsome men, but I've always considered them a little feeble in that department. Now I found out that you're also quite gifted!"

In my soul I gave thanks on behalf of the Republic of Poland and its immortal symbol Joseph Pilsudski.

FOUR

Since that night no one has ever felt greater and more tender affection for the Anglo-American bombers than I, because the story would repeat itself like a musical phrase from a broken gramophone record: after the air-raid alarm and the corresponding switching off of the electric lights, the nibelung would go to his mistress and for this pay me one reichsmark; minutes later his Brunhilde would show up on her bicycle and later would also give me one reichsmark. From the point of view of commercial ethics, on which we really insisted in Kolodetz, this was a fair business transaction in which everyone was on the winning side and no one on the losing.

A similar transaction was offered to the banker Abraham Rosenbaum by our Mendel: "Mr. Rosenbaum," said Mendel, "we can engage in a wonderful racket, in which each one of us will make three hundred thousand rubles!"

"Interesting. And what's the racket?"

"I learned that you are giving six hundred thousand for your daughter's dowry."

"So?"

"Well, I'm ready to take her for half the price!"

So much for mutually beneficial transactions. As to my two honestly earned reichsmarks for every Anglo-American bomb attack, tell me, please, in which camp was what Jew ever better off during the Second World War?

But every beginning has an end too, as my mother Rebekha Blumenfeld used to say. And most often, the good beginning, unfortunately, as my mother also used to say, doesn't necessarily mean a good ending. And the bad ending began with that one morning after the military check, when four civilians in long leather coats came pouring out of two military "Steyrs," and quickly ascended the few wooden steps to the office. It was an icy February—that same February when the most frequently mentioned geographic locations in the world were the Volga and Stalingrad. I was diligently standing erect in the corner in my gray duck clothes; the civilians threw a quick glance at me and after an exchange of whispers with the Radish, who became visibly pale, went out.

A little after that three people were arrested—the senior-master Stakhovich and two Russians. I was freezing outside, on the small veranda in front of the office, when they were taking the arrested men away. The limping Stakhovich cast an indifferent glance at me, as if he had never seen me before, and then crouched down in order to place his large body inside the car.

Much later, from sketchy remarks of Oberlieutenant Brückner, who was feeling disgraced and discredited in front of the whole Reich—from the Atlantic, as he would put it, to the Russian steppes—I could form a picture of what had happened. And what had happened was something incredible: in the strictly secret and not less strictly guarded Special Site A-17, it turns out, a secret radio transmitter had been operating, and maintaining regular contact with Berlin—not of course with

Wehrmacht headquarters, but with other headquarters, you know what I mean. This equipment, in the form of a small wooden tool case and its electronic contents, had been home-produced by Stakhovich with the golden hands and hidden in the coke heaps of the blacksmith's workshop. After a few months of successful operations, however, it was detected by the new German contraption called "*Peilgerät,*" which with ingenious precision spotted its location too, and the rest you know. What my completely humiliated boss Brückner couldn't understand was the way in which the parts, the lamps, and the miscellaneous condensers and resistors had been delivered to the camp. As far as the Resistance was concerned, not in the electric but in the political sense of the word, I was partially up-to-date on a certain small package, handed to me by the German locomotive machinist, and the thought of it froze the blood in my veins. Because if the fellows who'd been arrested were to talk, I thought to myself, it was all over with me, and at the hands of the Gestapo, without any doubt, I'd shit my pants.

Soon after that, during one of my sleepless and fearful nights, I was again visited by Rabbi Ben-David.

"Are you scared?" he asked.

"I am," I admitted.

"I don't doubt it, but let's hope they won't say anything. And that you won't be arrested, and thus miss your only chance in life to become a hero. Don't worry, you wouldn't talk to the Gestapo anyway, not because you're strong but because you've got nothing to tell them. The machinist doesn't appear on the ramp anymore, does he? I hope he took off in time, so you can't tell on him either. Sleep calmly."

"Was it worth it," I said, "for three people to sacrifice themselves for something of doubtful benefit, that won't even scratch the paint of one of their tanks and will in no way determine the outcome of the war?"

"Who lied to you," said the rabbi, "that it won't determine the outcome? This small tool case is the overcoming of fear, a protest against submission to slavery, an act of resistance against the temptations of conformism. These chaps who got arrested, or the German machinist, aren't they planters of faith that the light has not gone out forever and that the men of Europe have not disappeared?"

"I know I'm weak and I'm ready to pay for it," I said, "but aren't they sowers of wind, because what's a pitiful handmade radio transmitter, buried in the blacksmith's coke heaps, in comparison to the might of their armies?"

"Shall I tell you what it is? It is the stubbornness of the slave and a challenge to inhuman shooting steel. I will tell you: it's nothing and everything—a finger to the Führer, but also an example, which the weak fellow needs, in order to believe the world can be changed. Then it will gain new meaning and then what's written on the gates of the concentration camps will come true: 'TO EACH HIS OWN!' Amen and *Gut Shabbos*, Itzik!"

It seemed to me that I didn't close my eyes all night, but I was awakened by the merciless sound of the piece of railroad track that announced the birth of another camp day.

FIVE

One law of nature, confirmed by science, as well as by clairvoyants, says that general awfulness has no day off. Or to put it in other words, when something bad happens to you, you can be sure it doesn't come alone, and that after it others will follow along like ducklings after their mother. In our case, it seems that no minor role was played by the collapse of our "Special Site's" prestige as something that had firmly supported the doctrine of the strictly guarded secret as a major element in national security. The situation was also influenced by a solitary bomb, dropped by an absentminded American, whether by accident or on purpose we don't know, that fell about twenty meters or so from the machinists' workshop, broke the windows of the surrounding barracks and, as a final strategic-military effect, made a hole in the sea. But the respective institutions also saw in this bomb evil premonitions and treason, which imperatively required that we purge our collective of poisonous weeds.

This is how we came to the lining up of the ethnic Poles—almost half the camp personnel—at the square in front of the commandant's, while the other—the Soviet half—remained in the workshops to maintain production. And as far as I was, at least on paper, a pure-blooded Pole, I found myself among those lined-up, and to my surprise, even Oberlieutenant Brückner didn't know the meaning and purpose of the telephone-transmitted order.

And so, we were standing in the square, with the Radish on the small wooden veranda in front of the office, as if he were going to receive a victory parade. He frequently looked at his watch, himself anxious by the delay of the parade, though pretending to be well informed and highly confident by asking strictly from time to time for silence. Of course, the gossip information agency, the one that every well-equipped camp possesses as well as the whispers crawling between the lines, had immediately set itself in motion and been informing interested parties that we would probably be released, a reward for labor honestly dedicated to the Reich.

Nothing could be further from the truth, because after a half-hour's eager anticipation, we were still standing there when two furious SS bosses stormed in and with an abruptness unsuitable to his rank handed over a written order to our completely confused commandant. Hurt to the bottom of his sensitive soul, Oberlieutenant Brückner, with a hollow voice, ordered us to count ourselves and after we did, the two cocky SS men passed quickly by the lines and harshly pulled out every tenth man to stand in front of the row.

You'll die laughing, but one of the tenths happened to be me—as they say, if Yahweh, glory to His name, has given orders for you to get into trouble, there's no way you can avoid it.

The whole business was about some big boss of theirs who'd been shot in the streets of Warsaw, and now they were looking for a hundred Poles as hostages. You know how it goes:

if the assassins do not surrender themselves by this or that date, this or that time, on the dot, the hundred Poles will be shot in legal and fully understandable retribution. Now, I ask you, in view of the existing situation, which was better—to remain a Pole or admit I was a Jew? The question hardly has an answer, because in the one case, as well as in the other, I'd end up, as the saying goes, pushing up daisies, but I personally preferred to be a Polish Jew—a sweeper in the New York subway. My boss, Oberlieutenant Immanuel-Johannes Brückner, to his credit, tried to get me out with the reasoning that he needed me in the office and other things like that, but nothing helped, and New York, unfortunately, was a pure adolescent dream, too far away from the dim reality of Oranienburg.

In this way a hundred of us turned up squeezed like matchsticks into the already overcrowded common cells of some prison—a sinister building of unpainted brick somewhere in Berlin. In it there were Jews and Gypsies, some Montenegrins quietly singing sad songs, some homosexuals, and other beings harmful to the Reich.

Since we were a hundred Poles, and the kitchen hadn't planned for those who had poured right out of the blue onto the heads of the prison management, they forgot to feed us, maybe with the hope that it wouldn't be necessary. And I, exhausted from the hard, worry-filled day, tortured by the journey in the trucks, in which we were packed so tightly that we couldn't even sit down, soon fell asleep folded up on the floor—there weren't even any cots, let alone that blessed iron bed in the office.

And here's what happened, my dear brother: I dreamed I was in my hometown Kolodetz, at a Jewish wedding. I was playing the violin, and the rabbi Shmuel Ben-David was circumcising giggling Jewish boys. We were all happy and singing Jewish songs, our good neighbors, dressed in caftans tailored by my father, were clapping their hands in rhythm, and in the middle of the circle of people the old postman Avramchik and Esther Katz were dancing the *cracowviak*, stomping with heavy shoes.

It turned out that the stomping wasn't from the shoes, but from guards who were loudly banging their keys against the opening cell doors and shouting "*Juden raus!*" which means "Jews out!" And I, the idiot of all idiots, still sleepy and confused, completely forgot that I was the Polish pan Heinrich Bjegalski, a doorman at the Lvov ophthalmology clinic, and dazed by the merry Galician wedding, went out with the other Jews. Along the endless corridor, lit up by naked electric bulbs, sleepy and frightened people crowded together from the neighboring cells, and I was maybe the only one without a yellow cloth star on my breast. Later I figured out what was happening and wanted to explain the apparent misunderstanding, and even showed the identification papers proving me a legitimate Pole, but the doors were closing, let's go, let's go, don't dawdle! In such cases no documents help, I had admitted to being a Jew by merely going out of the cell, and the guards apparently shared the Soviet state accuser Vishinksi's view that admitting guilt—in any circumstances, even under pressure—is the queen of evidence.

It was useless to resist, because it has been said and seven times seven proven: to be a Jew is a life sentence without the right of appeal!

Again crammed into the horse wagon, this time I learned that they were deporting us to the camp Flossenbürg, Oberpfalz, where a typhoid epidemic was raging, and where we were going to be asked to take care of our dead brothers, very touching! At least this is how the problem was explained to us by the transportation boss, some *Gruppensturmführer*, so there wouldn't be panic and attempts to escape. In other words, we were on our way to certain death in the typhoid apocalypse of Flossenbürg and there was no doubt about it.

And now, brother, let me remind you again that the human being is a helpless little ant in the powerful and irreversible games of fortune and to it—the ant—it's not given to judge if the trouble afflicting him is God's punishment or His secret caress. Because that same night the remaining ninety-nine Polish hostages, brought from Special Site A-27, were shot dead, as I learned after the war. The hundredth of them, according to the diligently compiled list, remained unfound, and this was me, Isaac Jacob Blumenfeld, at that moment traveling to distant Oberpfalz.

SIX

A completely dazed, exhausted crowd, surrounded by soldiers with dogs—this is what we were, when we went through the camp gate, framed by two square brick towers, while above our heads hung the arch-shaped metallic sign with the sacred words: "TO EACH HIS OWN."

And now, please, save me from the memory, heavy as a hundred-ton cast-iron mold, and allow me not to describe to you the hell in which we ended up! Many people before me have done it, and truly much better, too, than I would do it. The times of the first shattering discoveries have passed, those waves of horror have died down that, like a tsunami, flooded the world's conscience after the war. Millions of meters of film and photo reels have been rotated, mountains of court files and memories have been accumulated, in which everyone could see his piece of the truth through the keyhole of his own experience. It became a profession to put systematically in drawers the self-admitted guilt of the repentant and the ambiguous blather of unrepentant butchers; filed away and numbered in protocols and shorthand records was the subdued weeping of the survivors, and from it, from this crying, some people erected an impressive and invisible pantheon of the Holocaust, while others built for themselves also impressive, but quite real, villas with swimming pools and two satellite dishes. Words like "Zyklon-B," "gas chamber," or "Final Solution" gradually lost their original demonic unreality and became a daily ingredient of indifferent newspaper articles dedicated to commemorations and the like. In short, save me, please, because of the requirement for the completeness of the plot, as we were instructed during our creative writing classes by Eliezer Pinkus, may his soul rest in peace, from repeating to you things that are already painfully familiar, and that you are already maybe even fed up with.

Suffice it for me to say that typhoid had flared up to the scale of a pandemic and that the camp management was faced with a nightmare, because Flossenbürg was not technologically prepared to deal with so many dead, being far from the perfection of the big death factories in Poland. This had necessitated the building of pyres of human bodies whose size would have won the envy of the Holy Inquisition from the most glorious period of its existence. Gasoline, mixed with used motor oil, finished the job, as huge columns of sooty smoke rose up to worlds beyond, so they could also learn how far in its evolution this amphibian had reached, who once upon a time crawled up into the cave and from there, already a two-legged creature, sneaked out again in order to paint the portrait of Mona Lisa and create the Ninth Symphony. The incompletely burnt remnants were shoveled away with bulldozers into huge ditches, the sandy soil discreetly and forever locking within itself destinies, laughter, ambitions, lumbago, I love you, what grade did you get in geography, or to whom is Aunt Bertha writing. Farewell, brothers, and rest in peace!

Together with three Jews from Zagreb, I pushed a wheelbarrow full of corpses, which were in almost skeletal condition, loosely piled every which way. From the wooden partitions of the wheelbarrow legs and arms stuck out like broken branches. The most horrifying thing was that I soon turned into a thick-witted drudge, who stopped feeling terror and got used to his work in the same way as my former fellow campmates from Special Site A-17 got used to pushing wagons with the cast-iron molds.

And still, my soul probably wasn't completely dead, because there amid the hellish congregation of the sick, the dying, and the dead, amid the moans and the foul stench, I met—and I swear this is exactly what happened—my dear rabbi Shmuel Ben-David and the last seed of emotion, surviving by a miracle in the folds of my desert indifference, bloomed like a peony. The rabbi was playing the role of physician, helpless to heal anyone but capable of alleviating the suffering with either a good word, or a moist compress, or a good old prayer. And so among the doomed, and we ourselves were doomed, we could see each other briefly, and I don't know if these momentary encounters of ours brought me more joy or sorrow. Such disasters the rabbi had survived, that if I were a writer, to describe them I would have to put them in a separate novel. He'd sneaked into our occupied Kolodetz, to find out that all, literally all our close ones had been deported or shot dead there on the spot, in that ravine above the river which I loved so much. What had happened to Sarah and the children he didn't know and he couldn't know, because instead of fleeing east to save himself, he'd made his way to Warsaw, where he tried to steal into the Muranov neighborhood, surrounded and fighting to the death, or in other words the Warsaw ghetto, when he got arrested. What saved him was having a fake ID as a Polish doctor, head intern, and as such he'd ended up here, in order to help those who were dying in his hands.

From Rabbi Ben-David, who was himself nothing but skin and bones, I received strength or, as he used to say, two handfuls of hope like spring water. From him I learned that the Allies were already in Europe, and Soviet troops had crossed the Oder and were following our sometime road that was to lead us to the heart of the thousand-year Third Reich.

"Vengeance," the rabbi once said, cradling someone who had just died in his arms, "is foreign to faith in goodness and has to be uprooted from the heart of humanity, even though now its unavoidable hour will strike. May God give seven days to our souls, just seven days, so that both the living and the dead will be at peace. Seven terrible days, seven flaming horsemen of retribution, and to each—his own! And I will pray to God to bless and forgive all those who will want an eye for an eye and a tooth for a tooth, life for a life, and death for a death! But seven days! And then—let ashes cover everything and let grass grow over the ashes. Because children will have to be born again in goodness and peace, and sowers will have to sow fresh seeds for the bread of the people. But before that let that which has been said come true—and to each his own. Amen!"

Thus spoke the former chairman of the Atheists' Club in Kolodetz by Drogobych, Rabbi Shmuel Ben-David, and his good eyes had opened wide and become fierce and evil. In his arms something that resembled a human being lay dead, and these words were maybe a curse and maybe a prayer for the peace of his soul.

SEVEN

The world is full of surprises and if only they were pleasant, the making of it would have been a magnificent and deservingly praised whim of God. But, unfortunately, it's not always like this, and our world—may the Creator not take offense—has too many lumps and cracks, even though neither Poles nor Russians took part in casting it. One unpleasant surprise, like a small bump in the perfection of creation, manifested itself in the moment when, pushing the two-wheeled cart crammed with the dead, we heard a voice shouting behind our backs in German: "Hey, you there, wait!"

The three fellows from Zagreb and I instantly nailed ourselves to the spot, blind obedience to any kind of order pronounced by anyone in German being an indisputable law in the camp. And one more rule, to which we had long ago been accustomed so that it had become second nature, in a way like the unwashable black spider's web on senior-master Stakhovich's hands, was to look at the bosses' boots and never in their eyes—a human privilege we were denied because of some suspicion on the part of the scientist-anthropologists about our racial adequacy, or even about the chances of our belonging to the species *Homo sapiens* at all.

"You!" said the boots. "Look at me!"

All four of us obeyed the order. In front of us stood a stout, rather round Sturmführer not in the prime of youth, who pointed his finger at me. "You! Come this way, but don't come close! The three of you, keep moving. Go, go, go!"

I came up closer, to a safe, so to speak, sterile distance, the three others pushed their burden away with difficulty, and I, with my cattle eyes fixed at the tip of the polished boots, indifferently waited for the next blow of destiny, for which I'd long ago stopped being anything other than a punching bag.

"Where do I know you from?" asked the Sturmführer.

I looked at him again but he didn't seem familiar. I shrugged my shoulders. "I really don't know, Mister Sturmführer, sir."

He thought for a while, knitted his eyebrows, and then his face brightened. "Of course, I know! When someone from the unit is imprinted in my memory, it's forever. Weren't you that nasty Jewish bastard who was playing tricks on me during the First World War, spreading around some little leaflets? Do you remember Lieutenant Schauer? And your sergeant major? Look me in the eye!"

Oh, my God, Zukerl! How could I recognize him after so many years, when, moreover, he had shaved his mighty-like-the-Austro-Hungarian-Empire sideburns à la Franz-Joseph and gone and stuck on his upper lip just a small hairy patch from the "Mein Führer" fashion line?! Now, on top of all my troubles, I was overwhelmed by this one too, because, if you remember, I was the emotional focus, so to say—the epicenter of his malice, which was related to his completely groundless suspicion that I personally had signed the capitulation of our unconquerable armies at the Compiègne forest, in the same lonely and historic railroad car-become-museum piece, in which during the present war the French had shat their pants, despite unequivocal instructions that such things were to be done only when the train was in motion. On the other hand, if you remember, I had no direct involvement with Esther Katz's leaflets, even the police bosses had indisputably acknowledged my innocence, but apparently Zukerl was right in saying that when something stuck to the folds of his brain, it was forever.

Probably by the sparkle that glistened in my eyes, he understood that I'd remembered who he was, because, risking his life, my former sergeant major stretched his arm and pinched that thin-as-parchment little skin of mine still remaining on my cheek. "Oooh, but you're so sweet! Come with me!"

He gave this order with an icy and evil look, waved his hand and turned around abruptly without even checking if I was following him—this was taken for granted. I dragged my feet after him, wearing tattered shoes already for a long time lacking laces but with tongues sticking out, gray duck clothes—remnants of those stellar moments in the Radish's office—that had turned into rags and were wrapped around some places, to the disgrace of the tailoring shop Mode Parisienne, with bits of string, other places with wire, and on my breast the obligatory yellow cloth star, which I had torn out of the clothes of a diseased corpse, myself almost a diseased corpse who couldn't remember the last time they'd given us the thin sour swill of rotten potatoes and cabbage.

I took a long time dragging myself after my former sergeant major, who was striding ahead with a broad and swaggering step, for I had a clear consciousness that for me this was the final section of the road called Life. Zukerl stopped in front of a long one-story building with multiple doors and started digging in his pants pockets until he found the key that he needed. Only then did he look at me with the same evil look and give me a silent sign with his head to follow him inside.

No, this wasn't the cooler or the gas chamber, as you're probably thinking, but a most ordinary office. Zukerl sat down behind a desk crammed with papers under the Führer's portrait, and I remained standing, waiting indifferently. The office was ascetic in a military fashion, lacking any trace of the Radish's abundance, like, for example, the iron bed or the little library with novels that filled up my Anglo-American vigils. But as far as having any memory of my former sergeant major, I don't think he needed any novels, because his literary interests were completely satisfied by the contents of the Military Field Manual, and the Internal Regulations Manual, and the little book *Mein Kampf* leaning against the window like an ornament—he'd probably leafed through as much of it as most Christians through the Gospels and Marxists through *Kapital.*

Zukerl was looking at me intently, and after contemplating me for a long time, during which he was probably trying to awake sleeping memories, as it goes in an old tango, he said, "And you, the Jews, what are you thinking, that you've already won the war? It's not going to happen. Is that clear? I'm asking you—is it clear?"

"That's correct, Mister Sergeant Major . . ."

"Sturmführer!"

"That's correct, Mister Sturmführer, it's clear, it won't happen."

"Have you heard of the Führer's new secret weapon?"

"Not at all, Mister Sturmführer."

"You will."

He opened his holster, but didn't produce any secret weapon from there, just a simple "Walter" revolver. This is it, I thought indifferently—this is the end. But it wasn't. Because Zukerl took the gun by the muzzle and broke a walnut with its handle and noisily started chewing the meat, observing me. And altogether unexpectedly he said with an almost tender voice, "If I was hard on you, it was because I wanted you to become a man. Because you come as cattle to the army, but you should go out as men. Isn't that so?"

I was of a slightly different opinion, but the Flossenbürg camp wasn't a forum for such discussions and I sheepishly confirmed: "Quite right, Mister Sturmführer."

"Well now, and you, didn't you become a man? Didn't you become at least a corporal?"

"Begging your pardon, sir, but I didn't become one at all."

"Is that right? So, why did we have two wars then, if you didn't get at least one decoration? What were the wars for, I'm asking you? You Jews are generally losers and good for nothings! Or isn't that so?"

"It is," I readily agreed.

He looked at me with contempt, even with slight disgust, because that was me all right—a ragged, dirty semi-human being, probably stinking of corpses and carbolic acid, with a graying reddish beard with dried bits of cabbage stuck to it. And right there at this place, something happened that I least expected: Zukerl opened the side door of his desk and angrily dropped on top of the file folders a loaf of brown rye bread, square like a brick, and on top of it—a decent piece of smoked lard. "Take this and get out of here! And if you ever show up in front of me again, I'll send you you-know-where!"

I could roughly guess where, but I didn't even try to play at heroic pride or incorruptible honesty, and quickly hid the newly acquired treasure under my shredded coat and, as per the order, got lost.

I'm ashamed to tell you, but I secretly shared my acquisition only with my rabbi—we broke everything into little pieces, hid them in our pockets, on the bunks and anywhere else we could find, and ate them crumb by crumb, with the exception of those portions, shared with the rats, with which the camp was overflowing. Unlike the outside world, where people live in communities but die each for himself, here we were dying communally, but surviving each for himself. It's shameful to admit it, but this is how it was with us people, as well as the rats.

I don't know if you got the clue about the deadly sin we committed by eating lard, forbidden by our faith! That's how it was, I'm confessing sincerely, and on Judgment Day we may have to answer for placing our pitiful life above the Scriptures. But after all, wasn't it the same sinful temptation to which Rabbi Ben Zvi submitted, when he looked around and sneaked into the Christan sausage shop, saw the pink and juicy Prague ham, and asked, "How much does this fish filet cost?"

"This is ham, sir," said the butcher.

"I'm not asking you the name of the fish, just how much it is!"

Sturmführer Zukerl had ordered me not to appear in front of his eyes again, but nevertheless I did, though it was sometime later—when I saw him hanging from the observation tower, while American tanks were smashing the gates with the arched sign "To each his own." I don't know if Zukerl had done it himself or if he'd been reached by those seven fearful days of Retribution desired by Rabbi Ben-David. In any case, I remembered the bread and the piece of lard, which had probably helped us survive, and I prayed for his soul.

EIGHT

Rabbi Ben-David and I hugged each other and wept for a while —two shadows that had once been men, in hanging rags that had once been clothes, and behind the brick tower one little American soldier was throwing up—back home in Oklahoma he hadn't seen such heaps of semi-burnt and still smoking human corpses. Probably at the same time somewhere in Treblinka, Auschwitz, or Maidanek, little Soviet soldiers were throwing up, believing along with Maxim Gorki that "human being" has a proud sound.

American nurses were walking up and down the camp, and nuns from some Samaritan order were carrying the dying on stretchers, here and there arrested SS men were being taken away, movie cameras were buzzing and photo cameras were clicking.

One American major solemnly ascended his tank to announce something to us, probably important and epic, or so it appeared, but I didn't hear him—a cold darkness crawled into my brain and I collapsed on the ground. That's the way it goes. Human perseverance is a great mystery and it's not hidden in biological laws governing the cell, just the opposite, it completely opposes them and submits to completely different, immaterial, metaphysical qualities of the soul, or, as the rabbi would say, its stubbornness. I have heard about people sick with incurable diseases, for example malaria or fainting, who in the face of formidable physical or emotional strain and despite the extreme exhaustion of their organism, have not even once been visited by the otherwise periodic, clockwork-like symptoms of their disability. But on the first day, when the gates of the camp or the prison remain behind their backs, people have collapsed and everything has started up all over again—as if the disease, mercifully gone on temporary leave, energetically spits on its palms and gets back to work again. Then follows the first seizure in years, or the malaria with the exotic name of "terziana" remembers that it hasn't tormented you for a long time with its fevers that are so high and so pedantically regular, like the ocean's high and low tides, that you could fry an egg on your palm. So much then for the stubbornness of the soul. I'll come back to it later.

I opened my eyes and looked around, without moving my head, and found myself in some kind of a yellow cloud. Light was beaming literally from everywhere and this light was making everything hurt—my eyeballs, every fiber, every little atom of my body. I tried to lift my arm, in order to block out this yellow luminescence, but it was immobile and heavy as lead.

Then I saw myself—you won't believe it, but I swear that's how it was—from the height of the square brick tower, below which the body of Sturmführer Zukerl had earlier been dangling from a piece of electric cord (but how much earlier—yesterday, last year, last century?) and I also saw myself lying on a folding bed in the huge yellow-orange medical tent with the two red crosses on it. How I could simultaneously be up there at the tower, and see myself from Zukerl's point of view inside the tent, I don't know, but that's how it was—I could see my arm, immobile and heavy, because it was tied with a strap to the folding bed, and drop by drop, through the transparent little tube inside its veins, flowed something glistening and yellowish—maybe from the yellow light, streaming in from everywhere, or maybe this was the color of life, I don't know.

Only when things began to take on realistic outlines and I managed to move my head did I come down from the tower and see Rabbi Ben-David, sitting on a folding chair, his eyes fixed on me with a worried look. "How are you?" he asked.

I moved, very slightly, my cracked lips—a sign that I heard him, that I was there, that I was alive, but even so much as a squeak I couldn't produce. The rabbi dipped a small handkerchief in the aluminum mug and wet my lips with it, and then my forehead too, burning with fever. I reached out with my free palm and placed it on his knee, clothed in ragged duck trousers. I did it perhaps in search of security and support, and he, my rabbi, stroked my hand. After that I again sank into darkness, bottomless and endless.

Time again lost its dimensions, I don't remember how many times I observed myself from the top of the brick tower and then again came down to the tent, to my body. My thoughts, shredded to rags, slid down the surface of my consciousness as if it were a smooth glacier and none of them could catch hold of anything, any kind of small jagged bump, to avoid sinking deeper down, into the darkness. But I still managed to crawl up stubbornly to one single thought, because I needed the answer: Was I alive? And why was I at the same time both up at the tower at Zukerl's wire, and down in the tent? From my height I was dispassionately observing the doctor, who in his white coat over his military uniform was listening to my heart and lungs, or my rabbi, who was trying to thrust a spoonful of broth through my spasmodically clenched teeth. I was sliding down the glacier, naturally it was cold, my whole body was shivering in spite of the clear sensation that I was sweating profusely.

One night, during a blinding full moon, I was sitting up at the tower, and right below me Zukerl was swaying in the breeze, whistling some tune from *The Merry Widow*. On such cloudless nights the Anglo-Americans don't fly, the moon was up there staring, and I was feeling light and immaterial, calm and good. I didn't notice when my former sergeant major sat down quietly beside me, loosened the noose around his neck, patted me on the shoulder in a friendly way, and said:

"But do you know why I love you? Because you're a dirty Jewish bastard!"

I gave out a laugh, happily: "That's what I am all right!"

"And now the two of us, are we dead?"

"Of course," I answered, still so happily.

"It's good to be dead," dreamily said Zukerl.

"Very much so, Mister Sergeant Major."

"Sturmführer!"

"I mean to say it's wonderful to be dead, Mister Sturmführer. You and I saw a lot of death, we were transporting death, burning death with gasoline, and burying it. Now it's our turn and I think it's fair."

"Naturally," Zukerl agreed readily. "As they say, 'To each, his own,' isn't that so?"

It was a nice, quiet night, but I had to excuse myself to Zukerl and go down to my body, because they were sticking in my behind some of those nasty and painful needles, after which a wave of heat ran through my spine all the way to my brain, and made me wake up and vomit some bitter green stuff.

I opened my eyes and whispered "water." This apparently was the end of both my painful crawling along the slippery ice, and my sweet nights on top of the tower in the company of the swaying Zukerl. I looked around surprised and saw above me the blurry face of Rabbi Ben-David.

"Am I alive?" I asked with difficulty.

"Probably," said the rabbi, "because the dead don't ask stupid questions."

"But I was dead," I said.

"Almost. But not completely."

"I think completely. Because my soul had left my body and was observing everything from above, from the top of the tower, with the hanged Zukerl."

The rabbi laughed quietly, "And what did your souls see from the top of the tower?"

"Everything. And me, and you, and the doctors. And that angel all in white, with a white halo, and a cross on the breast, who came to take me."

"Ai-ai, Itzik, you're dreaming Christian dreams!"

"It wasn't a dream," I insisted.

The rabbi tried to remember something, then asked, "And wasn't the face of this angel completely black?"

"I don't know. Maybe. I didn't see it."

"Because the angels from the cotton fields of Mississippi have black faces. And yours is even called Nurse Angela, a sergeant from the medical unit."

"Nurse Angela. . . . If that's so, why have I been then simultaneously here and on top of the tower?"

"This was a dream of your soul, Itzik. Just a dream for courage. Because every mortal is in his own way vain and wants to leave something of himself behind that is eternal and unchanging —if not a pyramid, at least an immortal soul. But even the pyramids get robbed a long time before the end of eternity. After death there's nothing left, I'm sorry to say. It's the same with humans and with worms; both of them submit to the same conditions of life—Ecclesiastes said it. Now sleep, my boy, and stop dreaming of hanged Zukerl."

Much later, during one of my next lucid periods, when I felt considerably better, I asked Ben-David, "When are we going back to Kolodetz?"

The rabbi was silent for awhile, apparently hesitating, then he finally said, "Itzik, you should be admitted to a hospital. Nurse Angela will take care of it. And to Kolodetz—I'll go alone, for now."

"Are you abandoning me?"

"We're all bound together in a chain, the dead and the living, the innocent and the guilty, and none of the links can leave the chain. I love you, Itzik, but I have to go—I have seven times seven accounts to settle and seven times seven thousands of dead to rebury. And to learn all the truths, and utter all the curses, and say all the prayers. Otherwise what's the meaning of all the trials we've endured? Stay here, I'll let you know when and whether to come back!"

"But I have to find Sarah and the children!"

"I'll tell you when to come back," the rabbi stubbornly repeated, "and whether to come back. Because the fruit of futile hopes is bitterer than even the saddest truth."

I stretched my powerless arm, took the rabbi's hand, and squeezed it while one single, lonely, hot tear ran down my cheek.

And so, my dear brother and patient reader, some took off to the east, with the military forces, to home and hearth, all in ashes; others took off for the west, to new shores. Who was wrong and who was right? I don't know. Right and pure remained only the dead, may God give them shelter in His boundless kingdom.

THE FIFTH BOOK OF ISAAC

"Shnat Shmita." Once More, from the Beginning. About the Black Sun and the White Nights.

ONE

Have you ever seen an idiot who carefully builds a house, paints it, plants three pine trees under the window, puts up a curtain with little blue flowers over the window and a pot of geraniums on the ledge, and, after he marvels at his creation, starts systematically tearing it down, stone by stone, until not even one is left standing? Then this fellow, the idiot, declares the day the house has been finally demolished a big family holiday and shoots fireworks in the sky, while his neighbors for a long time to come will be taking out pieces of brick from their soup and spitting plaster. Something similar was done by those friends who provided construction materials to Hitler and all of his *Mein Kampf*, and gave him money for a curtain with little blue flowers and even the pot of geraniums. They were numerous, these benefactors, acting sometimes discreetly, sometimes more obviously, but each one nurtured his own tender thoughts and his own tender hopes. Then all of them got together as a group and got angry at him because too often he refused to obey, and then all together they demolished the little house at the cost of fifty million dead.

This was something like Mendel, who was traveling in a third-class wagon from Berdichev to Odessa. In the compartment, in front of the eyes of his curious fellow passengers, he took down a basket from the overhead luggage rack, laid a plate and a napkin on his knees, and got to work most assiduously. He cut some boiled chicken, cracked and then with his pocket knife sliced into little pieces a hardboiled egg, two boiled potatoes and a red beet, found some onion in the basket, mustard, salt and everything else. Then he mixed everything well, poured some rapeseed oil on it from the small flat bottle that had once contained cough syrup, added a little sprig of parsley for decoration and marveled at his creation, while his fellow passengers were salivating. After that Mendel pulled down the window and threw everything out, wiped the plate and put it back in the basket, and put the basket itself back up again where it belonged. Then he yawned and looked out at the telegraph wires.

One of the flabbergasted passengers finally summoned up the courage and asked him, "Excuse me, but what is it you just made?"

"Jewish chicken salad."

"And why'd you throw it out the window?"

"Oh, there's nothing in the world I hate more than Jewish chicken salad!"

As far as that business of Mendel's is concerned, as well as those investors who demolished the little house and celebrated this fact with fireworks, now they pretend to be absentminded and forget whose genius idea it was to provide some kind of necessary support and stimulus for that former painter of baroque facades and, to top it off, give him a parsley sprig for decoration. And on his part the possessed maniac came to believe that he could give the finger to all of humankind, including the ones who planted the three pine trees for him. In fact this was precisely the fatal mistake of the aforementioned painter, and it determined the denouement of the fairy tale, about which everyone now swears that there's nothing in the world they hate more than the salad they mixed together themselves.

And in order to continue in the same spirit, I now offer you a joyful little problem to solve in the lazy Sunday idyll before lunchtime: for all of this construction, including the equipment for hunting and other types of weapons, about 270 billion dollars, they say, was spent. Deducting from this money the expenses for my delousing, about which I was given a timely warning from Commandant Brückner, known as the Radish, a sum of money remains, about which the problem arises: Where did it all end up? It could hardly have been deducted from the savings of that fat drug addict and lover of stolen works of art, who ended up on the gallows, and even less so from the dowry of that limping apostle of culture, with the looks of a professional gambler, who escaped justice, because, having been in that line of work, he anticipated the executioner, or from the speculations of Bormann, Eichmann, & Co. in unique artifacts of human skin. So where did it come from, then?

When you add up the many times greater size of the resources, in excess of a thousand billion, spent for the demolition of this same small house and multiply this sum by the cubic meters of bloodshed and suffering endured, the problem then includes the question: Who carries the main responsibility—the master or the slave? The initiator or the person who carries it out? The person who gives the order or the finger that pulled the trigger?

To this question for the time being only Abramovitch's answer has been received: "Oy-oy, don't ask!"

I don't want to bore you with puzzles of a higher degree of difficulty: the whereabouts, for example, of those seventeen tons of gold, collected in Auschwitz alone from wedding rings, dental crowns, and the like, including a small pair of earrings in the shape of a four-leaf clover that brings good luck, given to Lizochka Weissberg as a gift on her third birthday. I would ask where they are, as a mere particle of the infinitely greater quantity of things of similar gold origin, but in light of the sensitive peristalsis of certain bankers from neighboring and respected neutral countries, who would take this as a hint that might disturb their good manners and hearty appetites as they sit gathered around the table joyously savoring pheasant in truffle sauce, I withdraw the question. And besides, to tell you honestly, I don't expect an answer either, and on the other hand I'm in a hurry for the morning checkup in the American army field hospital, temporarily situated in the surviving wing of the bombed-out old-age home "St. Peter" in Salzburg.

The American medical authorities transported here a large number of gravely ill, though still breathing, camp inmates from the Oberpfalz region. The others, the lighter cases, stayed there, at the camp itself, inside huge tents, which in my hallucinations I used to see as yellow clouds of light.

There, after the respective medical treatments, the survivors were directed, just like my rabbi Ben-David, to their destination of choice—for some east, to their birthplaces, where very often there was no one left waiting for them, some—as I've already told you and they weren't a small number, those so-called at the time "displaced persons"—to new, unknown shores. We, the more serious and even hopeless cases, had been transported here and situated in the big baroque halls, with those touching plaster angels wearing garlands of roses on the smoky ceilings, which had once probably gladdened the eyes of the Salzburg elders. The beds were positioned so tightly that the poor doctors and nurses could only move through the sick by going sideways. Filled to the maximum was even the small stage, adorned with peeling gold, on which, in better times, His Majesty's imperial chamber choir, or even my colleague Mozart, had probably played. Those who hadn't found room there were jammed into corridors and stairway landings and I don't know who suffered more from this unimaginable discomfort—the sick or those treating them. You may have noticed that I'm reluctantly describing unpleasant or disgusting scenes and am in a hurry to get through them with the biblical strides of a hundred Roman *stadii*, which I've already mentioned to you, because life offers you nasty things in sufficient quantity without my assistance. But I can't pass by that feature of our Salzburg life, wherein from the far end of the hall the medical workers had to carry a dead body over the heads of the sick, who right at that moment were clicking their spoons against their aluminum bowls, filled with pea-soup, just as I'm completely skipping details from those cases when the inexperienced sanitary workers, volunteers from Minnesota or Ohio, squeezing between the beds, would drop the dead, may they rest in peace, on top of the living. And do let me remind you that a large number of us had been blasted by typhoid marked by the proverbial phrase "*Panta rei*—everything flows," so you'll understand why the rest is silence, to which I, in a most unservile manner, bow my head as a sign of gratitude and respect to the American medical personnel, who, with tight lips and without even realizing the magnitude of their silent heroism, sacrificially fought for the life of every single one of these human remnants.

Probably it was like this as well at many other places, where, staying awake and fighting to save human lives under the protective sign of the Red Cross, there were people in white jackets on top of their Russian, English, and French military uniforms and even without uniforms—just nuns, Samaritans and other organizations of Catholics, Protestants, Adventists, and atheists, to whom, as far as I know, up till now not even a humble monument has been erected anywhere in Europe, though they are no less deserving of memorials than the liberating armies, for whom I also feel unconcealed admiration.

In connection with the people in white I had quite a shock, which threw me off balance for a long time, but about this a little later.

If you're from the generation that still remembers that time, you must have noted in the matrix of your mind that those weren't simply days of grief for lost loved ones and villages and towns burned to ashes, but also of hope that the evil had ended once and for all and could never again repeat itself. "Never again!"—these are the words that were pronounced like a chant, without satisfying the thirst to say them again. That's how it is, naiveté goes with people, just like lice. But these were also days, let's say it openly, of hatred and fierce craving for revenge. These passions, as you know, make the human soul blind and often unjust; however, don't judge those by now distant bursts of uncontrollable fury from the perspective today of your table at the Café Sacher, where you've just been served your next martini with clinking ice and an olive.

At that time, if you remember, they were shooting fascist butchers and their accomplices all over Europe—sometimes with a trial, other times after a shorter procedure—and among the executioners there were not seldom some ardent truth lovers, who up until the day before had shouted "Heil Hitler," "Viva Duce," or whatever they shouted at other places. People exhibited an almost biological revulsion against anything that smacked of fascism; throughout otherwise freewheeling and tolerant Paris, always so accepting of any human weakness and passion, they dragged along the streets shamed and weeping girls with shaved heads, because they had danced with or maybe slept with German soldiers; they denounced and disgraced and even passed sentence on dumb journalists because of some little article praising fascism—as if similar writings don't pop up to this day. From all parts of Europe post parcels were traveling to Norway, sent by private persons and public libraries, containing the books of the Nobel laureate Knut Hamsun, which the shocked and indignant readers were returning to the author as a sign of protest and contempt for his pro-Nazi inclinations. The concept of "collaborationist" had acquired such fluid and unclear boundaries that in a number of countries it was even forbidden to perform music by the collaborationist Richard Wagner, and Friedrich Nietzsche, considered by some people a first cousin to the circle closest to Hitler, was said to be passing the hat to others, in this case one Zarathustra, who'd said to him, I told you so.

And after all, I repeat, don't judge with a high hand the passions of that time—some legitimate, some not altogether so, and some even at times tragicomic—from the point of view of today's well air-conditioned and aromatized criteria and values, but try to go into the worn-out and mangy skin of Europe of that time, in order to understand its tortured soul, which smelled like gunpowder residue, carbolic acid, and the unburied dead.

I've said all this not to bore you with old memories, but in order to understand the situation of Dr. Joe Smith, our magnificent physician—one of the not too small group of selfless saviors who dragged so many of us out of the black rectangular ditch toward which we were heading. "Doc Joe"—this is what both the nurses and the medical workers called him too, with that warmth and informality characteristic only of the Americans.

One morning I woke up painfully from the drowsiness into which I had sunk and which was at the customs office on the border between dream and afterlife—because someone was lightly slapping me on the cheek. I opened my eyelids and in the slowly condensing magma of light and shadow and the images starting to take shape within it—as if a photographic plate were being developed in my mind—I saw the concerned face of Doc Joe hanging over me. I moved my eyes, in order to discover in my range of sight that black angel, who once upon a time, if you remember, had come to take my soul and whom I'd been observing from the height of the tower, at which I had spent such blissful moments in quiet discussions with the hanged Zukerl. I've already told you that this was the angel's name—Sister Angela—and at that moment she was sprinkling in the air a transparent liquid from a syringe, with my behind the final goal of this exercise.

Doc Joe waited for the procedure to be completed and asked, "Well, how goes it? Are we alive?"

You know how it is, doctors always speak in the plural, including themselves in the case history out of solidarity, and this one, unlike Sister Angela, was expressing the aforementioned solidarity in a surprisingly beautiful and educated German. I tried to smile with my cracked lips, covered with crusts of peeling skin.

"Probably," I said. "Because not long ago a relative of mine explained to me that the dead neither ask nor answer questions."

"You mean the rabbi?" asked Sister Angela. "What a person, oh my God! Till the day he left he managed to tell me a hundred and one Jewish jokes!"

"Yes, that's how it is," I whispered, "with a man with no worries, that happy-go-lucky fellow. . . ."

The black-and-white Angela took my words at face value. Little did she know about the tribe of Jewish jokers, the Kolodetz brand, who at life's most hopeless moments will shoot out some droll story from Berdichev.

"You could sure envy a guy like that! A man with no worries!" she sighed. "I learned you were relatives or something."

"Or something . . . ," I said.

Sister Angela started looking in the pockets of her white medical smock, which looked whiter because of the contrast with her face, or maybe her face was becoming more black, framed by the little white starched cap with a red cross on it. She found something, handed it over to me—this was a pressed aluminum button from a piece of camp clothing, painfully familiar, because we'd had to strip the corpses before arranging them on those pyres, which I've mentioned to you, while from the next applicants for the pyre we piled up clothes with similar aluminum buttons for steaming and further use.

"Your relative, the rabbi, gave it to me as a memento before he left. Poor dear, he didn't have anything else and tore it out of his clothes. He said I could offer it as a model for a gigantic memorial to the humane twentieth century, this camp button."

I took it in my emaciated, yellowish-brown palm, dried as old parchment: a pressed aluminum circle, probably the wartime product of some "Special Site," because it didn't "breathe,"

the press hadn't done its job very well, and only two out of the four holes were punched through all the way.

"A strange idea," quietly said Doctor Joe. "A monument in the form of a button!"

"The rabbi Shmuel Ben-David always has such ideas in storage," I said. "They come to him while he's crossing the desert."

"Which desert?" asked Sister Angela, surprised.

"That one."

The sister cast a quick glance at the doctor. I had apparently generated in her some vague suspicions, and, moreover, she was familiar with my walks to the top of the tower.

"And for what will be the purpose of this monument?" I asked.

"To be a reminder of what happened in this century and not to forget it. That's what he said."

I looked up at her, shaking my head. "It will be forgotten, Sister, it will be. The rabbi is a terrible romantic. Monuments usually turn quickly into decorations, something like brooches on the breast of the town, to which the local people get accustomed and stop noticing them, and the tourists take pictures as souvenirs, using them as background, without knowing who or what is depicted by them. Believe me, this is how it is. Once upon a time in Vienna my Uncle Chaimle and I used to take pictures of ourselves with Shwarzenberg* in the background, without knowing anything about who was this fellow on the horse or what was his contribution."

---

* Karl Philip Shwarzenberg, Austrian general who commanded the united armies against Napoleon during the French campaign. [Mr. Blumenfeld's note]

And still, while Doc Joe, sitting askew at the edge of my bed, was listening to my chest whistling like an old kettle, I enriched the rabbi's idea with my own: Why can't they, I thought, in some museum, for example the Musée de l'Homme in Paris, about which I had read something in Kolodetz, and where behind glass windows they keep the preserved clothes of emperors, Madame Pompadours, and Venetian doges, display my shat-in pajamas from Salzburg? After all, they too are a symbol of a glorious epoch.

I felt shy about sharing my idea with Sister Angela, who was in a hurry anyway, she took the button as if it were made of gold, and went away with her tray, arranged with a rich assortment of tablets, droppers, and syringes for the next patients in pajamas, who, just like me, were expecting her visit with glassy eyes fixed on the ceiling, on which plump, light-winged angels were carrying garlands of roses.

With the tips of his fingers Doc Joe started to press painfully on my stomach and I even moaned. "Does it hurt?" he asked.

A little irritated by the sharp pain, I said, "What do you think?"

"I think the sickness is already going away. It's time for you to start going out to the park. You're fine."

"I'm fine?" I protested almost indignantly. "Do you know that in the Jewish cemetery of Berdichev, there's the gravestone of the shoemaker Uzi Schweitzer, which says: 'Leah, you didn't even believe I was sick!'"

Doc Joe laughed: "But still, keep it up and stop contemplating your belly button. Help me and try to exhibit your stubbornness in another area."

"The fact is, Doc, with the same stubbornness I resisted typhoid for a long time. It's now also probably paid for."

"Everything is paid for . . ." said the doc, falling into deep thought about something else, probably far away from here, because his eyes wandered in space.

With a touch of exaggerated joyfulness, he patted me patronizingly on the cheek—as if he were a pediatrician treating a willful child resisting recovery, and not me, the old fighter, who had lived through two world wars, one May 1st competition, two concentration camps, and, as a garnish for it all—like the parsley that we mentioned already before—the embarrassments of stomach typhoid.

TWO

However, my situation soon really improved quite a bit and, sometimes with Sister Angela's help, other times alone, I would lean on the marble banisters of the stairways and against the walls and go out for a short while and sit in the park of this majestic, half-destroyed building. The linden trees were blooming and flooded us with their sweet fragrance, which tenderly but firmly overcame in waves the sharp hospital smell.

Quite a long time had passed, and I still hadn't had any news from Rabbi Ben-David. I was looking forward to it, this news, about which I felt both horror and hope, and I kept looking into that secret fold of the human soul, in which the most mindless hopes are hidden. Mindless, groundless, proved by nothing and still longed for: maybe tragedy hadn't reached Sarah but someone else with the same name, and maybe it wasn't that sanatorium in Rovno, but the one next door, and maybe the ravine above the small river where the mass shootings had taken place was not in Kolodetz, but . . . I'm ashamed to admit to you that egotism with which I sacrificed all the others in my thoughts, in order to save my own. I'm ashamed but that's how it was. The only thing I firmly believed was that our children were alive—Ilyusha, Schura, and Susannah, and maybe they were somewhere close, in Germany or Austria, not as camp inmates but as winners in this grand and formidable Exodus.

The sands of the first month since the end of the war had run through what was sometimes called, in the little local newspapers printed on yellowish wartime paper, the "capitulation" or the "occupation," at other times the "liberation"—according to the political leanings of the authors. But in any case, the Nazis were being referred to as "those people," some alien, extraterrestrial mythical monsters from outer space, as if my once-upon-a-time Austrian compatriots had been seized by a heavy amnesia and had completely forgotten the diligence and even enthusiasm with which *Kristallnacht* here had been conducted, as well as many other not so crystal nights and days. And as if it weren't here but on some other planet, and as if there the Mauthausen camp hasn't existed, serviced by a staff speaking in Alpine dialects. Of course, compared to the four million victims of Auschwitz and the two million of Dachau, the one hundred and twenty-three thousand killed in this camp in this musical country were something like a minuet in three-quarter time, with curtsies and bows. Quite some time later, I heard respectable Germans saying both jokingly and half-seriously: "So cunning, these Austrians: they pushed Hitler on us, and took possession of Beethoven."

It's a pity, because I like Austria and its life-loving people—a wonderful mix of eastern and western winds and kitchen recipes, with a slight breeze from the Italian south! Now as I'm writing these lines and everything has passed long ago and turned into a memory, a relic, or a boring history lesson at school, I know that there's a time for throwing stones and a time for gathering stones and building—otherwise how can we all together sow the plowed furrows of Europe? But at that time—one month after the end of the war—every attempt to keep silent about the crimes and to transfer the guilt echoed painfully in our wounded souls more as a justification than as a generous gesture toward peacemaking. Because when the small village tries to be silent or to conceal the doings of a horse thief, the victims suspect the whole village of horse thievery. I'm sorry about my preachy tone, but that's how things are.

One day in June, bathed in the dripping fragrance of the blooming lindens, Doc Joe sat down quietly on the bench next to me, visibly tired by the hard work of keeping vigil over the convalescent and the dying. The doctor was a big, not-handsome man, with a meaty nose and heavy glasses, and despite his relative youth—somewhere in his mid-forties—his forehead was dented by two deep wrinkles. Two similar wrinkles vertically lined his cheeks and made him look rather kind and folksy, raising one's expectation of a smile, which wasn't long in coming, and revealed the strong but yellow teeth of a serious smoker.

"How're things? Are we recovering?" he asked, and patted me on the knee with his big hand, which was like a blacksmith's or a village barrel maker's rather than a doctor's.

"I'm getting there," I said. "But I was just thinking, Doctor, about this building—how's it going to recover? Just look at it: what a pity, really now! And why did it have to be destroyed? I just don't get all the military significance, so to say—the strategic benefit of bombing such an old city. Amadeus Mozart was born here, after all!"

"Everywhere someone's been born. War has its own scale of values and its own needs. It doesn't choose its victims according to human logic, neither does it distinguish the howl of bombs from the Magic Flute. Is it possible that the bullets will only hit the bad ones, or only the Catholics, only the communists, only the blue-eyed? And why was Dresden senselessly destroyed, can you explain that to me? It didn't have any military significance, and they had the Zwinger museum with Raphael's Madonna! And why did we raze to the ground Coventry, Oradour, and Lidice? Or half of Russia?"

I looked at him in surprise: "Why we? In what sense 'we'?"

He was silent for a moment and then looked me in the eye and said calmly, "I am German. A major from the medical services of . . . a certain German military unit. Haven't you noticed that under the doctor's smock I don't have a uniform?"

"To be honest, I didn't think it meant anything. Some of the military nurses not only skip wearing a military uniform under their smocks but also even a bra."

"Yes, that's a more pleasant sight."

"On the other hand, come to think of it, your German was immediately apparent. Unlike Sister Angela who uses about a hundred German words in an English syrup. I thought you studied it at college or something."

He shook his head. "I studied it with my grandmother in Ottobrunn, near Munich."

"I'm sorry if I'm asking inappropriate questions, but . . . it seems strange—a German major with a name like Joe Smith, who turns out to be in an American unit before the end of the war."

For the first time I saw him light a cigarette—indoors this was forbidden for everyone, including the doctors and the nurses. He didn't offer one to me. He said, "The English reading of my name is what does it and the American habit of reading Johann as Joe. I am Johan Schmidt, a citizen of the just-collapsed Third Reich. Whether there will be a fourth one—we don't know yet."

THREE

And so, my dear brother, who will read these lines, if you have the patience, learn also the story of the major from the medical services, Johann Schmidt, or if you wish, Doc Joe. It is all presented in exactly the way he personally told it to me in that quiet and fragrant dusk in Salzburg, before the blue shadows of the night started edging up the rocks toward the fortress.

And if I'm telling you, it's not to add one more drop to the overflowing well of memories of the Sinister War, but because the vignettes and caprioles of life are all tangled up in destiny, and as I've already hinted to you, we understood them in one way at that time, and quite differently now, years after the war.

The denouement was approaching and only complete idiots, among whom Doctor Schmidt was not at all included, were expecting a miracle in connection with the rumor of the Führer's new secret weapon. We know now that this was not idle chatter, and that Werner von Braun was feverishly preparing the atom bomb, but it was already late, and, moreover, a cat, thank God, crossed his path. Even the defeat of the Allies at the Ardennes did not paint a rosier picture of the imminent and inexorable end.

At that time the unit in which my doctor was enrolled was to be found somewhere in northern Italy, in the Dolomites, and the Americans were crawling unstoppably up the Italian boot. This was a rather small special unit, said Doc Joe, without clarifying what was special about it, which had been completely confused by the contradictory orders of the high ranking chiefs preoccupied more with saving their own skins than with the design of a systematic plan for withdrawal.

In this cheerful situation, Major Johann Schmidt decided to commit supreme treachery against the ideals of National Socialism, and, carelessly undoing his belt, moved off on the pretext of crouching behind the bushes, waited for a suitable moment of general disorder, and bolted down through the early crocuses.

He ran through bushes, snowdrifts, and creeks, until he heard laughter and noisy English speech. Ducking down in the low junipers, Doctor Schmidt crawled toward the sounds and discovered below him, in a small clearing, about ten American soldiers, who were boiling water for coffee on a small fire they had just made. It may not be decent to speak like this about the winners, but this team was no less disorderly than that which the major had just left without even bidding farewell, in that their weapons were hanging on the bare branches or were just lying on last year's grass. At this point our doctor jumped out from his hiding place and shouted out in a most cordial manner, "Hey, amis, Freundschaft! Hitler kaputt!"

It will remain unknown in history what exactly the Americans made of this diplomatic message, but all of them, as if by an order, threw away their metal cups and raised their arms. Some linguistic complications came up, while the doctor tried to explain that he was the one who was surrendering, and not the other way around. At this moment, from above in the bushes someone shouted: "*Hände hoch!*" which means "Hands up!" and the small representative part of American democracy turned out to be under the gun of a unit of SS soldiers, cleaning up the forest. The Americans had to surrender for a second time, but the exhilaration of the SS soldiers was beyond description when they found out that these ten Yankees had already been captured by one single major from the Wehrmacht, and a doctor at that! What more shining proof of the moral superiority of the German spirit over the rotten Western plutocracy!

The captured were taken to the special unit, in which Doctor Schmidt was enrolled, and he was personally given praise with the promise of being proposed for a medal of honor in the next report.

That same night, when the unit, completely soused on medical spirits, was snoring away, Doctor Schmidt unlocked the stone sheepfold, turned into a temporary holding cell for the ten Americans, and together with them fled, thus not hanging around to receive his medal of honor.

Since then, in other words, since the late winter of forty-four, Major Schmidt had been enrolled among the personnel of the American military field hospital and become "Doc Joe." He honestly and with his by no means negligible knowledge of German medical science, which, we must admit, has more than once also proved its superiority, tried to keep the thread of Ariadne unbroken in the wounded American soldiers, the civilian population suffering from battles, or, as in our case, the semi-humans dragged out of the stinking camps.

"Well, so what?" you will say. "What do you want to hint to me with this story? When the months till the end are counted, it's not such a big deal to act the way your doctor did. Especially if you have at least two grams of brain in your head!"

Yes, it's true, I have to hand it to you, but still most didn't do it, sometimes because of fear, other times because of useless hopes for a sudden change in the course of events or the imposing myths of a soldier's duty, fidelity to vows, and all kinds of high ideals for *Blut und Boden.* But let me remind you as well that the Soviet boys didn't do it either even when things seemed hopeless, or when freight cars were transporting the blocks of granite for a statue of Hitler on Red Square. There's a difference, you'll say, but please don't involve me in debates about just and unjust wars, because not every soldier, with his head stuck in the mud, can make a judgment about this from the high and strict criteria of history. I only want to say that complicated and mysterious are the ways of God, in which a life-defining choice reaches the brain and the heart, and with some this happens fast, and with others, I'm sorry to say, a little slower. Some, as we know, did not let fascism into their souls, others abandoned it—some on the first day of the war, others on the last one, and some never left it at all. For those who threw away by conviction the brown shirt of this somber delusion—no matter when, sooner or later, I'll remind you of the words of my rabbi, pronounced on a different occasion: "Let us understand them, without cursing them and without deriding them, let us leave some space, bread, and wine for them at our table." This is what Rabbi Shmuel Ben-David said and you try to understand it!

And this is not the denouement, or call it the punch line of my story, but rather that early morning, somewhere toward the end of June, where, in our hospital room, crammed with beds, there entered an American officer and a sergeant from the military police, "MPs" as they were called, accompanied by two civilians with red bands on the sleeves of their worn-out coats. One was a big, hairy mountain fellow, the other one just the opposite—a small fellow with wire-rimmed glasses, the way printers or history teachers in poor mountain towns look. Let me tell you immediately that red bands on sleeves at that time could mean a number of different things—from voluntary citizen police, trying to establish order in a country, where except for the occupation armies there was no other power, to representatives of committees, anti-fascist organizations and parties, or just self-appointed temporary community units, undertaking the responsibility for drinking water or bread for the desperate and disaster-stricken population. Doc Joe, sitting on the edge of the bed as usual with his huge body bent sideways, turned his head, looked at the newcomers and stood up, slowly taking down his stethoscope.

The little fellow with the wire glasses fixed his shortsighted eyes on him, then decisively stretched his hand and pointed at him with his finger—like a strict judge, a biblical prophet, the god Zebaoth himself: "That's him!"

FOUR

So Doc Joe was arrested and I never saw him again. One more time seized by doubts, as regular as stomach colic, about supreme justice, which eventually gives everyone what they deserve, I learned the truth from Sister Angela, and it was the following:

After the capitulation of Fascist Italy and the immediate German occupation of northern Italy that followed, a rather fierce partisan war flamed up in those mountainous places. Led by the insane paranoid idea of the "Final Solution," the Nazis undertook arrests of Jews here too, even though it is well known that some more sober heads from the Führer's circle were already sensing that the Final Solution was indeed not going to be late, but was moving in a slightly different direction. So somewhere in the region of Trento, a temporary transit camp was organized for Jews and other harmful elements, before deporting them. The major from the medical unit, Johann Schmidt, was taken off the rolls of his military hospital and enlisted in the "Special Unit" as a doctor who had to attest to and record in the documents the data about the medical status of the "merchandise." With respect to this some were sent to the stone quarries of Mauthausen, and those physically unfit for this heavy labor quite a distance further, to a resort in Poland, where despite mounting difficulties, created by the rapid advance of the Red Army, they were still well stocked with sufficient quantities of the round boxes of crystals under the code name of "Zyklon B." With the advance of the Americans the camp in Trento was quickly dissolved, and the unit was given an order to withdraw toward the former Austrian border.

This, more or less, is it. I don't want to and I can't judge either the degree of Dr. Schmidt's guilt, or the sincerity of his deeds given his forced participation in the nastiness, because years later I met some doctors in Kolyma, under a polar cap, and for some of them I kept in my memory a dose of quiet gratitude for their humane attitude or just professional conscientiousness, and for others—the most simple contempt. I only know that the finger with which the little Italian pointed at Doc Joe was the finger of Retribution, but such was the time—straight-shooting, without alleviating nuances and mitigating clauses.

Later on I learned that the doctor was sentenced to eight years in Milan, even the newspapers wrote about it—some with surprise, others with satisfaction—then that he performed diligently as a doctor in the prison hospital and was granted amnesty as soon as the third year. And if now he is a pensioner in Ottobrunn by Munich and if he by chance reads these lines of mine, I would like to tell him: "Hello, Doc Joe, I know that war is a nasty thing and makes the person an accomplice—sometimes conscious, sometimes unconscious. I'm not the institution that hands out sentences and that's why I only want to tell you that I remember good things about you."

I'm convinced that someone will furiously disagree on the above topic and I don't doubt the fairness of his disagreement, that's why I'll reply to him like the old rabbi: "You are right too!"

FIVE

On June 22, just like a caprice or game of chance—on the fourth anniversary of the moment when we were suddenly forced to interrupt our travels to the hills of Manchuria and our life unexpectedly went in another direction—exactly on that day I received a parcel mailed from Geneva, marked with the signs of the International Red Cross. Believe me, even before I opened the big envelope with trembling fingers, I knew that this was news from Rabbi Ben-David, and I knew what he was going to tell me. I was afraid to read it, I was picking the envelope up and putting it down, and up and down again, as if something in its contents could still change and improve. And it wasn't easy to read through the blur of my tears, because there was a document from the International Committee on Nazi crimes in Auschwitz regarding the person Sarah Davidovna Blumenfeld, maiden name Zvassman, who died in the camp on March 3, 1943. There was an excerpt from protocol 107/1944 issued by the Military Prosecutor of the Third Ukrainian Front for the mass shooting of peaceful civilians in the vicinity of Kolodetz, South Ukraine, U.S.S.R. In addition, there was a copy of the Order for the Posthumous Decoration with the "Red Flag" medal of the fighter Yeshua (Schura) Isaakovitch Blumenfeld and the radio operator Susannah Isaakovna Blumenfeld, from the Tarnopol partisan unit, who died in battle against the fascist occupier. And in addition, there was a notice on a standard form, quickly and carelessly filled in by an unknown bureaucrat, testifying that the guard-lieutenant Blumenfeld, Isaak Yacobovitch, had not returned from an intelligence mission to the enemy's rear in the area of Vitebsk, First Baltic Front, and should be considered missing. "This document is to serve his next of kin as . . ." Oh, God, for what other purpose could my boy's death serve, if it hadn't served already to speed up by one second, together with the other fifty million seconds, the end of this damned war!

My dear Itzik!

I managed to provide myself with the attached records, which with the generous help of a foreign correspondent you will receive through the Red Cross. I know how much you will be hurt by everything you will learn, but I've already told you that the fruit of empty hopes is more bitter than the saddest truth. This is how it is now all over our country, which is flooded by waves of bad news about the long-awaited loved ones who will not return.

I do not dare give you advice about what to do, because I myself am lost, as if in the bottom of a dark pit. Kolodetz is almost entirely destroyed and burnt, only its brick chimneys have survived the fire. This is what our miastechko is now—a dead forest of chimneys!

People are nonetheless beginning to return, here and there one of ours comes back. I am proud of them, because they come decorated with medals of glory in battle,

> but of our relatives, unfortunately, there are none surviving. Everything has to start from the very beginning, brick by brick. Because now it is Shnat Shmita.

I lifted my eyes from the letter and remembered the lessons from the Talmud: Shnat Shmita, the Seventh, the Sabbath year, when in ancient times the land was left unplowed, in order to rest and in peace to cover the dead with grass. Shnat Shmita—to everyone in the Seventh Year according to his need and everything from the beginning. This is what it had come to!

> That is why I will stay here, Itzik, with my people, because I am obliged to be with them! I want to help them understand that what happened was not inevitable and might not have happened, and that the quiet resignation with which many accepted it may conceal in itself the wisdom of the past, but hardly brings hope for the future. I am not a prophet, nor a tzaddik, but a simple rabbi in an ordinary small miastechko, myself confused and torn by doubts of both celestial and earthly truths, but I would like to help people grasp the meaning of what happened and liberate themselves from being hostages to resignation and biblical dreams—just like our brave Maccabees from the Warsaw Ghetto, eternal be their memory! They have the right, our people, to all the past of the tribe of Abraham, but the future we must enter awake, with eyes open and looking forward. This is what I think.
>
> And why am I writing all this to you? So that you know why I am staying. But you, my cherished and dearest Itzik, husband of my deceased sister and father of all my nephews and my niece fallen in battle, you are frag-

ile, and your soul is weak and wounded, and I don't want to see it broken like a cracked vessel in the Seventh Year. This is why I beg you: for the time being, do not come back. Settle yourself somewhere, by the side of a river, plant a piece of land and water it—let the grass grow.

Always yours,
Shmuel Ben-David

PS. I learned about Esther Katz as much as it was possible to learn: you remember that she was sent to take a cure, but, unfortunately, she will never return. I don't know where her grave is and what happened to her is a great, great injustice. But the traces of her steps on the sands of my life have remained!

Sh. B.

It's strange, but true—the stronger the blow, the weaker the pain, which comes later, much later. Maybe nature has encoded all this in the cell in order to preserve the life system. Have you noticed that at the funeral of a loved one, your mind drifts away to thoughts that are insignificant or quite inappropriate for the somber mourning ritual, as if the soul purposefully switches off its fuses, in order to avoid explosion. The sheets of paper from the big Geneva envelope were scattered on the blanket, and I was lying numb, with unblinking eyes. Indifferent grayness was stretching out in front of my inner sight—without a horizon, without a demarcation line between down and up, life and death, yesterday and tomorrow.

I don't know how long this lasted, but my black angel tried to drag me out from the depths of timelessness and took me for a walk up at the fortress. I submitted to her like a doll, without a will of my own. The small-track railway train was not working of course, but the angel had a friend in the supply unit, who drove us up in his military jeep. His name was Jefferson—that's right, Jefferson—and he was a hundred times blacker than Angela, but when he smiled, his white teeth flashed a hundred times whiter than her hospital smock. So, as I was saying, this Jefferson took us up, but delicately stayed with the car—maybe Sister Angela had wished it so.

Salzburg stretched down below our feet, squeezed between the forest folds of the mountains, with roofs here and there burnt from the bombings. Magnificent, royal Salzburg—reaching toward the Alps with its castles and squares, its churches and vaulted tunnels under the houses—here, from this height, looked like a model or a town of miniature beings from fairy tales.

Sister Angela stretched her arm out toward the hill in front, thickly covered with clouds of greenery. "Do you see that white house, with the wall that keeps appearing and disappearing between the trees? Do you know whose home this is?"

"How can I know?" I said indifferently.

"Stefan Zweig."

Something trembled in me, awaking memories of nights spent with his books, when my mother Rebekha would worriedly open the door to see why I hadn't switched off the petrol lamp yet.

"Stefan Zweig," I repeated. "He escaped to America, I think. Where is he now?"

Angela answered without taking her eyes off the white house: "In the heaven of the righteous. For a long time now. Actually, not such a long time, but time during war is thicker: In '42 he committed suicide with his wife in Brazil."

"My God, why?"

"Yes, why? I ask myself."

I started thinking, then quite some time later I said, "Maybe to avoid receiving after the war a letter like mine. . . . In fact, do you know that according to statistics, the Jews come last in the world in the number of criminal murders? And first in suicide."

"Does this mean something?"

"Maybe. As they say: as many Jews, as many opinions, as many differences. I don't know, maybe since the time of the Tower of Babel they've accepted different thinking and different tongues as something inherent in the tribe and don't try to eliminate their opponents through violence. This brought about the delusion that the Jews are adorably unified. As unified as the banker Rothschild and the revolutionary Karl Marx, who wanted to expropriate him. But on the other hand the deepest and most unsolvable disagreements the Jew has are with himself and suicide is the only way to get rid of that annoying Jewish opponent inside you, who is constantly nagging and contradicting you—"

"That's not funny," Angela said, drily interrupting my overflow.

"I'm not even trying to make you laugh. I just want to say that I fully understand Stefan Zweig. I even think this is the only sensible solution for me too."

She was startled, as if I had slapped her across the face, and gave me a furious, spark-flying look, and poked her finger in my chest: "Listen, you're really a nasty Jew! Don't you realize I dragged you out of the grave? I didn't sleep whole nights listening to hear if you were breathing! I held you in my hands, the way you hold a child—shitting in your pants, puking, scabby, covered in lice, and stinking! In order to bring you back to the world of people, you damned bastard! And now you'll be giving me your Jewish tricks with suicide!"

"This is my personal problem!" I screamed.

"Is this what you think? Then go screw yourself, you stupid jerk!"

"And you shut your black beak!"

Jefferson unhurriedly ambled over toward us. "Is there a problem?" he asked, without taking the cigarette out of his mouth.

"Get lost! It's none of your business!" Sister Angela angrily screamed at him. The young man shrugged his shoulders and obediently went back to his jeep.

Angela suddenly started to cry and this changed things. Overwhelmed by regret I caressed her on the head and said with resignation, "I'm sorry. I didn't mean to hurt you. It's Stefan Zweig's fault."

She looked at me and tried to smile through her tears. "Promise me you won't do anything stupid?"

"I promise," I said.

"And will you write me wherever you are? Wherever I am?"

"I'll write you," I said. "But is this address going to be sufficient: Sister Angela, the cotton fields by Mississippi?"

"Where'd you get this—about the cotton and all?"

"That's what the rabbi said, that that's where you come from."

Angela laughed sincerely, though her tears hadn't dried yet. "It seems in Europe you haven't read anything about America apart from *Uncle Tom's Cabin*! I'm from Massachusetts—Boston. I'll give you my father's address; he's the most famous Negro lawyer in New England. I studied medicine on the other side of the river—at Harvard. In my third year I interrupted my studies in order to come over as a volunteer to your damned Europe. So there. You'll write, okay?"

I had to stand on my toes in order to kiss this shapely, large-bosomed black woman. Sergeant Jefferson was looking indifferently and without a trace of jealousy, leaning on the jeep, because I could have been her grandfather, but from another, not-quite-up-to-par and significantly paler nation.

SIX

I don't know, have you heard about that Salomon Kalmovitz, the genius Vienna fur coat maker, who would make with imported rabbit fur magnificent women's coats of mink, otter, and even leopard? So this Kalmovitz, you know, returns to Vienna from his exile in London and moves again into his old apartment above Schwedenplatz. He can hardly wait for the sun to rise and immediately runs to the first newspaper kiosk where he asks for the daily edition of the official Nazi newspaper, the *Völkischer Beobachter.* Told that the newspaper is no longer in circulation, Kalmovitz gives a polite thank you and buys himself a bag of mint drops. On the next day he goes again and again asks for the same newspaper, in order to receive the same answer. And it's like this every morning, until on the tenth day the newspaper man tells him with irritation: "Dear sir, didn't you understand already that this newspaper doesn't come out and will not come out again anymore!"

"I know, my dear sir, I know. But it's so nice to start the day with good news!"

I don't really know for whom this news was in fact so good, and for whom not so good, but in any case I came to a Vienna different from the way I remembered it from the First World War—joyfully carefree, in love with itself, and prone to regard the blows of destiny as an historic *Auftakt* in the middle of its endless waltz—just a pause for rest and change of cavaliers. Maybe at that time it looked like this just from the outside, I don't know, but now the city seemed to me considerably more somber and confused, having lost its boisterous mood and with difficulty enduring want, destruction, and occupation. On the walls still hung the shreds of images of a manly Hitlerian soldier with a square face and a helmet stuck on his head, with his index finger held sternly to his lips: "The spies are on the alert!" and under these posters rumbled the heavy American, English, and Soviet trucks. Or little Russian soldiers would march in step, singing and whistling collective farm ditties about some Mashas and *mamashas*, completely foreign in this world, enticed as if by the embrace of the rainbow over the magnificent Hofburg. The Viennese would stop on the sidewalk to gape a little at these extraterrestrial visitors with Slavic snub noses or slanted Asiatic eyes, some looked at them with unconcealed curiosity, and others with covert mistrust, still not completely realizing what exactly had sneaked into their lives, like a black cat in the kitchen, through the crack between the two words "*Sieg*" and "*Heil*," in order to destroy everything, including Karl-Heinz Müller's plans for a stud farm or at least a small brewery by Rostov-on-Don.

This wasn't the case with Frau Sigrid Kubichek, who admitted me to the city commission for displaced people, located at the confiscated premises of the National-Socialist party, just behind the Burgtheater. To her I submitted the documents issued to me by the American military authorities in Salzburg, which indicated that as someone who had been born inside the borders of the former Austro-Hungarian Empire, I could be treated as an Austrian citizen, enjoying the privileges of the victims of Nazism and so on. She, this Frau Kubichek, was an extraordinary woman, fully dedicated to her mission, kind and particularly attentive to me when she realized that I had survived the Flossenbürg camp, from whence a comrade of hers hadn't returned. By a comrade I mean a member of the social commission at the destroyed and now recently revived Austrian socialist party, an act of political stubbornness that should have covered with indelible shame the Jewish social democracy in Kolodetz, if in the meantime it hadn't gone through events whose tragedy extends far beyond that memorable day at David Leibovitch's café.

This is how I happened to be accommodated in a small apartment in an old smoked-out building on Margaretenstrasse, which I have never left, except for the time when I had to take a stroll to the North Pole.

On the next day I dropped in again at Frau Kubichek's, in order to thank her for her generous compassion toward the former concentration camp inmates, and she treated me to carrot tea and Vienna croissants with nut filling—rare at that time. Real Krasnodarsk or Indian tea one could buy on the black market from Russian and English soldiers, but the socialist frau was a convinced and furious opponent of the black market—a quite dogmatic position that, to tell you honestly, I didn't fully share. And so, over a cup of carrot tea, I learned that her husband, Franz Kubichek, was a prisoner in Russia. She was ardently anticipating his return one day, but the fact of imprisonment in no way shook her belief in the just cause of the anti-Hitler coalition and the fully deserved trouble that had reached infantryman Kubichek.

"I am full of admiration for the heroism of the Soviet people," she said. "To tell the truth, in the thirties, before the Anschluss, my husband and I were convinced opponents of the cruel repressions of Stalin, but now I, as well as all of Europe, have quite changed our opinion."

"Is that so?" I said absentmindedly.

I, of course, shared her admiration. In this great battle my children had fallen too, hadn't they? But I didn't feel like arguing about the enflamed enthusiasm of Europe, because even from my pitiful observation point in Mode Parisienne at Kolodetz, three steps below street level, I could clearly see that same Europe, which could swing so easily from blind condemnation or indifference to blind adoration, and back again, in the same order. And about Stalin, who was wrongly judged by the family Kubichek before the Anschluss, I chose to keep silent and to take another croissant.

SEVEN

Sadness, like a morning mist, slowly dissolves in the cares of the day and the pain grows duller because life makes its own demands—like a leaf of grass that pokes through the asphalt and strives toward the sun and hope. In the same way, postwar Vienna quickly overcame its shock and its severest injuries and gradually started to regain its customary fresh mood. After all, bread had to be baked, children had to go to school, the rotten transport and medical institutions had to be restored—in other words, life had to be lived.

I've hinted to you about the black market, so firmly condemned by the socially conscious Frau Kubichek, but don't be too quick to make a superficial judgment about this postwar phenomenon. I'm not looking for paradoxes, honestly, but it was exactly these—the black market and speculation—that were the first to overcome, with their vitality and flexibility, the front lines, the borders, and the hatred; they were the first to melt the ice of frozen Europe. "Lucky Strike" and jellied ham in tins were the first American missionaries of good will, the time of "Yankee, Go Home" was still far away, because these Yankees were dragging in ham and bananas, condoms and medicines.

Human masses were moving and settling, like tectonic layers that are reaching equilibrium: displaced Polish Jews were buying destroyed houses and land for a song in the American section of Berlin, Bulgarian contraband cigarettes were being transformed into French contraband wine, green military English blankets were traveling a complicated road until they were changed into real estate not far from Vienna at Baden, and looted gold was turning into fake passports for Nazi military criminals, wanted under tree and stone both in Germany and Austria, but already drinking their gin-and-tonics with a lemon slice under the palms of Latin America.

I was forced to get involved in such affairs, smaller in the beginning, concerning coffee, chocolate, or the new American miracle, penicillin, but gradually the stakes of the game started to involve me, and one or two more significant and, to my surprise, successful coups laid the foundation for the dream of a small garment-manufacturing business. I was aware that the time of tailoring workshops such as Mode Parisienne was irreversibly over, and I plunged head over heels into making a new living in my fifth motherland, which was closing the dance line of motherlands and ideals. At least this is what I was thinking at that time, without suspecting that I would get caught up in matters pertaining to various pretenses and claims for restitution of old national property, but don't let me run too much ahead of events!

Sometimes I would stop by the City Commission for Relocated Persons in order to help Frau Kubichek as a volunteer translator from Polish, Ukrainian, Russian, and Yiddish to the crowds of immigrants who were flooding the Promised Land of Austria, where that Danube, which was still flowing with the delusion that it was blue, was cast as the modest understudy for the Holy Jordan.

On the banks of this new Jordan, beyond the desert that the war had left behind itself, you could find Mexikoplatz—the core, the pulsing heart, and the indefatigable quintessence of speculation and black marketing. Here from morning till evening, and from late night till early sunrise, people in all languages and dialects were buying, selling, and exchanging everything possible—from family relics and Orthodox icons to beat-up "Austrofiat" military trucks, from Swiss condensed milk to original Russian vodka. And don't think I'm talking about a bazaar where the offered commodities were displayed! None of these could be seen, people would stroll around or sit all day by their long-finished coffee and seemed to have no other care than to wait for the rain. Especially immaterial was foreign currency, exchanged in complete conspiracy, with the exchange rate here always more favorable than the official one, and if someone happened to dump phony English pounds on someone else, he could have found out without delay that the dollars received in return had not been printed in Turkey either. They even tell a story about two Romanian Jews who put on the clothes of a dead man who had been either half a meter shorter or fifty kilograms fatter, but, skillful in small currency operations in the dark, they used to pass each other in the morning and one of them would ask with his mouth half-open for information from the other:

"How much?"

"Five," the other would whisper.

Then the two of them would go to either end of the square and when coming back, hands seemingly stuck carelessly in the pockets of their shabby trousers, they would again pass each other like two ships in the ocean, and the first would discreetly inquire:

"What five?"

"And what what?"

In connection with this deadly passion that had taken over Mexikoplatz—the passion to buy, sell, and mostly exchange everything possible for anything else, someone had named this remarkable operation in economic rejuvenation "Little Odessa." This was certainly fair, because here was present that commercial aggregation of ethnicities and languages, with an apparent European presence, characteristic of Odessa before the Nazi invasion. They even tell the following story about a train that made a long stop in the middle of the night at some station. A sleepy passenger put down the window of the compartment, leaned outside, and asked the passing railway worker:

"Excuse me, what station is this?"

"Odessa," said the other one.

"And why are we staying so long?"

"They're changing the locomotive."

"With what they are changing it?"

The railway worker looked at him in surprise. "What do you mean with what—with another locomotive!"

"Then it's not Odessa!" said the passenger and put up the window.

With the above I hope I've explained to you clearly enough what Mexikoplatz was all about—arena of my first, initially shy and awkward attempts to get involved in the Marxist cycle of "money-commodity-money," though quite often this took the form of "commodity"-pause—and on the next day, "Where did that Croat disappear to?" which meant that the final "money" had evaporated.

Of course, Frau Kubichek had no idea about this activity of mine and was thinking that I was making some money as a cantor in the synagogue, destroyed during Kristallnacht and now rising from its ashes—a stupid lie of mine that I now admit with repentance. But otherwise, you understand, I would have sunk with embarrassment about the origin of my money, drinking tea not from carrots but from real tea and with walnut croissants, which I would bring now in my capacity as an independent economic unit. The tea was clearly from Mexikoplatz, and the croissants from under the counter of a small bakery in front of St. Stephen's Cathedral, which the Viennese affectionately call "Steffel," with the bell tower stuck up into the sky. My breath was always stopped with adoration in front of this mystic Gothic prayer of stone, although poor Saint Stephen looked like a one-legged war invalid, with its left tower swept away by a bomb.

Late one afternoon, duly equipped by the aforementioned bakery with the traditional croissants, I took up my battle post with Frau Kubichek, in order to help her on the difficult road through the language immigration jungle. From the moment I entered, I caught the strange look of my frau and the brief, troubled glance that she cast at a Soviet captain, sitting at the side on a worn-out couch and leafing through some magazine. The captain lifted his eyes, and Frau Kubichek chokingly said, "Here he is, Mr. Officer, that's him."

I was anxiously reminded of that little Italian with the wire-rimmed glasses who, pointing his Zebaoth's finger, had pronounced, "It's him!"

The captain stood up and in habitual Russian soldier's habit pulled his tunic below his belt. "Citizen Blumenfeld, Isaac Yacobovitch?"

"The same," I said, throwing a puzzled look at the pale Frau Kubichek.

The captain switched to Russian. "Follow me."

"Where? . . . Why?" I asked in Russian too.

"For a check at the Soviet military command. Please, in front of me, Citizen Blumenfeld."

I knew the difference between the cold "citizen" and "comrade" and it was this exactly, this difference, that froze the blood in my veins.

Outside a Soviet military vehicle was waiting to take citizen Blumenfeld, Isaac Yacobovitch, who at that moment hardly suspected that the Soviet command would only be the first stop in an unrepeatable and exciting trip to the White Silence of the North.

Farewell, Vienna, farewell Mexikoplatz, farewell Frau Kubichek and croissants with walnut filling! Farewell to you too, my poor invalid St. Stephen!

EIGHT

The whole business became rather complicated when the Soviet military investigator gave me an icy look, moved his eyes to the open folder with typed sheets of paper, sighed, carelessly leafed through the contents of the folder, and fixed his eyes on me again. I was standing in front of him and couldn't understand at all whether I was under arrest or most politely requested to give some kind of information. Finally the investigator said, "You have betrayed your Soviet motherland! Why?"

"What are you talking about, Comrade investigator!" I said with sincere indignation.

"Citizen investigator! I am no comrade of yours," he corrected me.

"In what sense have I betrayed it . . . Citizen investigator?"

"Why in the questionnaire did you deceive the American authorities and claim that you were born in Austria-Hungary?"

"Because I was born in Austria-Hungary."

"The district of Lvov is in the Soviet Union!"

"But when I was born it was Austria-Hungary."

"Maybe you'll say it's Canada? Or the Azore Islands?"

"I'm not claiming that . . ."

"Your last residence was Kolodetz, Union of Soviet Socialist Republics!"

"My last residence was the concentration camp Flossenbürg in Oberpfalz!" I insisted.

The investigator seemed highly satisfied with this confession of mine, because he leaned back in his chair and with a triumphant voice said, "Well, well, we come to the main subject. And now tell us about your treachery in the camp called Special Site A-17."

"What do you mean?"

"Do you know someone named Stakhovich?"

"Of course. He was arrested with another two of our men, Soviets."

"Oh, is that right! Now the Soviets become 'ours.' Did you know they were shot dead?"

"I didn't know, but I suspected."

"You betrayed them!"

"I?!"

"You!!!"

"I?!!!"

"Yes, you!!! Are these your initials?" He extended an order for arrest, signed by the Radish with the three letters I.J.B.

"This is the signature of the commandant Immanuel-Johannes Brückner."

"And not Isaac Jacob Blumenfeld?"

"My God, how could I sign a document from a Nazi concentration camp? I'm a Jew!"

"Treachery has no nationality!"

He was right, the citizen investigator, treachery, as well as idiocy, has no nationality, it's the most international thing, deserving its own Fourth or even Fifth International!

And further on what's the use of telling you and boring you with details about the investigator's sensational discovery, with which he intended to lay me flat and defeat my resistance once and for all, namely, that in the camps I was enrolled under the false name of Heinrich Bjegalski? For him, I mean the investigator and not the doorman of the Lvov ophthalmology clinic, this circumstance, adding to the weight of my guilt, was indisputable proof that I was concealing my Soviet origin. Forget the exact and indisputable information that I had lived in a concentration camp and played chess with the Radish. Was there any point in explaining that in this whole business Johann Wolfgang Goethe and Eliezer Pincus, my dear teacher of German and of all other aspects of knowledge, may his soul rest in peace, were also directly involved? Really, was there any point?

I, my dear brother, am but a speck of dust in the glory of the Creation or, say, an insignificant ant in the multibillion human anthill, and history will hardly pay attention and go back to my case, which is nothing more than a drop in the vast ocean of events. But she, the ant, has her own worldly vanity and would like to leave a good account of herself, which is why I'm sharing with you the protocol of the inquest, personally signed by me in the presence of the investigator. A copy of this protocol I managed to receive quite some time later from a filing officer at the court in Kiev, in exchange for two packets of American chewing gum and a pair of nylon stockings—in those years the tender dream of every female Soviet worker. Excuse me if you occasionally get a whiff of that youthful habit of mine of playing the fool, but insofar as the citizen investigator actually did regard me as a fool who could contribute to his rapid career advancement, why shouldn't I provide some pleasure to the good man?

PROTOCOL

I, the undersigned Isaac Jacob Blumenfeld, born on January 13, 1900, in Kolodetz by Drogobych, the Lemberg *voevodstvo*, or Lvov, a Jew, hereby declare that I have never and under any circumstances betrayed my Soviet motherland, or any of my other motherlands, because, excuse me, they are five in number. I was born, as I mentioned above, in the wonderful town of Kolodetz by Drogobych, and grew up as a faithful subject of the Austro-Hungarian Empire. The aforementioned state, which, for your information, no longer exists, I consider to be my first motherland and I think this is fair.

Later on, and in circumstances that I shall describe in court, when the time comes, without leaving my hometown of Kolodetz, Poland became my motherland.

I am grateful to this motherland of mine, because during the time of my Polish citizenship I married Sarah, about whom I will also give account, and she on her side bore three children of mine—two boys and a girl. I served Poland faithfully till the day my motherland was changed again. This happened on September 17, 1939, quite abruptly, when without leaving my hometown Kolodetz, the great Soviet Union became my motherland, which I served faithfully, regularly paying my trade union membership fees, participating in the First of May and the November Seventh demonstrations, and also congratulating my female co-workers on Women's Day, March 8th. But then certain events transpired in which, I most responsibly declare, I had neither personal participation nor committed a fault of any kind, and the German Reich became my motherland, which, as a Jew from a proven impure race, I must admit did not warm my heart. This for the first time forced some changes in my permanent residence, as well as in those documents concerning my nationality, and after illegally residing—I honestly admit—in Lvov under the name of Heinrich Bjegalski, my address was initially Special Site A-17 in the Oranienburg forest, then the Regional Command in the above-mentioned town of Oranienburg, Berlin district, and finally I resided in the concentration camp of Flossenbürg (Oberpfalz), under the number of U-20-05765, where, despite some material and other inconveniences, of which I do not complain, I awaited the end of the war.

At the time of this interrogation I live in Vienna, on Margaretenstrasse 15. I live alone, because Sarah and the children never came back from the mineral baths, to which I personally sent them in June 1941. I am also obliged to explain that I have a permit for permanent residence in the territory of the Republic of Austria, as well as a receipt for paid taxes and fees in compliance with the laws of the country, but I would be grateful to God if I would be given the opportunity to visit one more time my hometown of Kolodetz by Drogobych, Lvov region, USSR.

I declare with the utmost responsibility in front of the respected citizen investigator at the Soviet Military Command of the city of Vienna, that the initials of my name Isaac Jacob Blumenfeld (I.J.B.) and the initials of the commandant of Special Site A-17 Immanuel-Johannes Brückner (I.J.B.) coincide simply by chance, and that therefore I am not, please excuse me, a military criminal.

Personally written and signed by:
ISAAC J. BLUMENFELD
City of Vienna, 12 September 1945

And so, my brother, the dark clouds at my horizon became thicker, because besides the evidence of high treason, an additional devastating claim was presented to the national court that I was a military criminal, who with my personal signature had sent three people to their deaths. Except for the rejected request of my court-appointed lawyer for a handwriting analysis, which was said to be a useless waste of time, you understand the contradiction of the case: I was either a Jew or a Nazi military criminal! But major Gribov, the military prosecutor, was a very experienced person—the lessons of the great Soviet state prosecutor Andrei Yanuarievich Vishinski were apparent, and he managed to reconcile the irreconcilable.

I did not pronounce myself guilty, which was probably my most fatal mistake, because sincere repentance would have warmed the hearts of the court threesome, who, without faltering, and seized by revolutionary fervor, stuck me with ten years of rehabilitation labor camp.

And so, Shnat Shmita, once more from the top!

And you, Lord God Yahweh, master of Jewish destinies, who stretches Your hand out in protection above Your chosen people, would You please whisper to me, where are Your windows?

NINE

And now, brother, unfold the map of Eurasia and find Ural—the border between the two continents. Then take a stroll east and cross the river Ob, the first of the three great Siberian rivers. Continue to the northeast and try to cross also the second great river—the powerful Yenisey, and then further to the east the Lena too. Follow my road still further on, to the northeast, beyond the gold-bearing river Indigirka, until you stop at the rugged banks of the turbulent Kolyma. Take its rapids toward the Arctic Ocean until you reach Nizhni Kolymsk, in the foothills of the wild Kolymski mountain ridge, which, you might say, is where Soviet geography comes to a stop. Beyond the mountain ridge are only Ust-Chaun and Chukchi at the Bering Straits, and don't go any further or you'll find yourself penetrating the territory of the United States of America. The 70th parallel passes through here and if out of curiosity you follow it clockwise, you'll make in the opposite direction a mighty polar roundtrip of the planet, passing through the Barents Sea first and then crossing Novaya Zemlya in the Kara Sea. Then you'll touch the North Cape—the northernmost point in Scandinavia—cut through the middle of icy Greenland and when you get into the legendary route of Amundsen and pass by the Yukon fort, which is still dreaming the golden dreams of Jack London, through the Chukchi Sea, you'll come back home to where, just opposite the Bear Islands, the constellation of labor camps shines bright. When I say "constellation," I mean the red five-pointed stars above their strictly guarded entrances, with watchtowers made out of untreated pine-tree trunks. And that unsightly wretch perched on rocks fiercely blown by the icy wind, with eyes staring at the white vastness of the North, that's me, ZEK-003-476, or to say it more simply—prisoner Blumenfeld, Isaac Jacobovitch, a traitor to the Soviet motherland and simultaneously a Nazi war criminal.

Forgive me for repeating myself if I tell you that I won't undertake to describe or judge all this camp archipelago, with its unimaginable colorfulness and diversity, rendered in so much detail by the Russian fellow Solzhenitzyn, and by others, better authors than I, and I cannot swear that what I personally saw and experienced there is the same that someone else saw and experienced there, in the other camp, at a distance of fifty, five hundred, or five thousand Russian versts. Because the camps were quite different in regime, as well as composition and designation, and sometimes the workers, for example, in the tungsten and gold mines of the Northern-Anuyski mountain ridge were freer and better fed than the aging invalids—civil war veterans—from some rotten communal housing unit on the outskirts of Kostroma. From other places we would get visitors, according to mysterious schemes I never understood for dislocation and regrouping, inmates with loosening teeth and gums bleeding from scurvy, let alone those with hair falling out in clumps and swollen glands who were coming from the uranium mines, in which only a minority survived. And I'll immediately point out to you the idlers, who, as I've already mentioned, had, according to the Geneva Convention, a special status as bearers of the Iron Cross of Oak Leaves, the camp aristocracy, so to speak, whom I served for awhile when they were working in the "mailboxes"—secret cities in the taiga for super-secret research, technology, and production that had neither a geographic indication on the map nor an address, just a postal code.

You'd be mistaken if you thought that all of us were punished for political activities: in this camp cocktail were flowing powerful streams of Siberian and Caucasian bandits, Georgian speculators and Abkhasian contrabandists, professional pimps and gamblers or simply incorrigible Moscow streetcar pickpockets, declassé types from the swamp of society, and next to them, prostitutes and mamashas from secret brothels and gambling houses. And with them, in the same cocktail, poets and philosophers, biologists and world experts on the reactionary, bourgeois pseudo-sciences genetics and cybernetics, theater directors and movie stars. And you'd be wrong again if you looked for a common trait and perceived all of them, say, as just anti-Soviet elements: there, in the camps, sometimes former participants in the civil war would grab each other by the throat in endless and irreconcilable fights and arguments, one on the White side, the other on the Red, who for the past couple of decades had been free and then, on some convenient occasion, had again been hauled in. You could have become a witness to raging theoretical disputes between Trotskyists and Stalinists, sleeping together in the same bunk, shoulder to shoulder, engineers from the great construction sites of the first five-year plans and sincere saboteurs from the same construction sites, inflexible anti-Communists and cadre Bolsheviks, collaborationists who had served the Nazis but stopped short of being willing to take a bullet, and participants in the resistance movement in the occupied territories or, say, in the Spanish Civil War, who found themselves here for reasons about which they hadn't the slightest idea.

"Don't try to comprehend the scheme, the hidden logic in all this mess," said Mark Semyonovich Lebedev, my new friend and bunkmate, sitting on the rocky ledge polished by ice and winds—a young man whose musical comedies I had seen in Kolodetz, his hair now turned completely silver. "There aren't any schemes, if the mess in itself is not a scheme, a genetically laid foundation of the regime. Not only in the camps but just in general. Unlike the German camps, in ours there are no rules of the game, and there aren't any outside either, in society. The Nazis announced their ideological menu ahead of time and followed it strictly till the last second: which nations were to be subject to the Final Solution, which ones would be the manure of the Aryan race, and which ones faithful allies. Clear and precise criteria, announced in advance. True, inhumane and idiotic, unspiritual, barbarian—but criteria nonetheless. And we announced the building of a society of brotherhood, humanism, and justice and started singing that there was no other country where a man could breathe more easily. Then according to the Marxist theory of freedom as a conscious necessity, we realized the necessity of camps, all-around informing, and terror. I'm telling you, there are no rules of the game. But this can also be a rule, I even think—a rule for saving the nation. Do you get it?"

"No," I admitted sincerely.

"Institutional chaos, the anarchic movement of particles and the natural instincts for survival take up in lifesaving fashion the energy of the super-centralized postulates and democratize them, if you know what I mean. In fact, this Soviet element of spontaneous democratization in the final account destroyed the systematic Germans who have known since they were children that on the chessboard there are two black and two white horses playing. Against all the rules we put in a third horse and this is how we kicked their asses. Am I clear now?"

"You're clear. Go on."

"What did *Parteigenosse* Hitler expect when he launched a blitz war against us? That the oppressed Soviet people would rise up against their oppressor? That the panicky military specialists, technologists, and engineers liberated from the camps would seek the first opportunity to go over to the side of the Germans? Hell, no! That the population from the territories which the Hitlerites were declaring free from Bolshevism would greet them with bread and salt? Again, hell no! Listen to me, I was there and can testify: the fall of Moscow was inevitable, a mathematical axiom, check and mate in three moves. But the dancing party didn't take place! Why? General Winter? Bullshit for suckers! After that came General Spring, and General Summer, didn't they? No, we just put in front of those fieldmarshals a third horse, a fifth ace, and played poker according to the rules of football. Our strength lay in the caprice of chaos, the amateurism of spontaneously moving particles, the game without rules. In other words—in surprise, whose results, by the way, very often surprise even us. For example, to surprise the enemy, who expects you to trump him with the card of internationalism, but you pull out of your sleeve your most traditional, monarchic, Orthodox, and Great Russian nationalism, greasy with use. And to everyone's astonishment it functions perfectly, despite the party schools and the strict study of the Short Course in the History of the Bolshevik Party."

"So, in your opinion," I said, "everything is chaos and chance. But I have a rabbi who believes in the mystery of the road and in its final meaning. He believes that the goal is predestined."

Mark Semyonovich shrugged his shoulders. "Rabbis are by presumption religious believers. I'm not."

"And you don't believe in the final victory of a new society of Reason and Justice?"

"What does the Soviet Union have to do with all that? Have you seen the Moscow metro?"

"I've never been to Moscow," I said.

"What a pity. It's the most beautiful metro in the world. The deepest escalators take you up and down mechanical stairways. We are rushing up, as they say, toward the shining peaks of communism. But we're on the wrong escalator, which requires us to run and run, swimming in sweat, up the escalator that leads down. And so we move in place, singing rousing songs until we're out of breath. But one day we'll be dead tired of the senselessness of this movement, we'll stop running, and the escalator will take us down to the place where we started out. Mark my words: the Soviet Union will collapse inevitably. It has to. But this will also happen in the same abrupt, illogical, and unsystematic way, in order to generate new chaos, full of new joyful surprises."

A strange man was this Mark Semyonovich and strange were the reasons that had brought him to the camp. If I had to sum it up in one word, it would be "love." He was maybe the only one of this colorful tribe who had turned up here accused of love—love toward the daughter of a high-ranking (almost as high as the Kremlin clock) Bolshevik and state functionary, who through his people had more than once warned the movie director to take his dirty hands off this enchantress, promised to the son of a still higher ranking—say, almost at the height of the red ruby star—*tovarishch*, after whose name they had already christened one average Soviet town, one island, one canal, two dams, one tractor factory and some schools and kindergartens. And when this enamored movie fool didn't get the hint and continued to meet in secret with his goddess (so he naively regarded her), the father and future father-in-law got upset and, heaping on citizen Lebedev all the rage, vengeance, and moral decay of power, sent him for nothing, literally nothing, here to the 70th parallel.

In this connection I remembered a camp joke—because it may seem strange to you—but the most beautiful jokes and the most beautiful songs were born in the camps or their ideological vicinity, which at least in this respect, and not only in this, made them different from the Nazi ones.

A camp boss is interrogating three newly arrived prisoners: "How long is your sentence?"

"Ten years."

"Why?"

"Because I said that Stalin is leading the country to its death."

"And you?"

"I also have ten. I declared that the Short Course in the History of the Bolshevik Party is a complete scam."

"And you?"

"Also ten."

"For what?"

"For nothing."

"Don't lie!" said the boss, getting angry. "For nothing we give five years!"

Such jokes don't reflect the whole truth, or at least the truth exactly as it was in life—because the movie director Mark Semyonovich Lebedev, called by fellow inmates simply Semyonich, hadn't been sentenced to ten years, or even five—he was just staying there without a sentence, with limitations in space but no limitations in time, and such victims of lawlessness, who were not small in number, were constantly bumping up against the Great White Silence of the GULAG.* The only hope of Semyonich was some kind of miracle, for example, that the newspapers—and here, even with delays, an occasional issue of *Pravda* arrived for the local bosses—would announce, seemingly casually, that the tractor factory, named after the aforementioned father-in-law from the Kremlin, had been renamed after this and that congress of the party or this and that anniversary of the October revolution. Whoever was able to decipher the codes of such announcements would understand that the position of the aforementioned boss had started to wobble, and, following the laws of chaos, Mark Semyonovich, like a rabbit out of a hat, could jump out in the center of Moscow. Of course, he had no illusions that the enchantress would throw herself on his neck, because by now she had a three-year-old son and was pregnant with a second child—a future builder of shining communism, kingdom of Equality and Justice. And by that beautiful time the child would be in the hands of the nanny, the three servants, and the cook in the dacha just outside of Moscow with eighteen rooms, beautifully located by the dam, still carrying the name of the father-in-law, who was renowned and beloved in

---

* GULAG—*Glavnoe Upravlenie Lagerei*, which means Camp Management Headquarters, but I hope you realize this is an understatement and I mean the whole camp system of course. [Mr. Blumenfeld's note]

the area with his merry homespun character and his record catches of pike and rudd. I'm sorry about the long sentence, but the road to communism isn't short either!

TEN

I was arrested, as you know, in Vienna at the beginning of September '45, but don't get the idea that the Soviet court authorities were dying to see me. They had quite a lot of other, considerably more pressing work with former policemen, activists, and all kinds of assistants to the Nazi occupation authorities, and my case was dispatched helter-skelter in April the next year. And so it was off to Kolyma that I was transported at the end of May with a group of prisoners who were at first like slender creeks that merged into streams at different regional command posts and railway junctions, until they gradually grew in size to a great Siberian river. They were reinforcements for the copper and the lead–zinc mines, for processing lumber liberated from the camps and cutting stone—reinforcements for the seriously thinning camp ranks, on the one hand because of the massive release of prisoners who were to be included in the alarmingly dwindling army units at the fronts, and on the other because of the devastating consequences of the Great Hunger that had affected in different degrees the whole country, but which had inflicted particularly serious human losses in the Kolyma Constellation. It was then, they say, that the guards' shaggy Siberian shepherds began mysteriously disappearing, and in the deep crevices of rocks—the work of ice and the untamable element of the sea—even during my time one could see bones picked clean and traces of fire. Here the prisoners used to kill seal pups in cold blood, to which the guards as a rule closed their eyes, especially since the locals were also doing their part in the collective diminishment of the population of Greenland seals.

And so, I happened to arrive at the 70th parallel in the second half of May and for the first time tasted the charm of white nights, when the sun does not go down and only the hanging piece of iron that painfully reminded me of Special Site A-17 and the Radish divided conventional night from day, the time for labor and the time for rest.

After it became at last clear that a former typhoid patient could no longer make his contribution to the mines, Adonai again—for the nth time!—placed a sheltering right hand above my head, on account of which I apologize to Him for the hot threats, made by me from time to time, to break His window panes, and I was included in the group of translators who were facilitating contact between the guards and the low-ranking German POW's, who were occupied mainly with logging.

Here's the place to inform you that as a result of in-depth historical research, it has been indisputably established that since the time of Nebuchadnezzar and Amenhotep II until today, all through these years of war, slavery, and revolution, the Jews have made pronounced attempts to exchange healthy physical labor for translation or editing activity. The multi-ton basalt newsstands with the latest headlines, inscribed by Jewish slaves with cuneiform Babylonian signs or Egyptian hieroglyphs, testify to the present day about this inclination of the Jew toward the more intellectual variants of slave labor. To say nothing of the Jewish translators without whom the emperor Vespasian could have hardly made his way with the large numbers of prisoners from the Judean war, who couldn't curse in any language other than Aramaic, since Russian was still out of the market. But this is a different issue, let's not digress.

This is how I got to know Mark Lebedev, who spoke German badly, but had enough to get out of the copper mines. And maybe above him, the mischievous fool, there was also laid an invisible protective hand, I don't know.

So, Semyonich said, resting his arm on my shoulder, with eyes fixed on the melting midnight silver of the ocean: "Watch and fill your soul with light. Because then the time of the Black Sun will come, when you will know if it is day or night again only by the clanging of the iron. Here we call it 'St. Peter's Bell.' Because when you hear the iron for the last time, you're already there with the good sergeant Peter, guardian of the celestial concentration camp, no matter what it's called—heaven or hell. So, this is how it is, old boy, at the 70th parallel: an endless white night when the sun doesn't go down, and an endless black day when the sun doesn't rise. If you like, you can exchange them and in biblical style call the light day and the night darkness, but in that case it will also be conditional and change nothing, because if you had a watch you would've learned by now that it's three after midnight, for example. And your nose is at the moment being burnt by the sun and will soon look like a peeled snakeskin, if you don't put seal fat on it that I'll give you."

"And how do you know what time it is?" said I naively.

He patted me on the shoulder. "Cheer up, pal. When you spend some white nights here, you'll learn to tell time by the unsetting sun. It's harder during the black days, but you'll get good at that too—when there are no clouds, the stars will become a

Swiss Omega for you with twenty rubies, because the sky also rotates around us. Galileo has the opposite opinion, but let him mind his own business, I have my personal observations! . . . I'm telling you this to give you courage, because according to your sentence you have altogether ten days and ten nights to serve. Where else in the world do they give shorter and more merciful sentences?"

A pair of patrolmen passed by us and the senior sergeant whistled deafeningly: "Come on, hurry up and get inside, the sun will be rising soon!"

Lit by the rays of the bright midnight sun, we obeyed the order and went in to sleep a little in one of the dozens of monotonous brick buildings of the camp town, above which dominated the three-story headquarters with its offices, infirmary, radio station, and everything else needed by your average Soviet camp set up at the 70th parallel south of the Pole.

Don't be surprised by such midnight walks, because the wire fences of the camp were far from here and with Siberian generosity delimited a rather large space, within whose boundaries there was relative freedom of movement. Of course, it wasn't like this everywhere—there were camps with a considerably stricter regime, close to hard labor, according to the gravity of the actual or imaginary crimes, but I've already told you that everyone sees his little bit of truth through the keyhole of his own experience. That's why the memories and judgments of the Soviet camps are so diverse and even contradictory, which is natural for a country in which even more all-embracing than the Stalin constitution was the Law of the Spontaneous Movement of Particles, creating a saving chaos, and formulated in the middle of the twentieth century by the movie director Mark Semyonovich Lebedev.

This was an endless, blinding silvery night, in which there were no events or signs of any kind to separate one segment of camp life from another, with the exception of the clang of the "morning" iron and the repeated, monotonous, and lengthy crossing over to the Germans, who lived at the far end of the camp in four dwellings, segregated from us, with three hundred people in each.

When the water of the melted snow that had turned the taiga into a boundless swamp withdrew to the layers of permafrost and made room for the passionate northern spring, we, along with five hundred Germans, were transferred to a temporary summer bivouac—a vast meadow with thirty or so wooden barracks and a field kitchen, the so-called *Kommandirovka*, or "Business Trip." This considerably shortened the road to the wood-cutting area in the taiga, where the diesel tractors, trucks, and all kinds of machines rattled and smoked night and day—if the concept of "night and day" is applicable, month after month, to one single, long, glowing white night.

The work wasn't heavy at all, far from it—what was unbearable were the clouds of mosquitoes, huge as flying elephants. In order for you to understand this page of the apocalypse, I'll tell you that we became witnesses to the panicked flight of a flock of many thousands of northern deer from the thick clouds of mosquitoes chasing them, called here "The Abomination." A flight north and further north—to the cold. They, the pathetic deer, hadn't eaten for days despite the abundance of fresh vegetation nor could they take a rest, but just ran and ran in their drive to dip into the iciest river waters and plunge into the thickest ooze of the swamps. And if some poor sick female, just skin and bones from this constant running, lagged behind, she was immediately surrounded, completely covered, suffocated by the thick buzzing of the mosquitoes. Then literally in front of our eyes, the poor animal would bend its front legs, as if falling on its knees for mercy, but there was no mercy and soon, completely drained of its blood, the animal breathed its last on the damp moss. The huge carnivorous Siberian ants finished off the rest.

Our situation was relatively lighter, because the bluish diesel smoke, mixed with the smoke issuing from the fires all around and hovering over the camp, created considerable discomfort not just for us, but, thank God, also for the mosquitoes.

Like the camp, some kind of rhythm to our life here was also provided by the "Bells of St. Peter" and the brief lunch break, with the invariable oatmeal, and, rarely, some bone, whose meat had gone to the pot for the guards.

On paper, they were considered free people, these uniformed guards, and this was also one of the great Siberian delusions, the northern *fata morgana.* Because a guard in any kind of prison, say in Moscow or Rio de Janeiro, when off duty is free to walk around town, gape at the shop windows, and even occasionally buy an ice cream. Here, at the 70th parallel, the concepts of "on this side" and "beyond" the wire fence were as conditional and illusory as the concepts of "night" and "day." Because what was there beyond—in the free world, outside the "zone"—if not thousands of kilometers of tundra, wild rocky mountain ridges, endless swamps, taiga, and again mountain ridges, and again swamps? And what differentiated the camp inmate from the guard apart from the right of the latter to run over to the nearby completely alcohol-soaked settlement of Yakuti, Chukchi, Nenzi, or other similar revolutionary Eskimos, to get completely smashed on thick *samogon*—a secretly produced vodka from all kinds of junk, rotten potatoes, and, people would say, editorials from *Pravda* to "raise the degree"? And if, in the low log cabins, amid the stinking smoke of *makhorka*—something like wild tobacco—there happened to be some equally soused female guard from the neighboring women's camp, one could expect in the foreseeable future the appearance in the world of a new Soviet citizen. He would grow and mature politically like many similar beings around his alcoholic parents, in the free swampy territory between the two camps, covered in the summer with red berries and impassable in the winter, when even the short-legged northern deer, adapted to everything and taken in by the deer raisers to spend the winter in fenced enclosures, snuggle together to warm themselves with their breath.

But gradually the sparkling silver magnificence of the white polar night started to fade; the shadows, quite short in summer, began to lengthen. As soon as the snow began falling, we were brought back to the main camp, and, imperceptibly, the Black Sun returned, when for a long time thick darkness would embrace the Siberian North.

It was December 24, that night when the Catholic and Protestant world prepares to celebrate Christmas. Insofar as Orthodox Russia celebrates this event the night of January 7th, one could not rely on mercy from the bosses; moreover, the Russian Christmas was not itself an official holiday. Nevertheless, to everyone's joy, and as a sign of God's hand, people received the news that the thermometer at the entrance to headquarters had dropped to 43 degrees centigrade below zero.

This meant that on the next day there would be no work and that in fact the holiday with which the German, Baltic, and western Ukrainian prisoners were concerned had been declared by nature itself, since, according to regulations, work could go on down to minus 40 but not a single degree lower. "That's how it is with us here," explained Semyonich, who continued to introduce me in a patronizing manner to the secrets of camp life. "Not only here, but all over the Soviet realm life goes on normally in the range between minus 40 and plus 40 degrees."

"What's this plus 40? The Karakoum Desert?"

Semyonich looked at me in surprise. "What desert are you dreaming about? I mean the Soviet standard for the degrees of vodka!"

How could I have known that this would be our last conversation! But the iron struck, and for Semyonich this was indeed the bell of St. Peter. The doctor, a mild and sad Armenian, Robert Boyadjian, also a prisoner, diagnosed a massive heart attack. This was the end of a naive and amorous movie director, who tried to jump higher than the Kremlin wall!

"And what now?" asked the doctor in confusion.

"Leave it to us, you're a novice."

The body of Semyonich was laid in his own mattress, emptied of straw, and made out of burlap for sacks. Taken outside, at a temperature of minus 43 degrees, it became stiff fast and we, six prisoners, guarded by a little soldier, carried him away on our shoulders beyond the wire fence, to the camp graveyard. For hours on end the surrounding darkness was broken by the flames of the fire that was needed to soften up a little the earth turned hard as granite; for hours on end we silently warmed ourselves by lying on the snow sack with The Person Who Made Movies. Finally we managed to dig a shallow hole and laid in it the stiff body, covered it with earth and piled up stones to keep predators from digging it out. We doffed our caps and the icy wind like boiling water burned our ears.

"Farewell, Semyonich. May you be happier there!"

This was the whole of the funeral speech of Doctor Robert Boyadjian, pronounced with a strong foreign accent.

The little soldier bent to my ear: "Wasn't the deceased Mark Lebedev, the movie director?"

"Yes, it was him."

"I've seen his movies. Nice, joyful movies."

"Yes, nice and joyful."

The boy took down his military cap with the red star and crossed himself. For this they would expel people from the Komsomol, and in the army punish them severely.

As we came back to the camp, the flames of the pitch-pine torches were throwing light here and there on the stone-piled graves—some with crudely nailed crosses, some with the hammer and sickle, drawn with red paint, the same that marked the cut trunks. There arose and then disappeared, swallowed by the thick darkness, some Stars of David and even one Islamic crescent. "We will renew the world with the International. . . ."

Before going into the lit-up entrance of the camp, we extinguished our torches in the deep snow. The air, saturated with icy crystals, was forming around the electric bulbs a dense rainbow-colored glow, and in front of the German brick buildings there shone a Christmas tree with some candles—made by the locals out of whale blubber.

It was Christmas, 1946.

ELEVEN

Finally, I saw the aurora borealis! Dazed, I stared with eyes wide open at this miracle of nature: the spreading out through the sky, the interwoven and splitting ribbons that opened up to us like colorful peacock feathers, and then contracted and slithered low above the horizon like a multicolored snake, and I don't know if the quiet harmonic sounds of a tender harp were reality or the tremblings of the soul itself.

I was sitting on some smooth black rock, the glistening surfaces opaquely reflecting the glow, while beneath us the frozen ocean had become silent.

Did I say tremblings of the soul? Too poetic, thanks all the same. This was more of a cry, because loneliness was grabbing my throat, suffocating me with icy fingers: everyone was disappearing from my life, one after the other, and why was I, the fool, holding on tooth and nail to this shitty, senseless, unspiritual life, stuck in it like a parasite? Where was my good rabbi Shmuel now? He could probably decipher the meaning, the secret messages, the hidden high goal of Nature that created life, but forgot to explain to us how it's supposed to be used.

I was sitting on the rock and, without knowing it, started to cry. My tears were rolling down my cheeks for only a few millimeters and freezing in layers, one on top of the other. And then a miracle happened: in the glow, she herself all radiant, appeared Sarah, her wide open grayish green eyes, which reflected the entangled lights, fixed on me! She came up barefoot on the frozen ocean, bent over, kissed me on the forehead and whispered:

"My poor, my dear Itzik! Are you cold?"

"Yes," I said. "Very."

She undid her braid and covered me with her hair, and at that moment a blissful warmth poured over me. Sarah sat down by me, took my head in her lap, started rocking me and caressing me like a child to the rhythm of the celestial music, and a growing bliss, sweet and warm, began to flow through my veins. I was falling asleep happy in Sarah's warm embrace, but she suddenly shook me up roughly and spoke in a male voice:

"Come on, come on, wake up!"

Painfully I opened my eyes. Three people were leaning over me, fixing the round eye of a flashlight on my face, and Doctor Robert Boyadjian was rubbing my ears with snow.

Then I was lying on the old sagging couch in the doctor's cabinet and he said, "Were you ever lucky, comrade! You almost lost your ears and your nose. Do you know what the temperature is outside? Minus 52 degrees, a hell of a time for a walk!"

"And I was dreaming of warmth . . . ," I whispered guiltily.

"Of course, it saved you. The soldiers had come out to take a piss and one of them, while pissing on you, had the feeling that there was someone lying below. Sorry if that bothers you."

And the Armenian laughed; he didn't know that at this moment he was pissing on my loveliest dream.

And now, while I'm drinking my tea from the aluminum mug the doctor gave me, let me tell you a few words also about this quiet and almost unnoticeable man, with the constantly sad face of a clown—even when he smiles.

He was born, this Robert, in Paris, that's right, not in Kolodetz, but in Paris, can you imagine? His parents were well-to-do people, refugees from the massacres in Turkey. They had their own jewelry store or some other kind of store. But they couldn't get used to France and yearned to go back and die in their own Armenia, in Erevan. And while young Robert, in spite of the German occupation, was taking his medical degree at the Sorbonne, very far from the river Sena, on the Volga, the fearful battle of Stalingrad was raging. On a wave of general exhilaration with the heroism of the Soviet people, old Boyadjian sold everything and by secret means, with the help of his partners from the diamond business, managed to get through Sweden to Erevan with his family, in the foothills of Ararat—holy for the Armenians—which was standing white beyond, in Turkey. There, in Erevan, the yearned-for city of pink tufa, the old man donated all his money for the purchase of a tank that was going to be named "Ararat," and his son went to work for the Erevan city hospital. The tank Ararat, after heavy fighting, reached Alexanderplatz in Berlin, and the son Robert the Kolyma camp, opposite the Bear Islands, because of his immoderate talk about freedom and democracy.

So that's that, since for simple cases one doesn't need complicated explanations.

TWELVE

Mark Lebedev, our departed Semyonich, taught me not to look for meaning in the meaningless, or logic in the spontaneous movement of particles, so that's why I'll spare you my pitiful attempts to explain what remained an enigma for me too, namely, why, given the availability of so many camps dispersed all over our great country, were a thousand Germans and a not inconsiderable number of us, the others, picked up from Kolyma and sent south? "South" will hardly ring a bell for you, until I show you the dizzying route that lasted for almost a whole month and started with the rusty freighter, "North Star," filled to the brim with prisoners and guards. So, this star, I say, took us inland, by Cape Dixon, to the mouth of the Yenisey River, and from there by tugboat, dragging barges, also crammed with people, for twelve days against the stream until we reached Krasnoyarsk, where we were transferred to a train—from Barnaoul to Akmolinsk, Kazakh Soviet Socialist Republic. If there's anything unclear, call me.

Far from being despondent, the Germans were singing, because among them a rumor had spread that they'd be taken back to their motherland, while we were not singing, because we'd already learned that in the region of Karaganda, there were mighty bauxite mines. For your information, bauxite equals aluminum, which equals not only airplanes but also other, even starrier industries. And in order for you to finally understand where we happened to be, I'll give you the hint that a good deal later you would hear the geographic names Semipalatinsk and Baikonur—the first becoming after my time a nuclear base, and the second sometime even later laying the foundation for the Space Age.

And exactly here, in this Tower of Babel-like camp, amid the cries and the chaos, I literally bumped into—you've already guessed it—my good rabbi, my dear Shmuel Ben-David! And again we cried, and we embraced, and we couldn't believe, that we—two particles wandering in space—had met for the second time, that for a second time our camp paths had crossed, one time somewhere in Oberpfalz, in distant Germany, and now at some random point in endless Asia, the mother of geography!

We sat on the burnt steppe and couldn't get enough of looking at each other.

"Why are you here?" I asked.

"Because of my relationship with Esther Katz."

"They thought of it only now?"

He smiled sadly. "God's mills grind slowly. Let it go for now. Are you going to tell me about the North?"

"There's no point. In the North it's like the South. Like the West. Maybe like the East, I don't know—I haven't been in a Chinese camp yet."

The rabbi was silent for awhile, then lit up a Soviet Belomorkanal *papirosa*, with the cardboard tube resembling a cigarette holder, and a tobacco tip. "Did you learn to smoke?"

"No," I said.

"What did you learn?"

"Not to look for meaning in the meaningless."

"Then you've learned nothing, because everything has meaning. Everything leads somewhere, but it's not always given us to know."

"I don't even want to know. I put period to everything."

"From such a period the Big Bang started, the beginning of our planet. Humankind has always put a period after a road traveled, but it's never been the end."

"Shnat shmita?"

"Yes, everything from the beginning. But I'll let myself argue with my favorite Ecclesiastes: this time what will be has never been. And what has been, will not be. Everything new, otherwise what's the point?"

"That's exactly what I'm asking, Rabbi: Is there any meaning at all?"

"Of course. The meaning is in the road to the period. The next sentence others will write—the ones who'll come after us. I hope they follow our faith, but they have no right to repeat our delusions."

I looked at him, and didn't respond. I remembered Semyonich: Rabbis are by presumption believers!

At dawn we kissed each other, when his straggling gray column headed up the dusty steppe road, accompanied by guards on horses. He seemed to me bent over and sad. I was crying.

The columns went away in the dust, but my rabbi didn't turn around even once—maybe he was crying too, and didn't want me to know. Something was telling me that we wouldn't see each other ever again. This was just a premonition, at that time I couldn't know that from here began his long road to the construction of the White Sea–Baltic canal, bearing the name of the immortal leader of nations Joseph Vissarionovich Stalin.

The same immortal leader died, as you know, on March 5, 1953, but this was not the rabbi's dreamed-of period, not at all—just a comma. Because when the general grief after the irreparable loss faded away and people took a deep breath, at some meeting in Berdichev a fervent supporter of the new beginning declared:

"Already we can say with conviction, comrades, that in the years to come we will live better!"

"And us?" asked Mendel, the fool.

FINAL APOCALYPSE OF REVELATION

All of this, my brother, happened so long ago, it's as if it had never been. And it may indeed have never been, does anyone know what in our life is a dream and what reality, when life itself is a momentary vision, a mirage in the desert and chasing the wind?

I'm living in Vienna again, my eternal beautiful dream, I'm already more or less an old man and let me add relatively wealthy, if this matters at all. Because does the soul satisfy itself with what it's won, if it's hungry for what it's lost?

Yesterday at dusk I passed through the City Park, sat for a while by the little pond by the gilded Johann Strauss—that merry man with the violin—and threw pieces of croissant to the ducks. Then I dragged my feet along Wollzeile to my old friend St. Stephen, with its magnificent Steffel. Just opposite, at the corner of Graben and Kärtner, a girl with an indecently short skirt approached me:

"Hey, Uncle, shall we have some fun?"

"No." I was shy. "Excuse me, thanks."

She waved her hand and approached another uncle.

Loneliness.

What did that comrade from Berdichev mean by a "better life"? Really, what did he mean—it's been written that one cannot live by bread alone, hasn't it?

I made my way on foot to Margareten, passing through the luxurious underpass, which was crammed with drug addicts. What a calamity, my God, these poor boys and girls! At home, on the TV they were showing the next stupidity, meant for the other—the TV—addicts. It may not be such stupidity, but I don't understand it—I'm like the old Boyadjian who felt lonely in Paris and eventually bought a tank.

Sister Angela from the cotton fields by Mississippi will have to excuse me, but it's worth thinking about that Exodus from Egyptian slavery chosen by Stefan Zweig. I also have it in my bedside cupboard, this Exodus, three flasks of Dormidon, twenty pills each, for a good sleep. "You will sleep like a bathed child"—this is what the doctor said. Three by twenty makes sixty. Sixty bathed children.

Maybe before that I should've gone with the girl to have some fun?

No thanks.

I lie on my bed. What's so difficult? One glass of Evian water, thirty pills. One more—another thirty, this makes a whole kindergarten of bathed children.

I close my eyes and I'm young again, and I'm in my hometown Kolodetz by Drogobych. I'm playing the violin and my world comes to life again, swirling in a merry Hasidic dance. Here they are—my mother Rebekha and my father Aaron, he's in the red uniform of a *hussar* from His Majesty's Lifeguards, here's Uncle Chaimle and the old postman Avramchik, here are all the old soldiers from David Leibovitch's café, who are rolling and unrolling the ball of yarn of poor Rothchild's unsolvable problems. Here's Pan Voitek, the mayor, who's presenting a bouquet of yellow flowers to the Radish, yellow flowers like yellow stars. Do you see—Esther Katz is dancing with Liova Weissmann, our Catholic priest is clapping, happy as can be, in time to the Jewish rhythm, and there he is, my Zukerl, thumping with heavy boots in front of smiling sister Angela, my black angel! Doc Joe is secretly smoking in his palm, this is forbidden, and the little Italian with the wire-rimmed glasses is pointing his finger at him and shouting: "It's him!" The Polish pan ophthalmologist is hugging with two hands Frau Zigrid Kubichek and crazily whirling her around, my three children—Ilyusha, Schura, and Susannah—with Kalashnikovs on their shoulders and their arms crossed, are squatting in time, the dear movie fool Semyonich is filming all this, probably for television, and Doctor Robert Boyadjian is drawing hammers and sickles on the whitewashed walls. The little soldier is looking at him sadly, takes off his cap, and crosses himself—for this they expel you from the Komsomol, and in the Internal Forces they punish you. And up there, on the stage with its peeled gilding, where my colleague Mozart once played, proudly standing and conducting all this is the chairman of the Atheists' Club himself, Rabbi Shmuel Ben-David!

And where is Sarah, you'll ask, where is my Sarah? Here's my Sarah with the grayish-green eyes—like reflections of the water in the lake of Genezareth. This is she, I tell you, although she is so young! Of course, it's she! I quietly put the violin down on the wooden floor and hug the girl with the grayish green eyes, I hug her and the two of us suddenly become light and fly up. And here we are, flying above our homeland and it's painted now, this region, in the colors of this fellow Markusle Segal, or if you like, Chagall. Here, look, he's painted us, Sarah and me, flying in love above our miastechko, here below is the Orthodox church, here are the Ukrainian women with their white feet, here's the pregnant mare with a foal in her womb, and here are Sarah and I, flying away to the future, may it be good for everyone, amen.

I open my eyes. In the bedside cupboard the three flasks of Dormidon are sitting, still packed, I haven't even touched them. Excuse me, Stefan Zweig, you sly old fox, who were teaching the others how to live, but yourself ran away! If life was given us to live it, we will live it, there's no other way.

Laila tov, or in your words, good night!

Author's Acknowledgments

The author sincerely thanks all known and unknown creators, collectors, collators, and publishers of Jewish jokes and anecdotes, through which my people have turned laughter into a defensive shield, and a source of courage and self-esteem through the most tragic moments of their existence!

Translators' Acknowledgments

We wish to thank Angel ("Jacky") and Zora Wagenstein for their warmth and hospitality during the preparation of this translation. To William Weaver we are grateful for sharing with us his great store of wisdom on the art of translation. In the process of transforming Isaac's vigorous and colorful Bulgarian into American-flavored "Yinglish," we received suggestions and advice, for which we happily give thanks, from the distinguished Bulgarian translator Jeni Bozhilova, Professor Andrew Wachtel, who is the Bertha and Max Dressler Professor in the Humanities and Chair of the Department of Slavic Languages and Literatures at Northwestern University, Tzveta Petrova, Gina Cherkelova Brezini, Valentin Belinski, and Lydia Belinska. For responding so readily and fully to our endless queries, we would like to give special thanks to Elizabeth Frank's Bard colleagues: Professors Susan Bernofsky, Hezi Brosh, Yuval Elimelech, Franz Kempf, Marina Kostalevsky, Cecile Kuznitz, Natan Margalit, Jacob Neusner, Joel Perlmann, and Gennady Shkliarevsky. To Al Zuckerman we offer a million thanks for escorting our friend Isaac to American shores.

Lastly, we wish to dedicate our translation to the memory of

Dimiter Simeonov and Boncho Belinski, who valiantly took part in the Bulgarian antifascist resistance during World War II.

Elizabeth Frank and Deliana Simeonova
Sofia, December 2007

About the Author

Angel Wagenstein was born in the city of Plovdiv in 1922 and spent his early childhood in exile with his family in Paris. Upon his return to Bulgaria as a high school student, he joined an antifascist underground group. For taking part in anti-Nazi sabotage during World War II, he was sent to a labor camp from which he escaped to rejoin the Bulgarian partisans. Arrested, tortured, and condemned to death, he owes his life to the arrival of the Red Army in Bulgaria on September 9, 1944.

After studying filmmaking in Moscow, he went on to become one of the foremost screenwriters in Bulgaria, with more than fifty credits to his name, including the original screenplay for the film *Stars*, which in 1959 won the Cannes Prix Spécial du Jury, and tells the story of a German soldier's doomed attempts to rescue a young Greek-Jewish woman and her family, who are all being transported to certain death in the "Eastern Territories" of the Reich.

He has in recent years written three novels on the fate of European Jews in the twentieth century, of which *Isaac's Torah* (*Petoknizhie Isaakovo*), which has already been translated into French and German, is the first. His two other novels have also been translated into French: *Far from Toledo* (*Dalech Ot Toledo*), under the title *Abraham Le Poivrot*

(*Abraham the Sot*), winner of the Prix Jean Monnet de Littérature Européenne in 2004; and *Farewell, Shanghai* (*Sbogom, Shanghai*), published in English by Handsel Books in 2007. Wagenstein wrote the screenplay for the film *After the End of the World* (1998) while simultaneously working on the novel *Far from Toledo* on which it is based—a singular case, it would seem, of an original screenplay's simultaneously giving birth to its adaptation as a novel and vice versa.

Wagenstein resides in Sofia, where he takes an active part in Bulgarian culture and politics.